The Lady Dragon of Chinatown

The Lady Dragon of Chinatown is a work of fiction. Names, characters, places, and incidents are the product of the author's imagination or are used fictitiously. Any resemblance to actual events, locales, or persons, living or dead, is coincidental.

Willow River Press is an imprint of Between the Lines Publishing. The Willow River Press name and logo are trademarks of Between the Lines Publishing.

Copyright © 2023 by Noel Plaugher

Cover design by Cherie Fox

Between the Lines Publishing and its imprints supports the right to free expression and the value of copyright. The scanning, uploading, and distribution of this book without permission is a theft of the author's intellectual property. If you would like permission to use material from the book (other than for review purposes), please contact info@btwnthelines.com.

Between the Lines Publishing
1769 Lexington Ave N, Ste 286
Roseville MN 55113
btwnthelines.com

First Published: January 2023

ISBN: (Paperback) 978-1-958901-11-3
ISBN: (Ebook) 978-1-958901-12-0

The publisher is not responsible for websites (or their content) that are not owned by the publisher

The Lady Dragon of Chinatown

Noël Plaugher

A selection from a modern bestiary

In the cool morning air, the hawk glided swiftly and silently through the Chinatown gate. He sped through the plaza, navigating at low altitude, and high speed, deftly between pillars and stone sculptures. He purposely overshot his usual perch to make his presence known and scare off other predators in the territory.

Once in his hunting ground, the hawk always tried for a quick and easy meal. His eyes darted from the high rooftops to the low open range of the plaza. Skirting the red outcropping eaves of a triple-tiered pagoda, the hawk landed atop one of the fearsome dragon statues mounted on the structure. The winged predator immediately began scanning the area below from his ostentatious perch.

The night creatures were seeking shelter from the unrelenting crawl of day. Rats and mice headed back to their nests, and cockroaches sought cracks and crevices to melt into. Before long, the sunlight would completely take hold, and the hawk would have limited time before his prey were safe in their shadowed lairs.

A small movement drew the hawk's attention. With a lightning-fast twitch of his head, the hawk's gaze found two large rats racing for shelter. One rat was slightly smaller and presumably younger. With millions of years of evolution making the hawk's choice for him, the smaller rat became the prey.

The hawk opened his wings and took to the air. The avian executioner became silent death as it dove toward the prey with increasing speed. The smaller rat, moving quickly behind the larger one, had not yet noticed the impending death falling fast from the sky. Assuming an attack posture, the winged hunter arched his body and aimed his talons to strike. He then opened his wings to slow his descent. The hawk let its full body weight hit the rodent to stun its thoughts of escape, and to impale the prey onto its spiked talons. The vermin protested impotently with a chirp, but in an instant, the hawk pulled himself mightily back into the air, the prey tightly grasped in his talon's death grip. He flew into the morning sky high above the gray cement and shiny steel rooftops below. The morning death ritual was over, and in a few moments, he was gone entirely from view.

As the sun devoured the last remnants of night, the city became restless. Chinatown uncoiled, raised its head, and breathed in deeply the air of the new day. It would live this day as it had been living for generations. Like the Tai Chi practitioner's effortless strength, the town was not to be judged by its appearance. Beneath the pagoda facades and brightly decorated streets were deadly consequences. While the ways of the world changed around it, Chinatown, as if preserved in an oasis of time, stayed the same.

Part 1

Part I

Chinatown, 1965

Maggie Long shifted in her chair, trying without success to find a position that wouldn't put her legs to sleep. Though the weather was warm outside, the hard steel folding chairs in the lobby were cold and uncomfortable. Attempting to look studious, she pretended to read her well-thumbed copy of Sun Tzu's *Art of War* while her eyes peeked over the top of the pages to observe the kung fu class in progress in front of her.

It was sparring day. Maggie watched as her brother Sam prepared to spar with his nemesis Chad, the big blonde kid from the affluent enclave of Argent Hills.

Chad was stocky, arrogant, and typical of what one usually found in Argent Hills. Maggie's brother, Sam, couldn't have been more different than his opponent. Sam was small for his age, soft, and wore his defeated posture uncamouflaged. His size and cowering appearance made him a prime target of some of the boys in the class, especially Chad.

Sam looked nervous. He had trouble getting his gear on. His fingers couldn't find the securing straps for the pads, and when he did, they slipped from his grasp as if coated in butter. He dropped his mouthpiece more than once, and he took longer than it should to get his gloves on properly. Maggie sighed, as she imagined trading places with her brother, even if it was just for a moment. That was never going to happen

1

though. It was forbidden. She placed the book on her lap. She would watch the match closely.

White tape, irregularly applied to the floor, outlined the ring on the school's worn carpet. Sam and Chad were in opposite corners of the makeshift ring. After a short warm-up of bouncing from foot to foot, dramatic shoulder rolls, and theatrical head tilts, Chad punched his gloves together, grinned maniacally through his mouthpiece, and went to work.

Chad moved forward jabbing with his left hand and throwing quick stabbing snap kicks, checking Sam's reactions and distance. Though he'd done the drill many times before, Sam reacted to everything like a rookie. Rather than gauging the distance to counterattack, he jumped back and slinked away from everything Chad threw. He was scared.

Chad faked a back-knuckle to Sam's face, but it was too high. Still, Sam reached to block and left himself open. Maggie wanted to close her eyes, but her need to know the outcome wouldn't let her. With his abdomen exposed, Chad landed a spinning sidekick into Sam's midsection. Maggie heard the breath leave Sam's body with a labored wheeze. His eyes squinted with pain and his mouthpiece nearly leaped from his mouth upon impact. Sam staggered backward as his body absorbed the energy of the strike.

Chad giggled sloppily through his saliva-filled mouthpiece and bounced back to his ready position at the top of the taped ring. Sam tried to recover his breath, but he wouldn't have long, his attacker was moving in again. Chad threw a steaming left hook to Sam's temple and followed it up with a right uppercut to his chin. Sam's head ping-ponged off Chad's gloves, and his balance slouched toward defeat.

Maggie watched with anxious frustration. Her hands gripped the sides of the seat, tightly. The book slipped from her lap and landed unnoticed on the floor, as she shifted forward in her chair.

"C'mon Sam! You can take him!" Maggie's outburst brought a quick double-take from Chad. He took out his mouthpiece, slurped the clear viscous excess, and stared at Maggie as he spoke, still bouncing.

"Hey, stay out of it, Haggie! Unless Sam's gonna have his sister fight for him! Too bad we don't allow girls, huh? I'd beat the whole friggin' family." Chad put in his mouthpiece, punched his gloves together, and went back to work on Sam.

Maggie stewed angrily. She hated being called Haggie. Not because it was offensive, but because it lacked imagination. Chad truly was a small-minded fool. She had thought of plenty of creative names for Chad.

Wishing the sifu would intervene, Maggie knew that it wouldn't happen any time soon. The sifu was distracted working with his assistant and the younger kids at the other end of the large mat area. Sam was standing, but unsteady. Maggie bit her lip and clenched her fists, as she watched nervously, knowing that Sam was in peril.

As the match wore on, Chad looked even more confident, as he landed kicks and punches with ease. With his guard up, covering his face, Sam looked like he was just trying to make it through the end of class. Maggie's frustration was turning to anger with each passing moment.

Chad, breathing heavily, let his mouthpiece hang half out of his mouth. He was unconcerned about getting hit, as he pushed harder with his onslaught, and made Sam retreat from the marked-off sparring area. With his gloves covering up his face, Sam tried without success to avoid the pummeling. As Sam turned his back, Chad, with a gloating grin, delivered a heavy kick to Sam's backside producing laughter from the students nearby.

Maggie's eyes narrowed and her teeth clenched.

"C'mon, Sammy! Throw another sissy kick!" Chad taunted through his drool and half-hanging mouthpiece.

As if on cue, Sam rushed forward and threw a roundhouse kick with all his might. Chad evaded to the side and blocked Sam's leg with an elbow to the middle of the soft flesh of his thigh. Sam collapsed as he fell to the red carpet of the school floor, wincing in pain.

Maggie watched her brother try to get up but knew he couldn't stand on his stricken leg. Sam stayed on the floor rocking back and forth in the fetal position. The pair of students sparring close by registered little surprise as they watched Sam helpless on the ground. Chad stood over Sam, craning his neck down, with his gloves parked on his hips.

"That didn't hurt too much, did it? Pussy!" Chad declared, wearing a bully's grin.

Maggie had seen enough. She looked surreptitiously over her shoulder and out the window behind her, checking to see if her mother was coming back into the school. No. She was still engaged in her usual chatter. Maggie doubted that her mother would understand the subtle nuances of the confrontation between the boys. She wouldn't understand why Sam couldn't just shrug off the pain the way his father would. Or better yet, attack and defend himself, but alas that would never happen, and Maggie knew it. Sam was caught in the victim's cycle of wanting things to change but being unwilling to do anything about them for fear of a greater retaliation by his abuser. He didn't believe another outcome was possible, and so he locked himself in a behavioral cage never understanding that he alone held the key.

Maggie watched as her brother struggled to get up. Chad, still standing over Sam, stomped a foot on his downed opponent's torso. The stomp forced Sam to heave out his air

4

and make his legs and head snap up. Chad kept his foot on Sam's abdomen, holding him in place, and then raised his hands in the air, flexing his biceps, in a victory pose.

He started to look around the school, holding the pose, with one gloved hand clutching his drool-filled mouthpiece as it dripped clear liquid onto the fallen opponent. Chad looked around and spotted Jimmy, another kid from the Argent Hills, and called out to him.

"Hey Jimmy, I dropped Sammy again!"

Jimmy didn't say a word. He looked concerned. His head jerked around as if he was trying to find the sifu. Maggie suspected he was less than impressed with the bully's behavior, but like the others silently acquiesced.

"You don't belong in this school, dork. I don't care if you live in Chinatown or not. Why don't you quit, man?" Chad gave a shove with his foot before finally stepping off Sam and turning away to swagger toward the water fountain across the room. He took a long, noisy drink from the fountain, rinsed his mouthpiece, and then wiped his mouth with the back of his hand and sleeve before heading back to the spot where he had left Sam.

The sun shined brightly through the window and onto the worn sparring area. Chad walked back to the square and his eyes squinted at the bright afternoon sun coming through the window. Sam was gone, but someone had taken his place. A small shadowy figure carved from the sun's beam stood before him. Maggie was about an inch shorter than Sam. She had two long braids on either side of her face and a solid blue skirt that stopped just at the level of her knee. She was a girl, and Chad was going to have to fight her whether he wanted to or not.

Her hands and fingers twitched and shook with readiness like a gunfighter. She flicked her hands as if flinging water from them. Chad noticed she didn't look scared of him.

Maggie watched Chad's gaze as he scanned the lobby chairs and saw that Sam was now sitting on the chair where Maggie had been. Sam had his legs up on the seat, rubbing his injured leg. His tear-soaked cheeks and reddened eyes were hidden strategically behind his knees. Chad looked back at Maggie, unable to conceal his surprise at the turn of events.

"I can beat you," Maggie stated flatly, in a slightly lower voice, as if she was saying it to herself. She dropped back into a fighting stance, with her legs bent and her hands molded into little iron fists.

The realization that he was being challenged by Sam's little sister, knowingly crept across his face. Maggie saw him gulp before he started looking around the room to see that the whole class was looking at him and watching what would happen next.

"Are you kidding? *A girl?* Get off the floor!" Chad pointed to the lobby with a gloved hand. The other students started moving in closer.

"You're afraid to fight a girl?" she taunted calmly. Some of the students laughed. "Go ahead, Chad…Try me."

She tucked her chin and shaped her arms into a boxer's guard position, determined to make herself look like she meant business. She knew Chad, like all bullies, would be afraid of someone who showed no fear. Though she projected bravery, she had her concerns about squaring off with the miniature Viking. It was too late though. She had stood up and made her declaration. She had to see it through.

Ever wary, Maggie glanced out through the window to see that her mother was still speaking to the woman outside the school. Then she glanced over at the far end of the mat where the kindly, but inattentive, sifu was working with the younger kids on a block-kick combination that had him completely preoccupied. So far, so good, she thought. She had no time to lose.

"Okay, you want me to teach you a lesson?" Chad said, shaking his gloved fist toward her. "First one's free!"

He put in his mouthpiece and started bouncing excitedly from one foot to the other, and then on both feet simultaneously. To Maggie, it looked more like a showy stall, rather than some kind of extra preparation for readiness for the confrontation. He was vulnerable to the unexpected. Chad quickly looked around himself, and his manner made him appear a little anxious. Was he looking for someone to intervene at the last moment?

Hitting his gloves together, as he did before, Chad then tilted his head quickly from side to side. Maggie knew he was trying to mimic fighters he'd seen on TV. It wasn't going to do him any good though. He would underestimate her. She knew he would and so he had already lost.

The air became heavy and soundless.

"Aaaiii!" Chad yelled, a muffled battle cry through his mouthpiece, as he rushed in aggressively with a flurry of punches and kicks. Maggie stood her ground before she dodged the assault with a sidestep at the last moment. The force of Chad's momentum met with a deft spinning back kick squarely to his groin. It dropped him to his knees. He hit the ground hard and rolled on the floor with his hands covering his genitals, as he slowly rocked from side to side.

Silence saturated the air. Maggie inspected the group of student on-lookers and noted their looks of astonishment as the students' gazes alternated between looking at the much larger Chad rolling on the ground, and back at her.

"Wow, that little *girl* beat Chad!" yelled Jimmy. Chad, rolling on the ground, surely overheard. Maggie smiled. She could hear the murmuring of the other students grow louder and fill the air.

"You can't…hit…in…the…groin," said Chad, gasping for air through his mouthpiece as he rolled back and forth. He was trying, unsuccessfully, to rock away from the pain.

Maggie made her expression as innocent as she could, "Really? Well, they won't let me train, so I don't know the rules," she answered with a wry smile.

"What the hell happened?" the sifu yelled angrily as he ran upon the scene. "Where's Sam?"

Before anyone could respond he barked more orders, "Maggie! I've told you before, get off the floor!"

The sifu knelt and checked on Chad. He looked at Chad's eyes, pulling his eyelids back one at a time intently, seeming to study the reaction.

"His eyes are fine…I kicked him in the balls," Maggie said, dispassionately.

She knew that the sifu was angry with her, judging from his gritted teeth and his squinted expression as he jabbed his index finger into the air in the direction of the mirrors and yelled to the class, "LINE UP!"

The students quickly stowed their gear and put back their gloves and mouthpieces into their duffel bags. They straightened their uniforms and began lining up by rank in front of the large mirror that occupied one wall of the school.

Maggie walked assuredly back to the lobby area where Sam was sitting. Upon her approach, he relinquished his perch and walked off to get in line with the other students for the end-of-class salute. He started toward the mat area but stopped and looked back. He gave Maggie a conflicted look of disappointment and appreciation.

She knew that it was tough for a boy to have his sister stick up for him, but she also knew that she couldn't resist the urge to prove herself. *Was it wrong?* Probably, but choices in the heat of the moment are rarely plentiful.

The sifu stood in front of the two rows of students and led the formal salute to close the class. Maggie sat back down on the cold steel folding chair, now slightly warmed by Sam, picked up her book from the floor, and went back to reading *The Art of War*. She glanced up once to see that Chad was moving with a limp away from the line-up, and for a moment their gazes met. His face was twisted into a mask of hate tamed slightly by humiliation. Maggie gave him a knowing smile and continued reading until her mother came back in to collect them both and go home.

"Maggie!"

She heard her mom's voice booming from the kitchen and knew that she had to join the family for dinner immediately. Maggie had little fear when it came to opponents, but a healthy respect for the will and commands of her mother. She had been raised with love, but she knew that to anger her mother was not wise.

The table was set, and Sam and her father were already seated. There was a space left for her and one for her mother, but her mother's seat was rarely occupied. Mother always started the clean-up during the meal and only ever sat for a short time while she picked at the food she made for them.

In the center of the table was a large bowl of spaghetti with seven golf ball-sized meatballs. Mother used the big white bowl with a blue dragon circling the exterior, that she had picked up at the restaurant supply store years ago. It was her favorite bowl. She used it for the family's main dish each night. Flanking the main dish was a bowl of green beans and a basket of garlic bread.

Sam and their father sat stoically. Father watched mother finish her meal preparation awaiting her declaration to eat. Sam stared out the nearby window into the moonless night as if it was playing his favorite movie.

"All right…Eat!" Mother commanded.

Father grabbed a plate for Sam, filled it, and handed it back to him. He did the same for Maggie. He filled his plate last.

"Pass the green beans," Father said to Sam. Sam, mutely obliged, never looking in his direction.

"Bread," Father asked, with a nod in the direction of the basket.

"Here, Sam," Maggie said, handing the basket to Sam to hand to Father. She studied Sam's expression. He was still dealing with the event that happened earlier in class. It would be an awkward meal if it was discussed. Hopefully, no one would ask.

"Everyone has everything?" Mother asked the family as they all began to eat. Maggie and her father nodded. Sam was eating with little enthusiasm. Maggie noticed it, and knew that soon…

"Sam, you sick?" Father asked.

"No, just not very hungry."

"Did you eat that candy I brought home? I told you it would ruin your appetite. One piece a day. Your mother cooked this for you, for *us*, you need to - "

Sam interrupted, "I didn't eat candy. I'm just not hungry, that's all. No big deal."

"Hey, don't talk back. I know your friends talk that way to their parents, but that isn't the way we do things. I don't care what the goddamn Beatles and *bitnecks* say."

"Yes." Sam acquiesced.

"*Beatniks*," Maggie corrected.

Father glared at his daughter.

Taking in her father's reaction, she looked down at her plate and studied it as if it held inscrutable interest.

"He's probably just tired." As the words left Maggie's mouth, she wished she could take them back. She knew her comment would eventually lead to questions about the class. It was exactly what she didn't want to happen. Sam knew it too, as he shot her a modest cringe of frustration.

"Did class tire you out, Sam? That's good...Don't just concentrate on forms though, be sure and spar. You need to be able to apply your kung fu. The streets aren't like the movies."

"Yes," Sam replied quietly without looking up.

"Is that why you were sitting in the lobby, Sam? I looked through the window and saw you sitting in Maggie's chair during the class." Mother questioned Sam as expertly as an attorney cross-examining a witness as she stood holding the back of her chair.

"Why were you in the lobby?" Father tore a bite of the garlic bread with his teeth and chewed as his gaze bore into the top of Sam's head.

Maggie looked at Sam, back at her father, and then glanced back to see her mother had gone into the kitchen to get a plate. She was going to join them at the table after all.

"I got hurt. I had to rest up, ya know?" Sam explained.

"Hurt? Did you fall? Have an accident?" Father took another bite.

"No, I uh, was with Chad and he uh, he's bigger, and..."

"Jesus!" Father slapped the table. The force of the strike spilled the milk from the glasses and shook the utensils. An expectant silence hung over the dinner table as Mother and Father exchanged a flurry of looks back and forth at each other: Eyebrows were raised and lowered between them. Dramatic lips mouthed silent words.

Their unheard conversation dissolved as the space over the dinner table filled with silent anticipation.

"What happened? Did he get carried away? Did sifu see?" Mother questioned in her reasoned tone and ate her spaghetti as if she was only moderately interested in the answer.

Sam sat in silence; his face fixed determinedly on his plate.

"I saw what happened," Maggie interjected. "Chad was getting out of hand, but Sam took care of it. He got a little banged up, but he took care of it. It was very…good." She took a bite of green beans hoping to earn some goodwill from her mother with her choice.

"So, Sam took care of it?" Mother asked with no inflection in her voice. She pushed her food around on her plate and without looking up questioned Maggie.

"I thought I saw you on the floor, but I know sifu told you to stay off the floor during class time. Were you in the – "

Maggie jumped in before her mother could finish, "I had to use the bathroom, so I had to go in the back of the school, across the mat…" She took a larger forkful of green beans and carefully fit them in her mouth.

"The bathroom is in the lobby," mother stated.

"They were out of toilet paper, and I had to go number – "

"Hey!" Father objected with a mouthful of garlic bread.

"Sorry…Anyway, that's what happened." Maggie cleared her plate and took it to the sink in the kitchen, something she usually forgot to do.

"Is that it, Sam?" Mother asked without looking up.

He took a long pause before he answered, "Yes."

"Okay," mother concluded and continued eating.

Maggie walked by the dinner table on her way back to her room and watched the trio express silent understanding as they looked at each other without saying what they were thinking. If Mother saw Sam on the chair, she probably saw the whole thing, but Maggie knew she would not tell Father.

Father was tough, but not cruel. He had grown up on the docks, and though he wouldn't talk about it very much, it seemed obvious he had fought and got into trouble. The fairy tale they tried to sell their kids about meeting at a party on New Year's Eve, at an upper-class downtown nightclub didn't seem believable anymore. Maybe they understood the need to let Sam keep his story, even though they knew the truth because they had their own legends to protect.

She could hear Sam walk by her room on his way to the bathroom, and the low murmurs of her parents talking at the dinner table.

Maggie lay on her bed and wrote in her composition notebook. It was full of carefully notated pages. Blocks, strikes, techniques, combinations. She made a list of every kick that she could remember from the lesson in the class that day and used stick figures to illustrate the details. She noted a spin kick to the groin is an effective technique.

The wind blew gently through Maggie's hair and softly touched her skin as she stood in the warm sunlight on the schoolyard's basketball court. She took a breath and then with the studied movement of the Tai Chi practitioners she had watched in the park, her arms moved upward in a grand sweeping motion before floating down to her abdomen. The movement was graceful and served as the opening to her solo practice.

She faced her imaginary opponent, a thick metal pole used to hold the basket. With a deep inhalation, she let her arms float up from their low resting place close to her abdomen and rise to a guard position. One hand settled in front and the other rested closer to her face. She took another breath and began stepping carefully around the pole, never letting her gaze stray from it as if it was about to attack.

With each step, she began to lightly strike the pole with a chop, hammer-fist, ridge-hand, and other assorted hand weapons she learned from watching the classes of the internal martial art schools in the park. Afterward, she wrote everything she observed from the class in her composition book. She had assembled nearly all the eight palms of BaGua and their applications as well as the five elements of Xing Yi Quan. After witnessing the pole exercise, she started practicing it, similarly, to apply what she had learned. She tried to concentrate and execute each movement as closely as she could.

She breathed slowly, moved determinedly, and in time she was lost in the exercise. In her mind, she put a face and body to the pole and deftly avoided imagined punches as she countered with her carefully placed hand strikes to visualized targets: solar-plexus, neck, temple, and face. Occasionally, she would hit the pole harder than she anticipated, and a jolt of pain would shoot through her hand. When it happened, she tried to ignore the sensation and continue breathing, stepping, and attacking.

As she gained proficiency, she began to add low kicks and crossing steps that she had seen the BaGua practitioners use. The movements became an endless cycle of motion with her static steel partner taking the punishment without protest, as she moved around the pole in one direction and then changed and moved in the other. Her mind was pleasantly lost in her solitary battle as she pictured the opponent's endless attacks and her reactive responses in the form of counterattacks. Breathe, step, strike...

"Hey, I'm not sure how long that takes, but we have dibs on the court, so..." Maggie was startled to attention, as she snapped out of her meditation and saw a tall boy standing only a few feet away with a basketball resting under one arm flanked by two other boys. There was no telling how long they had been standing there. Maggie was a bit embarrassed and felt exposed. What would they think she was doing?

"Oh, sorry. Yeah, courts all yours," Maggie replied, trying to hide being startled.

"You can have it back when we're done, for your...dancing."

"Dancing? Well, I have to get going anyway, but thanks." Maggie knelt down and closed her composition book and placed it carefully between the pages of her math book before she picked up her sweater, pencils, and all of the rest of her belongings cradled in one arm and started home.

The boys were already dribbling and shooting before she had gathered up all her things. She was halfway across the schoolyard when she heard the boy's voice again.

"Hey, you dance real good!" He yelled.

"Thanks!" She said, never looking back.

The white powdered soap never really dissolved in the running water. The granules felt gritty, like little pebbles, against her skin as Maggie washed her hands in the school's restroom sink. For a reason never explained, there was never any hot water in the restrooms. The cold water seemed to make the rocky soap more abrasive and leave her hands reddened. She was preoccupied with her thoughts and sensations when she looked up in the restroom mirror and was startled to see three girls standing behind her.

They stared with blank faces and eyes that gleamed like a cat on the hunt. *Where had they come from?* Their image was unsettling. Looking back at her were three white girls. A brunette standing between two shorter, younger blondes. The brunette was wearing make-up. It was garishly applied. It looked as though she had decided that if a little was a good thing, then a lot was a whole lot better. She had the appearance of a bizarrely painted doll.

Maggie knew who the trio was. The brunette was a notorious bully from the seventh grade, Debbie Jenkins, and her two blonde confederates, Holly, and Christine. Their intentions were clear. Maggie knew that she was outnumbered and outmaneuvered.

She finished washing her hands as naturally as possible. Her back was still to them. Taking in a big breath and letting it out slowly, Maggie flung the water from her hands and stepped up to the bulky white wall-mounted paper towel dispenser. With each rotation, the mechanism generated squeaky acknowledgment that reverberated off the tiled walls and floor. Six eyes burned into Maggie's back.

She tried to act as if she didn't notice the three girls and hoped that they would just go away. She dried her hands slowly with the brown paper towel, watching the trio from the corner of her eye. A weighted silence hung from above as she wadded the towel into a dense ball and threw it in the trash can where it rebounded with a slight thud off of the side of the can and landed softly on top of the other debris in the echoing quiet of the restroom's tiled walls.

With a casual sigh, Maggie sought the easiest resolution to the situation and tried to walk past the three girls.

"Where ya goin', chink?" said the big brunette girl. She was more than a head taller than Maggie and outweighed her by more than ten pounds.

Maggie stared up at the girl's face. It was made up like a clown's, she thought, and it looked even more tawdry close-up, with those overly dark eyebrows and the heavy blue eyeshadow. The girl's cheeks were highlighted with red ovals, and the pink-painted lips seemed to jump out from the clown-white powder that covered her face.

"I'm going to my next class," Maggie answered, as she tried to walk by the other two girls who were blocking her way. They didn't move and their expressions remained unchanged until one gave a sarcastic smile.

"You're not going anywhere, chink!" The bully spat her words and drops of spittle landed on Maggie's cheeks. She struggled not to change her expression; it wasn't easy. The girl brought her painted face close to Maggie's.

"Your money, hand it over!" The brunette punctuated the order by giving Maggie a mighty shove. Maggie's body hit the tiled wall and the back of her head bonked against it. She winced in pain as the two other girls rushed to her flanks and held her arms to restrain her.

Her heart was pounding, she panted, and her hands turned clammy. Even though she could barely think straight, she had wits enough to remember something she read in Sun Tzu's *Art of War*:

"Attack him where he is unprepared, appear where you are not expected."

Calmed by the recollection, she realized there wasn't much she could do about what was happening now but take it. Though it hurt her pride not to fight back, physically, her thoughts roamed as she began planning her counterattack.

She didn't resist when the bully roughly reached into her pocket and pulled out the thirty-five cents that her mother had given her for lunch. She looked away from the robbery as if to deny it was happening, and looked down at the green-tiled floor, studying its cracks, soiled grout, and obvious wear from age and inattention. She tried to ignore what she knew was coming.

Standing before her, the trio looked to each other as if to confirm what was going to happen next, and then each girl hit her once in the stomach, a clean shot, as hard as they could. Though Maggie tried to prepare by exhaling her air and tightening her abdomen, she was still caught off guard by how hard the blows landed. Her face became pale, and her mouth gaped as she gasped for breath. They pushed her down fiercely onto the cold tile where she lay in a fetal position trying desperately to get back the air that had escaped. The attack ended abruptly, more likely from boredom than mercy. The three girls left the restroom with cackles of laughter echoing loudly even after the heavy restroom door closed.

Huddled on the floor alone, she waited for her breath to return, coughing as she tried to breathe deeper than her body was ready for. Amidst the pain and anger, she was grateful that it was over quickly and, even more so, that no one else saw. She sat up and held her stomach, still feeling where the blows from bony fists had landed. Before she had ever hit the floor, she already knew what she was going to do.

At lunchtime, Maggie entered the large, noisy, cafeteria, and immediately looked around to see where the three girls were sitting. She spotted them at their usual table seated in their customary places at the end of a long row. The dark-haired bully-queen sat on one side of the table, and the two blonde vassals sat opposite her where they could provide their liege with the requisite adoration.

The big brunette usually brought her lunch, but today she was eating the lunch du jour, which she had likely bought with the stolen money. The other two girls were eating their usual sack lunches from crumpled, occasionally stained, brown paper bags. The brunette was sampling the dessert before she finished her meal. Seeing her wolf down the formidably gelatinous bite of apple cobbler, made Maggie even more angered over having been taken advantage of. It was a horrible dessert, but it should have been *her* horrible dessert. The injustice of seeing someone enjoy what was rightly hers caused her wrath to stir. But she remained calm. She stuck to her plan.

Though butterflies were starting to take flight in her stomach, Maggie got into the lunch line with the other students. Her stomach growled and gurgled from hunger, but her emotions would not let her eat. The lunch money taker was a familiar old woman who sat at a small card table, with a gray cashbox. The students lined up dutifully before her and took their turn dropping their thirty-five cents into her cupped hand. Neither party seemed to give any thought to the silent transaction. Maggie approached and leaned over the woman close enough to her ear to be easily heard.

"I don't have any money," Maggie said, quietly, but as clearly as possible.

"What's that, honey?" the woman asked, squinting as she spoke.

"Money, I don't have any. I don't have thirty-five cents."

The cash-taker nodded her understanding, took a pencil, and marked a small tablet with a line next to ten others. "Oh, okay, tell *her*," She said, pointing with her thumb backward toward the first station in the line. Maggie gave her a nod in return, and the old woman motioned for her to move along. She stepped forward and grabbed a green rectangular tray and a white plate from one of three stacks.

Maggie surveyed the stainless-steel counter, ornamented with green trays, and got in line next to the other students as they sidled down the line toward each tray of food. The servers were a mixture of students and elderly all wearing white smocks and black hair nets. They stood at the ready with ice

19

cream scoopers poised to drop a dollop of their dish onto waiting plates with no comment or eye contact.

As she got closer to the first station, where the attendant would normally scoop out the barely identifiable entrée of the day, Maggie had to again explain to the server that she didn't have any money. In response, a peanut butter sandwich plopped, unceremoniously, onto her tray. She offered the lunch server an obligatory nod of thanks.

From the line, Maggie turned slightly to spy on the three girls. They were still eating at the table. Her body began to react to her anticipation. In addition to butterflies in her stomach, she had developed a dry cottonmouth. *Yes*, she admitted to herself, *she was scared*. But it didn't matter. She was ready. Her opponents looked relaxed, unwary. Good. She needed to act with cool decisiveness.

Walking at a slow and deliberate pace, from the line to the dining room, Maggie approached her adversaries. She zigzagged among the long rows of tables, and made small talk in short intervals with friends, sometimes only pretending to interact as she soundlessly mouthed words to the air. During it all, she kept one eye on the opponents.

A palpable escalation of fear coursed through her as Maggie started down the same row where the meanest of all seventh-grade girls sat. Her heart was beating in her ears and her breath became shallow. To get behind her opponent unnoticed, she turned her back and pretended to look for a place to sit while steadily closing in on her prey...a few careful steps at a time. Once Maggie could see the big girl's dirty saddle shoes from the corner of her eye, she knew she was directly behind her. Taking a deep, silent, breath, everything became still. All fear evaporated. All the sounds of the noisy lunchroom were silenced, and she became one with the moment. Time stopped for a second and hung in space. After a brief brush with infinity, time moved again and then accelerated. Faster. Her heart thumped loudly. Electric energy filled her body.

Attack!

Spinning around quickly, she let her food tray go, spinning as a flat missile toward the blonde girls, with a peanut butter sandwich, flatware, napkin, and milk flying in all directions— she hurled it full force at the stunned and disbelieving faces of the blondes. The tray hit one of the girls across the bridge of the nose, and the crack was loud enough to make heads turn. Surely, her nose was broken. The other girl was hit on the cheek, and she fell backward to the floor. Wasting no time, Maggie grabbed the big dark-haired bully's shoulders with both hands from behind, and pulled the girl backward, using all of the strength and power she could muster. The shocked girl flew backward, her eyes wide, her mouth full of apple cobbler and spaghetti, with an interrupted forkful still held aloft, idly, in mid-air, never making it to her red, sauce-stained lips. Forcefully removed from her regal bench seat, the petty tyrant landed on her spine, knocking out her breath and hitting her head with a loud thud on the highly polished linoleum floor.

Maggie pounced like a tiger and kicked the girl's body without mercy, randomly hitting any part of her torso that was exposed. She then leaped on top of her, straddling the girl, and rained blows on her made-up face.

She didn't tire, and she didn't let up until she felt the strong hands of the janitor pulling her off her hapless victim. As he dragged her away, she noted the stunned looks of the bystanders and the horror on the faces of the two blonde girls, each one nursing a wound from the impact of the tray. The defeated Debbie Jenkins, rolled on the ground, moaning, with eyes leaking blood and tears.

Maggie was sent home for two days as punishment. On the bus ride home that day, her mother was silent beside her. That night, her father never mentioned the incident over dinner. They just calmly passed the dishes to each other. "Bread?" She would say. "Yes, thank you" and father would take a piece without looking up. She did not know if they were too angry to talk about it, or if they were satisfied with how she handled the situation. She knew they couldn't come right out and praise her for beating someone up, but they didn't condemn her either. Eventually, the event faded from their thoughts with no words spoken between them.

The old man moved slowly in the level area of the park near the picnic tables. His movements flowed and unfolded in a kind of majestic meditative dance. The fluid circular movements of his arms, and the subtle shifting of his posture as he stepped, had a hypnotic quality when viewed over a period of time. It was like watching Jellyfish or Stingrays glide smoothly through the deep.

Standing close by was a young man, perfectly still, observing in rapt attention. His gaze never left the old man's movements. The old man would glance toward the student, and with raised eyebrows and wide eyes, emphasize a specific motion or form that should be paid special attention. Sometimes he would make a move and wag a finger and crinkle up his face showing mistakes to be avoided.

The old man brought the form to a close with arms circling up and then floating down. With a gracious hand of invitation, he exchanged places with the young man and instructed the student to perform the set he had just demonstrated.

From the far hill, Maggie watched the pair: Master and student. Their interaction was fascinating to her. The master was very interested in teaching his student to be as proficient as possible and to pass down his knowledge. The student would learn, become a master, and teach a student of his own. The cycle would continue as it had for decades, centuries, forever.

She hoped she would find a teacher someday. She wanted to be a part of this cycle as well: Student, disciple, master.

As the student and teacher began the set together, Maggie rose from her spot in the grass and slowly moved in time with the pair. She watched and mimicked their movements from her hidden spot on the far hill until the lesson was over. After making notes in her notebook, she took a moment to breathe, close her eyes, and picture herself with a teacher. She imagined them leading her in the form. They nodded and smiled as they moved. A smile surfaced and spread over her face. Still smiling, she opened her eyes, picked up her coat, and headed home.

After the last bell sounded, the children exploded from their classrooms. They streamed out from faded blue doors, stenciled with white spray-painted numbers, and into the grassy courtyard. The students moved quickly toward the various modes of transportation home.

The courtyard emptied as quickly as it had filled up. In a matter of minutes, the cement walkways were all but silent with only a faint echo of activity: little feet slapping against the ground rapidly, as a few children made late departures. As if on cue—and seemingly in unison—moments after the children left, the teachers emerged from their classrooms, closing, and locking the doors behind them. Soon the percussive sounds of high-heeled shoes against concrete and idle adult conversations about bills, car repairs, and dinner reverberated from all directions and then faded as the teachers left for the day.

Maggie crossed the vacant schoolyard alone on her way home. She often waited a while to avoid being caught up in the rush and the crowd of kids leaving for the day. Sam had already left with his friend Kevin to work on his science fair project, but also, he wanted to have some time to be himself. Maggie hoped he would find his place and where he fits in.

The quiet of the classroom's barren desks was something Maggie looked forward to. She would often spend her time reading, or sometimes she'd finish up her homework. Mrs. Workman, the homeroom teacher, didn't seem to mind Maggie staying after class at all. At least, until she wanted to get home herself. She would wait with Maggie until finally looking conspicuously at the clock and declaring: "I think we need to get going now, don't you?" Knowing that was the signal, Maggie would nod and smile, and then put her things in her backpack. Mrs. Workman, smiling, would already have her purse slung over her shoulder. As they exited together, she'd pull the classroom door shut behind them.

In the quiet of the schoolyard, Maggie casually surveyed the school's sports fields and playground, until something over at the baseball diamond caught her eye. She squinted for a better look. From a distance, she could make out three girls in a suspicious formation. Their body language signaled clearly to Maggie that they were up to no good.

As she turned and headed toward the ball field, she realized she recognized the three faces. Her response was visceral. Without even thinking, she rolled up her slender fingers into tight fists. Her pulse increased. Her breath became shallow as she instinctively readied herself for a potential clash. She ran toward them.

The trio circled like wolves around a pretty Asian girl, about Maggie's size, who was holding a big armful of books. She thought she'd seen her before a time or two in the hall or the lunchroom maybe. Maggie took her for a bit of a loner, much like herself. *Those that don't fit in, sometimes fit together*, her mother would say.

She knew the three girls accosting the new student all too well. It was Debbie Jenkins and her blonde minions. They were taking turns yelling insults and curses only inches from the girl's face. First, one blonde girl, and then the other one, and finally, Debbie took her turn and yelled *Chink!* at the small, pretty girl. A moment later, she pushed the girl down.

Maggie accelerated to a sprint across the field. Arriving on the spot, she caught her breath before she spoke.

"Hey!" Maggie yelled, from behind the three girls, hoping to startle them.

All three girls pivoted, quickly. Their faces showed their recognition and fear. Maggie was ready for them, firmly balanced with her right leg forward, guard up, fists at the ready. It wasn't necessary though. Without a word, the bullies each took two steps back, spun around, and took off.

With their hair trailing behind them, they retreated through the bushes to the empty walkways of the school. The tall brunette looked back once. Maggie watched them disperse and let a smile of satisfaction slowly grow across her face.

Once the threat was over, she turned her attention to the new girl, who had already stood up, dusted herself off, and was staring at Maggie with her mouth agape. She picked up her books, shifted them from one side to the other, and then started to laugh. The sound reminded Maggie of her mother's seldom-heard, but always entertaining, high-pitched giggle.

"I wouldn't have believed it," she said, "if I hadn't seen it for myself. You'd think Zhao himself was chasing after them!"

Maggie said nothing but continued to smile, as they both watched the girls run away until they disappeared from view.

"What did you do to make them run away like that?" the new girl asked with a nervous giggle.

"Well, they picked on me once, and it didn't go so hot for them. I think they remember it pretty well." She laughed a little.

Maggie's voice trailed off and she studied her shoes for an awkward moment. Although she was calming down from the adrenal rush, she had stumbled her way into a new kind of tension. Her confidence in fighting was one thing, but confidence in social situations was quite another matter. She had a hard time getting her thoughts out without getting tongue-tied, especially around girls. They made her anxious, although she couldn't say why. The pretty ones most of all.

"I'm Kathy. Thank you for helping me...you know, with those girls," Kathy smiled, as she too started studying the ground and creating designs in the soft dirt with the toe of her sneaker.

"Maggie," was all she said to introduce herself. She couldn't think of anything to add. She stared at Kathy's load of books. Action always seemed to help soothe her anxiety, so she reached out an arm. "I'll help you with some of those," she offered. Kathy, smiling, handed her books over. They walked from the school grounds to the street side by side. Kathy chattered on for several blocks, much to Maggie's relief: She didn't want to have to try to think of things to say.

When they were waiting at a corner for the light to change, Kathy gave her a sly grin and said, "You really won't tell me what you did to them? It's not some kind of secret, is it?"

Maggie relished the moment. She liked talking about fighting. That was something she understood.

"Well, one time, those girls cornered me in the girls' bathroom." She said nonchalantly, "They hit me. Took my lunch money, ya know?"

Kathy chuckled. "So, they're afraid of you because *they* beat *you* up?"

"Yeah, well, that wasn't the end of it," Maggie said, with her eyes blazing. Hardly able to contain herself as she relayed the story. Maggie realized she had quickened her pace as she talked about the incident, and that Kathy was hurrying to keep up with her. She hung on every detail as Maggie shared her victorious tale of the battle in the lunchroom.

Kathy laughed. "That's crazy!" she said. "I wish I could've seen it."

Maggie finished the story with a casual flick of her hair, as she clasped the books more firmly and confidently. She could see Kathy was genuinely impressed and it made her feel good.

"Man! You're pretty brave, huh?"

Kathy put a hand on Maggie's arm, stopped walking, and looked her in the eye. "You know what?" She paused. "You could grow up and be like a superhero, or John Wayne, or something."

Maggie noticed that Kathy's eyes were fixed on hers and she was suddenly unable to speak properly. Strange feelings had come over her ever since she met her.

"Say, do ya wanna come over to my place?" Kathy asked.

A moment of awkwardness hovered around Maggie's head as her feelings investigated the space between her and Kathy and sought to find a place to land themselves. She took a deep breath and then the strangeness dissolved a bit, and she felt better.

Maggie looked at Kathy and couldn't help smiling. She felt better than she ever had before. She knew Kathy was going to be a great and special friend. She could just tell.

"Yes, I do. Yeah, let's go."

The two girls walked together and talked the entire way. They followed the side streets as they snaked through

Chinatown to their neighborhood. They waved at the merchants and shop owners as they passed by, realizing they knew many of the same ones.

The girls lived close to each other, and when they arrived at Kathy's apartment building, Maggie marveled at how similar it was to her own. Once inside, Kathy's mother gave them a snack of almond cookies and milk. They talked for hours until Maggie realized, with a start, that it was getting dark and past time to get home.

"Crap, my mom's gonna be pissed," Maggie said a quick goodbye and ran outside, through the hall, and down the stairs. Kathy's mom's well wishes for a good night were silenced by the closing of their apartment door.

Once outside, Maggie saw the last rays of the afternoon sun fading to twilight. The streets were wet from a quick cloudburst. She hadn't even heard it raining while she was inside visiting with Kathy and her mom. Maggie had been absorbed in their conversation. The traffic was light, so she walked in the street observing the puddles, both large and small, that looked like mirrored holes in the earth.

Maggie walked quickly toward home, she was late, and her mother would be worried. But then inexplicably, she stopped to look into the largest puddle in the street. She approached it as if creeping upon herself and expecting to see something else. To her eyes, it was a brilliant image. Her reflection was colored with the fading twilight giving her skin a hue of gold. She studied the image. It was magical.

Her face was unblemished, and her black hair hung long past her shoulders. The colored lights of the neon sign above her gave her a green and yellow halo. Moving slightly without looking up, gazing deep into the puddle, she saw that her halo came from the neon sign of the Jade Dragon restaurant behind her.

She crouched down a bit more and tried to get the image of the dragon aligned with her own in the street's reflective water. When she stopped moving, she saw it: her face in the puddle with the dragon flying above her. She sensed the power of the omen, even if she couldn't quite understand it herself. Staring intently into the pool holding the image, she then felt a sober knowledge envelope her. The moment was significant, and she wanted to imprint it on her memory forever. When she felt it had been secured, she took a deep breath and then slowly let it out. She rose and ran as if flying, all the way home.

Sifu Chang watched the little girl walk from Chiu's kung fu school across the street, as she deftly negotiated the late afternoon Chinatown traffic. She entered the school with an air of confidence unusual in children her age. He wondered why she was coming from Chiu's school, and then he understood. He'd heard about this one.

As he observed his class executing a crane form in unison, the sifu noticed the girl in pigtails and a blue skirt now standing in the lobby. He could see with his peripheral vision that she was staring, expectantly, in his direction. He casually looked her way. She removed her backpack to give him the traditional salute of a fist in an open hand, representing the weapon and shield of combat. He saluted back and walked over.

"Hello, what can I do for you?"

"I want to study kung fu. Will you teach me?" She said getting right to the point.

Sifu crossed his arms and rested his chin on the "V" made from his index finger and thumb, "Well, do your parents know that you're here? They will need to sign you up, and get on a payment sched—"

Maggie interrupted, "They don't want me to learn. I will have to do it on my own." She glanced occasionally out the window at the school across the street. Sifu had encountered this situation before and figured that she was just another girl jealous of her brother. It was always the brother. She probably just wanted to do what he was doing. They were usually very forceful at first, and then when they began to see that it was not easy, the novelty wore off, and they quit and went back to the things girls do. He had no reason to think that Maggie would be any different.

The sifu looked around the room and then motioned with his hand for Maggie to follow him. He stopped by a wall adjacent to the training floor.

"Okay, you know a horse stance?"

"Yes," Maggie said, definitively.

"Get in your horse stance facing the wall," the sifu said with a waiter's gracious wave of his hand as if gesturing to sit at a table. Maggie got in her horse stance, with her legs bent, spaced wide, facing the wall.

"How long do you want me to stay here?" Maggie asked. Sifu's back was already turned as he walked away toward his class. She decided she would ask him when he came back.

The class continued behind her. Maggie listened to the sounds of the sifu's booming voice and the simultaneous execution of the commands by the students. Her eyes were fixed on the roughly textured and badly peeling yellow paint on the wall of the school before her. The well-studied spot held no more mystery, and so she closed her eyes and listened to her breath and the sounds around her. The instruction by the sifu, and then the rustling sounds of bodies moving into positions, inspired her imagination as she tried to picture the class's movements. She tried to ignore the mounting pain she was feeling in her legs from holding the horse stance for so long. After a few minutes, Maggie deduced that it was a test. She could feel sweat start to emerge on her back and slowly roll down her skin. Her legs were shaking, and she felt every part of them cramping up. Perspiration was accenting her face with a wet glow. She licked the beads of sweat from her upper lip as they accumulated and fell. The salty liquid was an ever-present reminder that tears and sweat tasted the same. Nothing is easy.

The class ended with a loud yell of unity that Maggie did not recognize. She heard the footsteps of the sifu approach, but she stayed fixated on the wall. She felt the sifu's gaze and tried her best not to look tired or weak.

"You've been holding that stance for a long time. Don't you want to quit?" Sifu Chang asked as he leaned casually against the wall, with arms folded, studying Maggie's face.

"If I quit, you won't teach me," Maggie said, never looking away from the wall.

"I never said I would or wouldn't teach you, I just told you to stand here."

"If I quit you won't teach me," Maggie repeated quietly, almost to herself.

The sifu walked away and Maggie could hear him making small talk with the mothers of the students and all of the other sounds associated with people leaving the class. She could hear the shuffling of feet and the sounds of the street each time the door opened, as well as feel the sudden rush of cool air, which was a welcome sensation to her overheated body. Once the school fell silent, she could hear the footsteps of the sifu coming back toward her.

"Okay, why don't you stand up and shake out your legs."

"Will you teach me?" Maggie asked, still in her stance with sweat and now tears slowly crawling together down her face.

Sifu Chang put his hand on her shoulder and nodded, "I will teach you. Stand up and shake out your legs."

Maggie stood up slowly, her strained muscles making it almost impossible to straighten her legs. She continued looking down not wanting the sifu to see her face.

"Here, use this," the sifu said, as he handed Maggie a tissue.

"Thank you," Maggie said, as she wiped everything but her eyes, not wanting to admit that she had tears.

"Come on Saturdays to my house. I teach in the garage around back. I can't teach students for free in the school. If the others found out it would ruin my business. There are a few other students that you will meet. Some have no money, and some have other problems, but I teach them. Someone did it for me long ago, and so I do it for them, and I will for you. I will say though. Most students study for a while and then quit. Very few reach a high level. I make no judgments. I have no expectations. I will teach you as long as you learn. Never ask about anyone else though. Quitting is common. You don't need to ask why, everyone knows why: It is hard. If someone stays and becomes a sifu, then it is worth asking them why they stayed. Learn the ways of persistence rather than surrender."

Maggie stood up straight, forgot her previous concerns, looked the sifu in the eye, and saluted. The soft snap of knuckles hitting his fleshy palm reverberated in the empty school as Sifu Chang saluted back. Maggie swept up her backpack and moved as quickly as her strained legs would let her out the door. Sifu Chang watched her from his front window as she jogged back across the street to the school where her brother studied. Sifu walked back to his office and sat at his desk. His eyes wandered to the small dragon paperweight near the edge, and he purposely turned it over.

Rising with a restless feeling, he walked to the now-empty lobby and sat in one of the folding chairs. His mind raced as he studied the unremarkable floor before him. She was the first one to ever pass his test.

"Where are you going?"

Her mother's question made Maggie stop in her tracks. With one hand on the door handle, and the other hiding her borrowed kung fu uniform inside a brown paper bag, she paused, still as a statue. Except for her eyes. Opened wide, they moved nervously about, searching for the source of the voice.

Sam peeked out from behind the thin, peach-colored drape that separated his bedroom—once part of the living room—from the kitchen and the small living area. He shot Maggie a questioning gaze. Maggie returned the look with pleading eyes, compressed lips, and a pantomimed kick of explanation. He gave her a knowing nod.

"Remember, I told you. I have to help Kathy study on Saturdays now," Maggie spoke to her mother, as if a ghostly entity, as she looked up, her eyes searching for the response on the ceiling above.

"Today you're supposed to help Sam at the library and help him write his book report." Her mother's disembodied words hung in the air.

"She already did that, Mom. We finished it early, um, on Friday," Sam said, as he gave Maggie a wink and another nod and let the drape fall back into place before his face.

"Okay, but you be back soon. You and Sam need to help your father unload his car. He works hard for us... Don't be late!"

"I won't. Bye!"

The door was already shut tight, and Maggie had moved fast down the corridor when the muffled sounds of another

33

question from her mother evaporated unanswered in the empty hallway.

She could see that the large garage door was open as she rounded the corner behind the school. The garage was connected to one side of a small, unimpressive duplex. The driveway was at an incline and crossed with cracks, both large and small, from age and use. The gray slope was flanked by big juniper bushes. A lone pile of neatly stacked cinder blocks seemed to be standing guard in a ready position by the walkway. The bushes made it difficult to see into the garage until she was right in front of it. The large, dark opening seemed at once inviting and a little scary. She was there for her lesson, and it was what she wanted, but sometimes there is nothing scarier than getting exactly what you asked for.

With each step she took up the uneven driveway the darkness of the garage brightened. Two heavy bags, hung from the rafters, swaying, as if from recent use. The creaky chains croaked to their pendulated rhythm. She heard murmurs of a conversation. Drawing closer, she saw two boys at the far end of the garage. Both were about her age—one maybe a year older, the other about a year younger.

The older one had on black kung fu pants and a gray sweatshirt with "Kung Fu" handwritten on it in a black marking pen. The younger one wore a proper black kung fu top with frog buttons and gray sweatpants. It looked as though they were sharing one uniform. They stood in an intentional pose with their feet apart and their arms embracing the air. It took Maggie a moment to realize that she had seen Sifu Chang standing that way during one of the many times she walked by his school. Both stopped talking, gave up the stance, and crossed their arms once she arrived at the entrance to the garage.

They stood looking at her in silence. Maggie took the moment to make a quick survey of the interior of the garage. It looked like a makeshift martial arts school complete with a small wall of full-length mirrors and many handmade contraptions lining the opposite side.

She wondered what the devices were for. She saw a dolly with a milk crate full of large rocks sitting on the hauling plate and a piece of rubbery tubing secured with nails to the wall. Leaning against another wall, was a long stick that looked like an upside-down "L" with a lightweight wiffle bat tied to one end and various-sized medicine balls corralled in a corner. Maggie was intrigued to think that in time she would find out what they were all for and learn how to use them.

"I'm here for a lesson," she announced to the two boys, trying to sound as confident as possible. They looked at her, and then at each other with big smiles before they burst out laughing. Maggie's anger grew and her body got hot. The older boy tried to calm the younger one with a slight move of his hand patting the air. He seemed to realize that it was not polite to laugh in people's faces, even if they were a girl.

"We didn't, uh, expect you," he said, as a little snicker escaped.

"Yeah! We weren't expecting you," the younger one contributed with a huge smile and a snort.

Maggie dropped her bag and not attempting to hide her anger, strode aggressively toward the laughing boys.

"I don't know what's so funny, but how about we find out, huh?" she said, challenging them both, and wearing a look of readied combat.

"And that will be the end of that!" Sifu Chang's voice came from above and behind, along with an accompanying hand on her shoulder to gently guide Maggie backward a polite step or two. "We are all students here," he said. "We are all equal."

Glancing back up at him, she saw Sifu Chang raise an eyebrow at the boys, and give a quick nod down toward Maggie.

"We're sorry," said the older boy.

"Yeah, sorry," the younger one agreed without stifling his laughter.

Stepping to the side and looking directly at her, the sifu gave Maggie the same lift of the eyebrow and gestured toward the boys.

"Yes," she said, "but they –"

"No! That is the end of it, and now we move on," sifu said dispassionately, quelling any further discussion or comment with his commanding presence. He moved to his position of authority and stood in front of the three students. "Now that we are warmed up, with that…we can do our morning run. So, you'll start at my word and get back here before the timer goes off."

He twisted the dial on the yellowed plastic egg timer, and then gave the command: "Go!"

The boys sprinted out of the garage as if being shot out of a cannon. Standing alone, facing sifu, Maggie felt her stomach drop at the realization that she would inevitably be last since she didn't know where to run to, and the boys were already gone. She bounced nervously from foot to foot while looking up at her teacher.

Sifu stared back at her.

"What are you waiting for?" Sifu shook the timer in front of her.

"Where do I go?"

"Follow the boys…if you can catch up!"

With sudden realization streaking across her face, Maggie darted out of the garage and down the driveway into the street after the boys.

Sifu leaned his back against the rickety stand that held the wooden weapons as he reached into his pocket for a cigarette and lit it.

The wind blew past her ears and through her hair as Maggie ran at full speed. *Now where the heck did the boys go?* She had to find them, and fast.

There! She spotted them, already way ahead of her. They looked like small dark silhouettes against the bright morning sky. She lengthened her strides and felt herself reeling in the distance between her and the boys with each footfall. The words of Sifu Chang rang in her ears and fueled her effort.

An oppressive heat grew in her chest as she pushed herself harder. She ignored it. Her thin-soled sneakers slapping on the asphalt were the only sounds louder than the wind in her ears. The once small and distant silhouettes grew increasingly larger as she gained on them. She tried to run lighter to quiet her steps, and hopefully hide the sound of her approach. She wanted to speed past them as if they were standing still.

The two boys were at a quick jog and didn't seem to hear Maggie getting closer. Though she was getting tired, she gathered up her energy for a burst of speed and ran between the two boys, almost knocking them over, provoking protests from them both. She continued to run as fast as she could. A smile of satisfaction bubbled up and widened across her face. The protests of the boys had quieted, so she thought that they were likely working hard to keep up.

She looked back to see how far the lead had extended from them and noticed to her horror that she was now suddenly alone. They must have turned down the street she just passed. Being in the lead was great, but it was difficult to keep it if you didn't know where you were going. She doubled back and came around the corner, to see the two boys were not that far ahead. Running faster still, she caught up and stayed close.

The boys looked back with expressions of disbelief at her sudden appearance. Sweat was beginning to run from her head into her eyes, and her feet were aching from the constant pounding on the hard asphalt. She ignored everything though, except the imperative to keep up with the boys.

Rounding a corner brought them onto a short section of Cabrillo Street, one of the busiest thoroughfares in Chinatown. As the trio tightly skirted the corner around a parked car, a noisy series of honking horns erupted, startling Maggie.

The boys seemed oblivious to the frustrated motorists and pulled slightly away from the relentless new girl. While they stayed on the street, Maggie cut between two parked cars and deftly sailed over the curb onto the sidewalk. Although she thought she could avoid the cars and make better time, she immediately regretted her decision. While there were no cars to dodge, there were plenty of other obstacles.

She evaded a woman walking with a small child, and ignoring her angry shouts, she quickly spun away from the near-collision, agile as a gazelle avoiding a predator. Upon coming out of her spin, she had to leap to avoid a man on a bike making deliveries from the Jade Palace restaurant up the street. Her quick jump to the side, out of the bike's trajectory, landed her squarely in the path of two garment racks in front of the Fancy Dance clothing store's sidewalk sale. As she slipped between the two aisles of silk blouses and pretty scarves, some of the garments caught her eye and she made a note to come back to the shop later with her mom.

Passing through the aisle of clothes, she almost ran into a vacant folding chair. She launched herself off the seat with a powerful driving push of her leg, hurdled over the back of the chair, and sailed over the A-frame sign announcing the store's name, artfully hand-painted in pink and green. She slid nimbly between a parking meter and an overflowing garbage can to get back out onto the street. Though greeted with the inevitable honking of the drivers' horns, she was able to make better time and soon began catching up with the boys again.

The last turn brought the trio back to the long alley that led to sifu's garage entrance. Thinking that they had left Maggie far behind, the boys were jogging along at a moderate pace. Maggie saw that the sifu's garage was close, so she dug deep and used the last bit of energy she had left, and sprinted past them, still hoping to be the one to get there first. Streaking by, she awakened the boys to the very real possibility that she could beat them.

Both boys immediately increased their speed and took longer strides, their arms pumping like pistons. Running three abreast, in a tight line, they were so close to each other when they reached the driveway to the garage, that their feet became entangled, and they all three tripped and fell like dominos at their teacher's feet. The tinny bell of the egg timer sounded. The three red-faced students looked up at their teacher's gaze, noticing it registered no emotion.

"All right. Cool down a bit. If you want, you can get a drink of water from the hose, and then let's get to work." Sifu Chang turned off the timer, and without further comment, walked into the dark garage. The trio rose slowly to their feet, helping each other up. They paced in circles until their breath returned, then walked together after their teacher. The door slid down, closing behind them.

"You've probably introduced yourselves already, but just in case, this is our new student," Sifu Chang said, looking at Maggie expectantly.

"Maggie," she stated with a nod to the two boys.

Sifu pointed with an open hand for the older boy to introduce himself.

"Yeah, I'm Dean, and this is my brother —"

"Jerry," the younger boy announced with a grin.

As the realization of the boy's names washed over her, Maggie did her best to hold back her amusement, but a loud snort escaped, and she soon found herself in a fit of nearly uncontrollable laughter.

"Dean and Jerry? For real?" She put a hand over her mouth trying to contain her reaction to the comedic association.

"I guess it could've been worse, huh?" Dean said, looking at the sifu for agreement.

"Yeah, you could've been called Bud and Lou," Maggie blurted out with another loud snort. Sifu Chang shot her a look of disapproval that made her quickly attempt to recover her composure.

"We all have difficulties, don't we?" The teacher stood with his arms folded, his gaze moving evenly over each of them, taking a moment to connect with each student individually. "You're all here for the same reason. At least I hope so, and that is to learn kung fu. For one reason or another, none of which we will ever discuss, you are here instead of in the school."

He looked once more at each student in turn.

"Although you are not studying in the school with the other students, and this setting may seem informal, you must always treat me *and each other* ... with respect. This is not optional. By studying together, you become like family, brothers, and sisters. You must always treat each other as you want to be treated."

The three nodded in agreement.

The sifu leaned in closer to them and pointed his finger to the rafters for emphasis.

"Listen, because without forming a common bond between us, and without seeking to develop our character, we have

40

nothing more here than some interesting punching and kicking combinations. And you can get that anywhere."

Sifu Chang reached past Maggie's head, grabbed a large black kicking pad from the wall, and handed it to Jerry. "You hold it for her, and Maggie will do twenty roundhouse kicks with each leg."

"But you haven't taught me anything yet?" she protested.

"From what I've heard, you know how to kick already." Sifu Chang gave a wink of acknowledgment and walked toward Dean. "When I finish with Dean, I'll come back and work with you two," he said, looking back over his shoulder as he stepped away.

"All right, let's see what you got," Jerry said, as he adjusted his grip and held the bag securely with both hands, and then gave a nod of assent.

Maggie squinted as she focused on the bag, her imaginary opponent. When just about to launch her kick, a grin erupted and spread from her face to Jerry's.

"Go on, kick it!"

She drove hard off the ground and her leg penetrated the bag with a thud. The impact caused Jerry to lose his footing momentarily. He nodded his confirmation of the power even as the second kick was landing.

The classes continued with each one building on their previous lesson. They ran, sparred, and learned techniques, forms, and weapons. Their teacher was always watching with his inscrutable expression, and only occasionally awarding a "good" with a slight nod of his head. For the students, it was the measure of success. Maggie acted like she didn't keep track of the approving gestures, but she remembered every one of them. She won more than she lost when sparring, and her forms were near perfect. Sifu Chang was regularly heard instructing the class, "Watch Maggie." Maggie was often chosen to demonstrate something new and was left in charge of sparring and instruction when the sifu stepped away. To all, it was evident that she was the top student.

"Do they still think you're coming over here on Saturday mornings?" Kathy spoke quietly, one hand shielding the mouthpiece, trying not to draw the attention of her parents watching the evening news in the next room.

"Yeah. I used your idea about tutoring you in math because my mom knows that's my best subject," Maggie spoke in a low tone directly into the phone. Her eyes darted periodically to Sam, and then to the balcony where their mother was barbecuing. Sam had reluctantly agreed to alert Maggie when she came inside by uncrossing his legs. In the tiny apartment, with its thin walls, it was easy to overhear conversations from the neighbors, let alone from someone in the next room.

"I wish I would have picked a better subject to be supposedly helping you with," Kathy declared. "I'm terrible at science. I don't know why I said that. It just kinda came out when your mom asked, ya know? If they ever ask me anything about it, I'm sunk!"

"Are you kidding? You know more than they do. They'll never know. Just use big words and a lot of scientific terms like *Newton's theory* and *thermodynamics*, and they'll be impressed." Maggie said confidently.

"I don't know, your mom's pretty smart. The last time I was over there, she asked about my dad's job, right? Well, he said that he ran into her on his route. What are the chances of that? I think she checks things out, ya know?"

"Well, maybe…Just keep the same story though, unless I say something…" Maggie stopped talking as she sometimes did when she felt an awkward moment coming on. When speaking to Kathy, she often became overwhelmed with feelings for her, and though she thought that Kathy felt the same, she was too uncomfortable to say anything, and so kept dancing around her emotions. It seemed to always be between them: unspoken but understood. The silence hung in the air for a few beats until Kathy spoke.

"All this crisscross stuff, just to cover our tracks, so you can become a kung fu master, and I can get out to see you when you're not...becoming a kung fu master. It's kinda wild." Kathy's words filled the void as Maggie stared off into the soft light of the shaded bulbs in the living room above Sam's head. "Still there? Kathy questioned. What are you doing? Thinking about everything? Kung fu stuff?"

"I guess, I was just daydreaming... I wanted to, ya know...Thank you for everything..." Maggie nervously wrapped the coiled phone cord around her fingers multiple times.

"It's fine, ya know? Besides, it's a gas being part of your secret life. You're like a girl James Bond or something...A *Chinese* girl James Bond...Who is secretly learning kung fu!" Kathy laughed, and she could hear Maggie laugh as loudly as she did.

"It's crazy, huh? I don't know why I've got to sneak around. Why can't I just go do it? I'm as good as anyone else, right?" Maggie uncoiled the phone cord and leaned her head against the wall.

"Better."

"Thanks." Maggie let Kathy's words soak in and was lost in the moment until she was startled back to reality when she noticed Sam uncrossing his legs in an overly dramatic fashion that would make Charlie Chaplin proud. "I gotta go. See you tomorrow though, okay? Same place?"

43

"Yeah, I'll be behind a newspaper with two eyeholes cut out."

Both girls laughed. Maggie hung up the phone quietly. She passed her hand over the receiver slowly one time, gently, as if petting a kitten.

The garage door was closed when she arrived, so she went around to the pedestrian door on the side to enter. The space was dark, except for the parallelogram created by the natural light through the window as it blazed brightly onto the cement floor. The dust floated in the light as if trapped like particles in space. It felt so different without Sifu Chang or the others present. It felt like she didn't belong there, alone. As if it should always and only ever be used as a shared space. She thought about waiting outside, but Dean and Jerry always waited inside, so why not her? Kathy called it "the girl thing," and reasoned that being held to a different standard by others inevitably led to doing it to yourself.

It was strange that Dean and Jerry weren't there yet. They lived close by, and ever since she started training with Sifu Chang, they had always arrived first. She took the small bag of pork buns she had picked up on the way over and set it next to the box with the wooden weapons. The four of them could eat them after class.

Out of boredom, she gave a light punch to the heavy bag. It quickly rocked back and forth, and the creaky sound was at first rapid and loud, then slowed down considerably, and soon the lone groan of the straining anchor bolt was the only sound in the garage. The light sound of footsteps approaching outside signaled someone drawing near. She decided to duck down behind the kicking pads piled next to the side entrance, and then jump out to scare Jerry. He said he hated it, but he always laughed. When the door opened, Maggie jumped out but was surprised to see the sifu rather than Jerry, and the instructor was not startled at all.

"Sorry, I thought you were Jerry or Dean."

"I'm sorry to disappoint you." The teacher let a slight smile cross his lips as he walked past and put his keys on a hook by the door.

"Oh, I'm not disappointed. I'll just have to wait until they show up, and then I'll get 'em!"

"Well, let's get started…" Sifu Chang took off his sweater and headed to open the garage door to let in the light and a breeze of fresh air.

"Aren't we going to wait for them?"

"No, I don't believe they're coming." The sifu sat down to change into his running shoes.

"Why not? Why aren't they coming?"

"I don't know. They haven't answered any of my calls, they didn't come by on Friday, and they're not here today. It's best to just move on." He shrugged his shoulders and continued putting on his shoes.

"I can run to their house and ask them what's going on. They showed me where they live," Maggie said earnestly.

"If someone is no longer around, regardless of what anyone says—especially that person—it means they quit. It's very simple. Quitting is common. Very, very common. You don't need to ask why. Everyone knows why; this is hard." Sifu Chang finished working on his shoes and then rose and stood there looking out the open door for a moment. He stood as if looking into an impenetrable void, and then he spoke.

"Oh, they may say that I'm holding them back, or they're just too busy these days, or they are not progressing as fast as they think they should, or give you one of a hundred other reasons why they quit. It's not even worth asking them why."

He turned to look at her and raised an eyebrow as if to emphasize his point. Maggie listened carefully.

"But if someone stays," he went on, "stays and becomes a sifu, then it is very worthwhile to ask them why they continued. What kept them going? Why didn't they quit? What made them different from the many that do?"

She nodded thoughtfully.

"I know it may sound tough to you now, but this is important, Maggie. Learning the ways of persistence rather than the ways of surrender is rare indeed."

She let a moment pass before speaking.

"Of all the students you've had," she asked, looking up into his eyes, "which one was the best?"

He laughed a little.

"My best student? My best student is one that didn't quit."

Sifu Chang jumped to his feet, pulled on his sweatshirt, and jogged down the driveway. Maggie waited a moment as it all sank in, and then she ran after him. She caught up but didn't pass him. She ran beside him the entire way.

It was a particularly cold and rainy Saturday, cold enough for Maggie to have put on her wool jacket before she ventured out. Underneath her gray umbrella, she was warm and dry, and she tried to keep her feet from getting wet. Once she turned down the alley and away from the bustling Chinatown business district, the broken ruins of old sidewalks stretched out before her. Random attempts to lay a new walkway, attempts that had remained unfinished, appeared and disappeared under her feet as she walked. Downtown Chinatown was like a movie set with its elaborate facade of bright neon lights, ornamental pagodas, and dramatic sculptures of dragons and lions, all masking shadowy back alleys, decrepit storefronts, and overgrown lots. The girl with the gray umbrella left the movie set world behind and walked into the gritty real world that she knew best.

The rain increased, and the downpour produced puddles everywhere, as water ran from small tributaries flowing down narrow side streets. Maggie delicately negotiated a path through broken chunks of asphalt and cement surrounded by pools of muddy water. She did her best to keep her shoes and socks from getting wet as she adroitly sidestepped, jumped, and skipped over the obstacles.

Her decision to incorporate a little martial arts practice into her journey helped to liven things up until she tried to execute a jumping roundhouse kick and it nearly ended in a messy disaster. Her legs catapulted her upward all right, but when she landed on a slick, oily, mini peninsula of asphalt, she lost her footing and almost fell on her behind. Trying to regain her balance, she dropped her umbrella and ended up looking like an imperiled cartoon character, as she waved her arms in big circles. Teetering, mouth agape and eyes wide, she finally centered herself and stood up straight again.

Retrieving the discarded umbrella, she looked around to see if anyone was watching. The idea of having to explain to Sifu Chang and Mike, the new kid, that she fell attempting a jumping kick in the rain was suddenly sobering. She decided to keep the journey to the garage more sedate, foregoing all the grand prospects of excitement, for the sake of keeping as dry as possible. Too late for her shoes though.

Walking up sifu's driveway, head down, watching her shoes squish through the rain-soaked gravel, mud, and grass, it was not until her hand was grasping the door handle that she saw the note hanging by a piece of clear tape.

At first, Maggie felt a twinge of disappointment, imagining that the new kid, Mike, leaving only a goodbye note in his wake, had already quit after just two weeks. But as she peered at the message, she saw that she was mistaken. It wasn't from Mike. The note was penned in her teacher's spiky handwriting, and though droplets left dark spots on the paper, it was still legible.

Students,
No lesson today.
I will be unavailable for a few days.
Sifu

While she was relieved Mike wasn't quitting, the message was disheartening. She always looked forward to her Saturday class. She read the note three times and stared at it for a while as if the words would change somehow. *No lesson today.*

They didn't change, and by the end of the third reading, she felt that something wasn't right. Not only had she never known Sifu Chang to cancel class, but she also couldn't imagine him canceling at the last minute. He kept to his schedule like clockwork. He always preached the value of consistency. It had to be something very important to make him cancel on such short notice.

Maggie peered into the garage. Though she knew no one was inside and there wasn't some secret class going on without her, she still felt the need to look and even be sly about it. Maybe there was a clue inside? She was good at surreptitious peeking, but the garage window was too high. She needed something to stand on.

Propping her umbrella under the eave, Maggie hurried over to the stack of cinder blocks near the garage door. Drops of rain hit her face and head sporadically, and then more consistently, as she tried to gain purchase on a slick block near the top with her small, thin fingers. She carefully pulled it from the top of the stack, but it was heavier than she realized. As it came away free, she lost her grip, and the block crashed to the ground.

"Crap!"

She tried to pick up the block again. Her hair and clothes were rain-soaked. With the block held in a close embrace, she walked, carefully, taking small steps, and then put it down gently close to the wall. Stepping, gingerly, with cold feet inside of rain-soggy shoes, she looked inside. *Geez, good thing this wasn't going to be on a test!*

Leaning close to the window, she peered into the dark garage and spotted a pile of broken wood in the middle of the floor.

The handle of one of sifu's long staves lay on top. It looked to have been snapped in half. The thickly lacquered black shaft was unmarked, but it was no longer in one piece.

She scanned carefully for anything else she could recognize. The trophy display shelf had been broken up and the trophies, covered in dust, along with other broken items, peeked out from the heap. A lone golden kicking-man statue, broken off its tall pedestal, was lying on its side near the pile.

She tried to make some sense of what she saw. Someone had smashed everything up and then put it in a neat pile. Had there been something that caused some fit of anger? She had never seen Sifu Chang out of control, but she supposed like anyone, he had his limits. Or did someone jealous of all his trophies and his good name, enter, and destroy the mementos and equipment in his garage? She touched her stomach as, for some reason, an uneasy feeling started to grow inside her.

She hopped down from the cinderblock and started for home. The rain pattered on the gray umbrella that she continued to use even though she couldn't possibly get any wetter than she already was.

As she walked, listening to her footsteps and steady breathing, louder under the umbrella, the image of the pile of broken things in Sifu Chang's garage stopped her in her tracks. The broken things she saw were personal. They were symbols of what he spent his time doing. Though she couldn't explain why, for some reason, she didn't think anyone had broken in and destroyed them.

She turned back and walked purposefully toward the school, crossing the backlot parking area, and passing through the alley into the street. The noise of the city filled her ears. Car horns, motorcycles, sirens, music from a restaurant patio, and loud conversations of passersby. She sighed, and then took a deep breath. As she joined the flow of the sidewalk, her mind suddenly shifted to something that Sifu Chang always said at the end of each lesson: *Take your kung fu with you. Don't leave it here!* Its meaning, though she had always associated with martial arts, seemed more applicable now: take the confidence, skills, and abilities that you acquire through training with you everywhere. Don't separate yourself into two different people, one who can do amazing things in school, but can't apply them in ordinary life. Be unified. Be one.

She approached the large front window of the school. *Chang's Kung Fu* was painted across the middle of the glass, in gold block lettering with black trim. The black shadowing gave the gold letters a three-dimensional look. She held the umbrella against the gray sky as she peered into the sifu's inner sanctum.

The interior was neat and orderly. All of Sifu Chang's things were intact, at least as far as she could tell from her vantage point of the sidewalk, as she gazed into the darkened school. It was still, and devoid of any sign of life, with one exception, the sifu's office door was open, and the desk lamp was on. *Was he inside?*

She checked the front door. Locked. Her mind spun trying to fathom the intentions and thoughts of her teacher, but she knew it was pointless. She wondered what had happened to make him leave so unexpectedly. If she could —

"Sifu gone today!" a loud voice proclaimed behind her. Startled, Maggie jumped, then whirled around to face the speaker. The owner of the produce store next door peered at her from where he stood next to his large wooden bins of fruits and vegetables.

"Do you know where he went?"

"Yes," the grocer said, nodding solemnly, as he placed an orange on the tiptop of the citrus pyramid he had completed. He admired his work, then grabbed a small empty box from the ground and turned to walk back into the store. Maggie followed him in. A giant white banner inside proclaimed: *Fresh Produce Arrives Daily!* The smell of citrus fruits perfumed the air

"Where did Sifu Chang go? Do you know if he's all right?" She spoke to the grocer's back as she pursued him to the counter. He lifted the hinged horizontal door of the countertop, slipped beneath it, and let it fall with a loud bang. A customer with a basketful of artichokes began speaking to the grocer curtly in Mandarin. In response, the grocer shook his head, then shrugged his shoulders, and pointed back to the far corner of his store. As the man turned toward the grocer's directive, the grocer turned his attention back to Maggie.

"Chang go to foonrul."

"Foonrul?"

"Yeah, lef' while 'go. To foonrul. Then bury in graveyard."

"Oh, funeral…"

"Yes, what I said: foonrul! Graveyard in T.P. Car come by and pick him up." The grocer's explanation complete, he came out from behind the counter, hoisted a heavy-looking box of potatoes with ease, and carried it toward the square crate that had been converted into a display with more potatoes piled high. Maggie followed him and watched him stack the potatoes the same way he had the oranges.

"Did he say who, uh, died?"

"Chang never talk much, you know? Talk less today." The grocer turned away from Maggie and returned to the counter. She exited the store as a cold chill crawled up her spine. Once out on the street, she looked for the nearest bus stop where she could catch the number 7 bus to take her to Terre Promise.

The bus stopped and its loud, percussive brakes shocked Maggie out of the daydream that she had been entertaining herself with while leaning under the covered bus stop. She snapped to attention. Once the squeaky doors opened, she entered following an elderly woman also waiting to take the number 7 bus on that wet day. Neither of them would have any problem finding a place to sit as rows of empty benches waited expectantly.

"Does this bus go to the graveyard?"

"Yes," the bus driver confirmed.

The ride to Terre Promise was going to take a little while. Maggie leaned back in her seat. The hard plastic wasn't comfortable, but that was a good thing. The well-heated bus felt a bit too warm and the hard seat would keep her from being lulled to sleep and missing her stop. She knew where the cemetery was. The whole family had gone there to bury Grandma the year before.

Her impending arrival made her question even more whether she should be going there at all. *Would Sifu Chang be mad at her?* Outside of martial arts class, she didn't know much about her teacher. She assumed the house attached to the garage was where he lived, but she didn't ask, and he never volunteered any information about his personal life.

She asked him once if he had any kids, and he told her that he had a whole school full of kids. Something seemed odd about the way he answered. He was evading the question, hiding something. She thought about asking again, just to clarify that she wanted to know if he had children of his own. But then she realized his tone of voice probably meant he wasn't interested in responding to any more questions.

Once, she had noticed a pair of pink slippers with white pom poms on the step from the garage into the house. When Sifu Chang saw her staring at them, he casually picked them up, opened the door to the house, and tossed them inside without saying a word.

The longer she studied with the sifu, the more she wanted to know about him. More than anyone else, he was helping her. She was grateful and wanted to show him her concern.

As she bounced softly in her seat, she thought of an incident that had happened a while ago. One day, she had gone with her mother to help carry bags of groceries and baby clothes to her mother's friend Vi, who had a new baby. Her mother told her that Vi's husband had been laid off from his job at the factory. When they arrived at the apartment, her mother quietly placed the bags in front of the door and then turned to leave. Mother gestured with a finger to her pursed lips for Maggie to be quiet and follow her back to the street.

Confused, Maggie asked her why they didn't go inside and visit Vi and see her baby. "Vi's too proud. She'd never ask for help," her mother said. "It's important to respect her dignity."

The scenery from the bus's large front window gradually changed from the Chinese themes of Chinatown to the boring architecture of Terre Promise, where all the signs were in

English only. The buildings, stores, and homes of Terre Promise displayed an approach toward modernity in an unregal and mundane past.

It made Maggie a bit uneasy to go so far away from Chinatown, especially realizing that no one knew where she was. Her mother would be beyond furious if she ever found out where she went. But then again, she would be furious about most things Maggie did, if she ever knew. That was the key then—she must never find out.

As the bus got closer, Maggie saw more open spaces, fewer buildings, and more grass, and trees. The landscape had changed. It was like an oasis of green in the middle of all the urban gray. The bus slowed and then stopped with an abrupt jerk. Outside, an expanse of stone monuments, evenly spaced, hugged the contours of the terrain. Patches of color—the reds, yellows, whites, and blues of memorial flowers—sporadically decorated the austere scene.

"This is your stop, little girl," the driver said, looking back at her in his large mirror. He grabbed a clipboard and with his head down began writing something. She nodded assent, and rose, remembering not to leave her umbrella behind. As she walked past the driver, she nodded again, and he nodded back and went back to his writing.

She held onto the handrail and stepped down carefully. Her feet landed on the wet concrete sidewalk, and the door closed behind her with a few squeaks and a clumpy thud. The engine roared to life and the bus rolled away. A dark exhaust cloud rose and slowly dissolved in the moist air.

Maggie stood alone with her umbrella. The rain had almost ceased, and only a slight mist and an occasional sprinkle remained. Keeping her umbrella closed, she held it across her body, almost unconsciously gripping it the same way she held a broadsword from the sifu's garage.

She had dried off some during the long, warm bus ride, and though a little damp, she didn't feel nearly as wet as before. The sun was now making an effort to break through the clouds. The odd mixture of soft golden light and misty air gave the cemetery an enchanted, dreamlike, quality. She surveyed the manicured field of mortality markers before her and spotted the only gathering of mourners visible atop a small hill. She set out on the path that led up to where they stood.

As she approached the modest gathering, she saw Sifu Chang, along with a few other people that she didn't recognize. He was wearing a dark suit and stood with his head bowed. She approached respectfully and took a place at the back of the group. She waited, head bowed, for the conclusion of the burial service. After a collective murmur, the group dispersed and meandered back down the hill. Sifu Chang remained, alone and motionless, his head still gazing as if at a mystery just before his feet.

Moving quietly toward him, she reached out and took his hand. He glanced down at her, his expression solemn, his eyes red-rimmed, and he gave her a nod before turning his gaze back to the gravesite. They both stood looking at the grave, holding hands, for some time before Maggie gently led him away, down the hill, and back toward the waiting car.

Maggie and Sifu Chang rode in silence in the back seat, still holding hands until the car arrived at his home and dropped them both off there. The sifu patted her hand softly, nodded slightly, and mouthed the words *thank you* to her, then disappeared into the house.

For the next two days, Maggie skipped lunch, and combined with her saved allowance, brought her teacher takeout from the Phoenix Garden restaurant up the street. Each time Sifu Chang received the meal that she brought, he only mouthed words of thanks. It was as if grief had temporarily stolen his voice and the magic from his eyes. She knew it would return. She hoped it would.

Maggie kept her silence about the events of the day and never repeated her discovery of the destruction piled inside the garage, which she assumed was from a fit of rage, or the graveside meeting. She kept the entire day's events in strict confidence. She knew he would want it that way.

"Move your head! Move it out of the way!" Sifu Chang's voice boomed at Maggie, as she squared off with Phil, one of the new students, as they sparred in the dusty garage.

The sifu shook his head. He had been telling her the same thing over and over. Maggie wasn't heeding his advice, she was trying to do things her way, and it wasn't going well.

Phil was a larger boy and had done some boxing at the YMCA. The one thing he could do was throw a jab, and he did it very well. Maggie was having trouble moving away from his punches. She got caught by his gloved left hand under her right eye. It made her stagger a bit. To her teacher's experienced gaze, it looked like her reaction was more from surprise than from the impact of his blow. Maggie, he knew, was not used to being dominated in a fight. She was having an emotional crisis; something she hadn't dealt with before.

They circled each other in low fighting stances. She kept wanting to square off with him, but she was having difficulty adjusting to Phil's reach.

"Slip underneath him. Use your size!" her teacher shouted. He could feel his neck flex and strain, as his instructions flew to Maggie with conviction only to bounce off her ego and fall, unused, to the ground.

"Kick low!" Sifu Chang watched dutifully for any attempt from Maggie. "Punch high!" Out of frustration, the sifu threw down the towel he had been clutching, and yelled, "Take out the legs!"

Maggie was determined to do it her way. Her gaze was locked on Phil. She made half-hearted attempts upon hearing her teacher's pleas, to do what he said, but although she could hear him, she wasn't really listening. And between hearing and listening, there was a difference. She was trying to meet force with force, which was a bad idea with a stronger opponent. She was fighting with emotion, losing her cool, rather than being tactical. That was unlike Maggie.

"Get close or get out of the way! You read Sun Tzu, didn't you? Evade! Duck! Don't be there. Move!" He was giving more coaching to Maggie than to Phil and he felt a bit guilty about it. Phil was new, and it probably seemed unfair to him. He would have to talk to him about it later.

More unanswered punches scored on Maggie's pouty face. She was used to being the best student, adapting quickly, and winning. This time, her opponent was larger than she and he was using skills that she was not used to countering. Phil didn't know very much about kung fu or Maggie, for that matter, except what he'd learned over the past couple of weeks. He was a worthy and unorthodox opponent for testing her skill.

It was the perfect opportunity for the sifu to find out what was really inside Maggie's head, and more importantly, what was in her heart. What would she do when things got tough? It was his opportunity to see her true character when she was in a situation where her best wasn't good enough. How would she accept failure and defeat? He let out a deep breath, crossed his arms, and let the match go on.

Sifu Chang watched as she was crowded by Phil and unable to counter with a strike of her own. The boy was a smart tactician. He had stuffed her snap kick and crescent kick by moving closer when she threw them. She was getting frustrated and began telegraphing her strikes. She then tried to move back to throw a big roundhouse kick. She did and it landed squarely. Phil winced from the pain, but it didn't stop him. He threw another powerful jab. Maggie stepped back to move away from Phil's punch. It was the wrong move. Phil took advantage of the distance to throw a roundhouse kick of his own. He followed it up with a big right hand that sent Maggie hard to the floor.

She stayed down. Normally, Maggie would have popped right up, but it seemed to be a few moments too long this time. Sifu Chang and Phil exchanged looks of concern. The teacher nodded to Phil, and the boy stepped forward and offered his hand to Maggie to help her up.

"I'm sorry," Phil said, looking down. His gesture was sincere. "I didn't mean to hit you so hard."

Maggie swatted his hand away without looking at him.

"All right, that's enough. Phil, go get some water. Let's all cool off." Sifu Chang looked at the boy, and with a meaningful gaze, quickly tilted his head toward the door. Phil took the hint and left the sifu alone with Maggie. Walking over to where she sat on the dusty floor, Sifu Chang lowered himself down on his haunches, balancing himself nimbly on the balls of his feet, with his hands hanging loosely over his knees.

"Hey, don't take it out on him. You should have done what I told you and moved your head."

"I did, didn't I?" Maggie's tone expressed her frustration. She took her hair out of her ponytail, shaking it out and letting it fall loosely to her shoulders.

"Not if you got knocked on your behind, you didn't." The teacher reached out his hand as he stood up. "Come on, it's no good down there. You get knocked down; you get back up again. It's as simple as that."

Sifu Chang kept his hand extended, but Maggie remained on the floor. Her posture was round, her body folded over with her head resting on her knees. Hair covered her face.

"You make it sound so easy," she said, speaking to her knees without looking at her teacher.

"I didn't say it was easy, but it is simple, there's a difference."

A beat of silence came and went before he decided it was the time to try to speak some wisdom to his defeated student, even though he thought, like most, she might be reluctant to take it.

"Sometimes you lose, Maggie. That's just the way it is. The only people who win all the time are liars. It's simple. Not easy. Don't confuse the two. Most people do, and that's the problem. If you want to be good, you put in the time, the effort, and you never give up, no matter what happens along the way. That's it." His hands parted for emphasis, like an umpire announcing a runner as safe.

She remained still as if in rapt attention with her knees.

"There's nothing mystical about it," he went on, "and there are no secrets to doing it. It requires commitment, dedication, and sincere effort…the rarest of all qualities. It is easier to hold a dragon's tail than to find a person with these traits, Maggie."

Her reddened eyes reflected the light as she barely turned her head and glanced up at him.

"Let's think about your parents for a moment. They provide for you because they know that they must, but it's not easy for them. Your father works long hours to support his family, works hard. When he gets up in the morning, it's a simple choice for him, because he's a good man. Some might say, *Forget it, I'll gamble today, or drink away my family's rent money*. And some do. You are lucky to have good parents."

She nodded.

"What about you now, Maggie? What will you do? Are you going to continue only as long as you win? When it's easy for you? Or are you going to continue after this loss, knowing it will be one of many to come, even though it would be easier for you to quit?"

Maggie took a breath, stood up, and pushed the hair back from her face. Her red-rimmed, glassy eyes told the tale that she was ashamed to admit. She brushed the dust from her uniform and took another breath as she looked at her teacher. The most humble expression he had ever seen appeared on her face. He gave her a slight smile.

"It is in the difficult times when we see ourselves most clearly. Didn't Sun Tzu counsel you to know yourself? Maybe you should be glad for this opportunity to get to know yourself better."

She gave him a reluctant smile.

"Stand right there. I want to show you something."

He walked over to a box on his workbench and retrieved a stack of the white postcard-size permission forms that parents had signed so that their children could study with him. He had written the word *quit* across each form in red ink.

"Look at all these forms."

Sifu pointed with his thumb, in hitchhiker fashion, toward the large garage window. Outside Phil could be seen leaning with his back against the wall drinking water from a white foam cup.

"I don't know what will happen with Phil," he went on. "He may stay. He may go. He may be the next kung fu movie star, for all I know."

He looked at Maggie to gauge her reaction to his words. Then he shrugged.

"Or he may quit tomorrow, and his mom will call me and tell me he feels *differently* now. Maggie, what are you going to choose?"

Sifu Chang walked back over to his workbench, laid the quitter cards down, pulled out the stool, and sat on it. The protesting squeaks rang out as the only sound in the quiet garage. He folded his arms and looked squarely at his student.

"I was just...surprised," she began, "that I couldn't do *anything* to him. He was stronger than me. Faster. He was using that boxing stuff mixed in with...our stuff."

Maggie finished her statement, at first folding her arms like her teacher did but then letting them fall. She held her wrist with her hand as she shifted her weight back and forth and alternated between looking up at the ceiling to down at the floor.

"Yes, he has had a little training somewhere else. That's fine. He will use what he likes and ignore the rest. We all do that. Even you. Someday you will learn other arts, at least I hope you do, and you will take from them what you like, creating an arsenal of motion that is uniquely yours."

Sifu Chang saw that the last tears were still wet under her eyes. He shifted on his stool, grabbed a tissue, and handed it to her. She quickly took it from his hand and dabbed at her eyes, then turned her face toward the window. Sifu watched as Maggie looked at Phil, who was by then looking their way. She waved to him. He waved back and smiled. It was an awkward and soundless exchange through the window.

The sifu got off his stool, gathered up the permission slips, and stacking them neatly, placed them back in the small box by his hanging tools. He then stood next to Maggie at the window. They both looked out into the afternoon sun.

"I know it won't be easy, but I don't want to quit," Maggie stated, not taking her gaze off the bright day outside.

Sifu was glad about her decision, but he knew that her words stood as a thin shield of protection around her. He hoped the shield would hold firm when the velvety seduction of surrender next tempted her.

"I've never lost a student because of an injury," he said, looking at her, sternly, "but a silky excuse wrapped in soft words will stop you quicker than any punch or kick."

Sifu Chang's words were rarely so pointed in their candor, and he caught, even himself, off-guard. As he looked down at Maggie, the one thing that he believed was that she was different. She was the one out of a hundred students who would go all the way. Still, he felt it important to make sure there were no fissures in her will.

"If you should decide to quit at some point, Maggie, say the word. Say it out loud. Don't hide from it. I will respect you more, and you will gain something at least by being honest with yourself."

He waited a moment and watched her reaction closely. She said nothing, but she nodded her agreement and her understanding as she looked up at him. Looking into her eyes, The sifu knew that he could trust her.

Feeling that he understood Maggie's determination, skills, and character, Sifu Chang realized that he was free to teach Maggie everything he knew. And that included the very unusual, unorthodox, and deadly, Mongoose style. It was rare. Mythical. Some things about it were even heretical to kung fu in terms of how the body's energy and power were used.

But for Maggie, he knew it would be ideal, as it especially suited a smaller person against a larger one, both in tactic and technique. Inevitably, all of Maggie's opponents would be bigger than her, so it made sense for her to learn it. It would make her unique. Powerful. And at that point, he was sure she had the strength of character to deal with such power. She made a decision that day, and so did he.

He had never taught it to anyone else. As they both gazed out the window to the bright day, Sifu Chang gave a light tap of his palm on her shoulder and a slight nod of his head toward the sun.

Chinatown, 1970

The air in the garage was thick with heat and sweat. The breeze from the open side door provided only occasional relief as the cooler air teased Sifu Chang's sweaty skin. Sparring with Maggie was proving to be a real challenge. She was keeping up well with the relentless strikes hurtling toward her. Hard fists and quick feet fired at her in a chaotic barrage. The sifu kept the pressure on. He wanted Maggie to react and not think. To achieve a detached calm. Zen. No-mind.

Sifu Chang pressed his attack, trying to disrupt Maggie's concentration with feints, jabs, and thrusting kicks. Maggie wore an expression of serene concentration. She appeared calm and focused. Aggressive but not angry. She looked to be in control of her emotions. She was blocking and evading her teacher's flurry of fast kicks and punches even as they came within inches of hitting their intended targets. Though Sifu Chang was close enough to touch her, he couldn't. Maggie was quick, cagey, and seemed to know when and where the next strike would come at her. She moved like a person possessed by the beast's spirit.

With an elastic elongation of her body, Maggie rolled away from punches, leaning back, yet still standing, as if suspended by invisible wires. She dropped under kicks so quickly, it was as if she disappeared. Sifu Chang knew that to Maggie, it was as if he were attacking in slow motion.

In the climax of their violent ballet, the sifu quickly faked low with a left punch and then threw a right. Maggie parried the punch, leaned back, and rolled her head and shoulders away. The evasion threw her teacher's attack off balance. His pride in his student was intense as she took advantage of the opportunity and moved into the tricky Mongoose roll.

Maggie spun behind her teacher and rolled across his back. It was a classic technique of the Mongoose style she had studied. The roll continued until Sifu Chang felt a dull pain in the back of his legs as Maggie corkscrewed her body downward and let her iron-like arm spin like a ball and chain into the back of his knees. The strike caused her teacher's legs to buckle, and he fell to the ground.

Her skill was uniquely developed. Maggie had taken the technique farther than what was taught. Her understanding of the Mongoose seemed instinctive. The fight was not over. Sifu Chang rose quickly, regained his balance, and then began to pressure her as before. Would she make a mistake? Or could she do it again?

In the small garage, Maggie had to economize her motion and change direction often or risk running into a wall, workbench, stool, or other obstacles. Knowing this, Sifu Chang used his larger size and tried to close off the space. Cutting off the ring, as boxers say. He kept attacking forward, keeping her from settling into any kind of set position. She had to move or be hit.

He suspected that Maggie was waiting for her next opportunity to get behind him in this game of cat and mouse, and then, by accident, it finally came. He jabbed hard and quickly with a left punch and extended his arm fully. His fist was less than an inch from her cheek.

She again parried the punch, rolled her body backward as if blessed with an elastic spine and then evasively stepped to the side. She used the rolling backward motion as a springboard to roll across the sifu's back again, landing on her feet, Maggie maneuvered into a striking position. She fired a short punch. Sifu Chang felt its biting impact to his ribs, and the force of the strike propelled him off center, making him lose his balance. Careening out of control, he could do nothing but try to avoid smashing headlong into a line of boxes stacked along the wall. His body landed with a crash and then a thud.

"Oh, Sifu! Are you okay?" Maggie asked, panting between her words as sweat rolled off her nose and drops landed at her feet.

"Yeah," he said, rubbing his head. "I'd say you've got the mongoose roll down pretty well since it worked twice."

Maggie rushed over to help her teacher up. He rose and began dusting himself off. Trying to help, Maggie left muddy handprints on his arm as her sweaty palms met the dirt.

"Do you think I'm ready now?" Maggie asked the air, not looking directly at him.

"Ready for what?" Sifu Chang wore a blank expression, acting as if he didn't know what she meant.

"The test!" she said exasperated.

She kept to herself the idea of opening a school of her own. It was a far-off idea, and possibly even dangerous, but one that she hoped to achieve someday. If she was good enough to be one of them, a teacher, they had to let her teach, didn't they? She returned to the thought often, and it was no small reason for her recent anxiety about nearing her most important test.

"How do you feel about it?"

"Ready." She responded, without a shred of doubt as she quickly tugged at her shirt to cool off her body.

"You know, Maggie, it won't be just about demonstrating pretty forms. This is big. You will have to show applications of techniques, combinations, principles of power, and you'll have to spar with one of them or a student of their choosing, maybe two…and because you're the first girl—"

The teacher saw the peeved look on Maggie's face and then quickly added, "I mean the first young lady to go for a rank this high… Well, you're the first one that I know of, anyway. I think because of that they may be a little harder on you."

Letting the sweat roll down his face, and only wiping it away when he felt it close to his eyes, Sifu Chang leaned against the open doorway to the garage. Her question still hung in the air, unanswered. He lit a cigarette and took a long drag. He slowly blew out a cloud of smoke. Removing the cigarette from his mouth and letting it dangle from his right hand, he looked over at Maggie. After a moment of silence and contemplation, he declared, "You're ready."

She let out a big sigh of relief that sounded as if she had been holding it in for far too long. The sifu watched her trying to contain her smile as she got ready to leave, acting as if his statement didn't carry the weight that they both knew it did. She removed her uniform top, pulled a black sweatshirt over the sweaty undershirt, then quickly pulled her hair back into a slick ponytail, securing it with a rubber band.

Appearing to study the cracks on the garage floor, she wandered closer to the open side door where Sifu Chang was still leaning on the doorway holding the cigarette. She looked like she was working up to something.

"I'm ready," she stated. Confirming it to herself as much as to him. "You know…I want to be like you, someday." She looked down as her fingers played with an extra rubber band, rolling, and stretching it determinedly. "I want to mean as much to someone as you've meant to me."

Silent, Sifu Chang took another long drag. The words clung relentlessly to the thick atmosphere. He thought about what they meant but only replied with a slight nod.

Maggie nodded back with a humble smile, then left.

He watched her until she disappeared, and then looked at his watch. He threw the cigarette on the ground, twisted it out gently with his foot, and shut the door. He went inside to make the call to set the date for the test.

Mr. Vargas' American History class was always a snooze-fest, but Kathy was in the same class, and that made it bearable for Maggie. They had grown close, closer than friends, since that first day so long ago. They often went shopping — really just window shopping — downtown on Saturday afternoons. That usually led to sleepovers, and discussions about life, the world, or just how to turn a thrift store blouse and scarf into an Audrey Hepburn look.

It was hard not to daydream about those fun times while Mr. Vargas was lecturing, especially given his odd speech pattern of strange pauses, particularly when the classroom became a bit too warm like today. On the spring days that skirted the cusp of summer, when the end of school was in the air, the class could become very warm and stuffy. The afternoon sun was shining through the clouded glass of the scuffed louvered windows, and the warm air didn't move.

An unexpected drop of sweat trickled from under Maggie's arm, coolly down her side, and suddenly she was alert. As she looked around the class, she saw the occasional head jerk, and sleepy eyes, and realized that the entire class felt the same way.

Mr. Vargas was writing out the key points of the causes of World War II on the chalkboard. His odd handwriting could be easily mistaken for Cyrillic script. Note-taking was impossible until he explained what he wrote.

Maggie glanced over at Kathy for her reaction to the scrawled list. Stifling a giggle, Kathy rolled her eyes up in her head, making a symbolic suicidal gesture with her hand holding an invisible rope, her head tilted sideways, eyes crossed, and her tongue sticking out of the edge of her mouth for the full effect.

Maggie giggled softly into her hand, hoping Mr. Vargas wouldn't hear her as he moved toward her desk in the back of the room. He was walking backward, arms folded, down the center aisle. As he walked, he twisted his body as if hugging himself in his olive-drab cardigan. He walked toward her desk in his strange, exaggerated gate, as he eyed his handiwork on the board through his wire-rimmed glasses.

"So, if there is one thing…that we have learned…from our text…about the Axis powers… it is that…it was an alliance…of convenience…Had they won the war…they would likely… have… turned…on each other...There is no honor…among… thieves. Don't you agree, Maggie? Mr. Vargas' gaze turned toward her.

"Uh, hmm, uh, so, okay, well, not entirely," Maggie stammered her response, surprised by the question. She cursed herself for not being ready since she had seen him moving toward her. Never underestimate your opponent.

"Really? Do…you think… that the… Axis powers were… honorable? I'm assuming…you…read…the…text?"

"No…I mean, yes. I read the text… But, no they, the Axis powers that is, entered into a convenient arrangement. That was the same thing as what the Allies did when they partnered with the Soviet Union. And then after the war, the U.S. and the U.S.S.R. turned on each other, and now we have the Cold War."

Mr. Vargas registered surprise as he raised both his eyebrows over his eyeglass frames.

"They all seemed to follow the belief," Maggie went on, "that *the enemy of my enemy is my friend*. It's an arrangement that doesn't usually work out well for anyone, uh, I mean, any party."

When she had finished speaking, she felt pleasantly surprised by her response. Had she really come out of her half-drowsy state and said all that? She looked over at Kathy, but she was turned toward the cheerleader who sat on the other side of her. Maggie filed away her frustration as she folded her hands on her desk and gave her staring history teacher a warm smile.

Let him stare. She had said nothing that wasn't factual. Even if she wasn't quoting something from her high school history textbook. She was just following a thought through to its logical conclusion, that's all. Kitchen table discussions with her father often touched on world events. Though he was a laborer, he was smart. He knew a lot about strategy, though she avoided asking him how he came by the knowledge. He would never talk about what it was like before coming to America. She speculated, and had her theories, but didn't really know. As far as the family was concerned, life started when Maggie and Sam were born.

The classroom had fallen silent. The drowsiness had vanished. Heads were turned, and all eyes were on Mr. Vargas in the back of the room. Most of the students were surprised by Maggie's answer and they wondered what Mr. Vargas would do next.

"Yes, well…" Mr. Vargas cleared his throat. "That was…more…or less, uh…that was…interesting. Wasn't it?"

Mr. Vargas looked up at the clock on the wall in a dramatic fashion, and then at his broken watch. He walked back to the chalkboard and began to write on it, pressing harder than usual. "Read the assigned chapters and bring in the answers to each of the chapter quizzes on Monday. All right, so —"

Brrnnnggg!

The bell rang, the class rose in unison, and the students began filing out the door.

"Maggie, come here, please," Mr. Vargas said, motioning with a single, lazy gesture of his hand.

Kathy moved past the teacher's desk with the rest of the students, without looking back.

Maggie stopped in front of Mr.Vargas' desk and stood waiting with her books embraced in front of her. Mr. Vargas erased the board quickly, but only in the middle, making a large swirl of chalk in the center of the chalkboard before he turned to Maggie.

"Yes, well, I think that....you are a...smart...girl...Maggie...but...you may...want to consider...not being...such a showoff...Nobody likes a showoff...Maggie." Mr. Vargas turned away and took a seat in his padded chair, ignoring her as she continued to stand before him.

She turned briskly away, striding over to where she saw Kathy waiting just outside in the hall. She had a great deal that she wanted to say but thought the better of it. The two walked away to their next class.

Mr. Vargas wasn't the first man to appear threatened by her willingness to confront them, or the first who mistook her confidence for arrogance, her ability for exhibition, and independence for insubordination.

"Ya know, you don't have to be Joan of Arc, Maggie," Kathy said, as they strolled together next to the busy street toward the bus stop. The bus to Terre Promise would be arriving soon. Maggie had decided to put flowers on the grave of Sifu Chang's wife as part of her own pre-test ritual. She thought it would be a nice gesture of gratitude and goodwill toward her teacher and whatever spirits governed the world from beyond. She wanted to be prepared in mind, body, and spirit. She felt that commemorating the personal moment that she shared with Sifu Chang, and honoring his wife, would fulfill the latter. One of her teacher's more potent maxims played in her mind: *"Always do things with a true heart, Maggie."*

"I'm not trying to be Joan of Arc," Maggie rolled her eyes, "but I don't want to be some broad that gets pushed around either, ya know?" The feeling of frustration was fresh. After Mr. Vargas' class, two boys in the hall told her to smile, and Maggie told them where they could go.

"Broad?" Kathy questioned with eyes wide before she turned and looked fruitlessly for a cigarette in her purse.

"Yeah, well, my dad says it sometimes, at least when my mom's not around. Anyway, I don't want some guy pushing me around," Maggie said, as she pulled out a cigarette from her book bag, and showed it triumphantly to Kathy. She tried to light it, albeit with some difficulty. Maggie was trying to balance her overloaded book bag under one arm, while she held the lighter steady at the same time. Kathy gave her a hand steadying the bag, and Maggie lit the cigarette carefully shielding the flame with her hands. Mission accomplished.

"Speaking of not getting pushed around..." Kathy gave a knowing wink, "your test is Saturday morning, right?"

"Yep," Maggie answered confidently, then squinted as she inhaled. She blew out the smoke attempting a smoke ring.

"Can I come?" Kathy asked, reaching for the newly lit cigarette in Maggie's hand, quickly taking a puff, and handing it back, while blowing the smoke from the corner of her mouth.

"Don't take it the wrong way, but I think I should go on my own, okay? I'll call you when I get back though," Maggie flicked the ashes from the cigarette with a deft and practiced technique, and then took a long draw from it. She was trying her best to look like Faye Dunaway, her favorite movie star, as she inhaled. The realization that she wasn't Faye Dunaway, and that any busybody neighbor could see her, made Maggie look around quickly to make sure that she wasn't spotted.

"As soon as I get home, I'll call you. I swear."

"You don't want me to go?"

"I just think I need to do it alone."

"Is Sifu Chang going?" Kathy questioned with inquisitive eyebrows.

"Don't be silly, he has to go. What am I going to do, test myself?" Observing Kathy's downcast gaze and sudden silence, Maggie felt the space become thicker between them. She stopped walking and reached gently for Kathy's arm. "It doesn't have anything to do with you, honestly. I just feel like this is important for me and I don't want to be thinking about anything else. I don't want to let my teacher down."

"You think I would be a distraction?" Kathy directed her query with her head tilted down, eyes looking up, and a forlorn expression prominently displayed.

"Jesus, I didn't mean it like that...it's hard to explain...I mean, I have to be completely focused, so I don't screw up, or get my ass kicked, ya know?"

Maggie watched as Kathy's face began to acknowledge her understanding.

"Yeah, I know...well, at least as well as I can, anyway, since I don't *do* the stuff...although I feel like I do, talking to you about it all the time."

"You think I talk too much about it?"

"It's what you love...so..."

Kathy's hand found Maggie's and held it, gently.

"There are some guys in my building. They seem to know about you. I heard them talking about a girl that studies with Sifu Chang. It has to be you right? I mean he isn't teaching any others, is he?"

Maggie shook her head, "Not that I know of."

"They were making fun of you, saying they could kick your ass, that you're a joke, and that even though they knew you were going up for a test soon, it wasn't real...it wasn't a real test." Kathy's eyes met Maggie's and unable to look away, she fidgeted with her hair, nervous to continue.

"I heard some girls saying that you were crazy, learning to fight, and that you were just trying to stir up trouble because you couldn't get a boy to like you." Both girls became quiet as they studied the stained sidewalk together.

The street sounds of cars, buses, and sirens filled their silence.

"Are you worried about what might happen? Does it bother you what they're saying?" Maggie questioned, with a steely gaze.

Kathy appeared still engrossed in the cracks in the sidewalk.

"I know what people say about me. I know the girls don't think I'm much of a girl and the boys think I'm a joke, but I don't care. I know who I am. This test is real. It's so real that they've created a rumor about it. I don't have anything to prove to them."

Maggie pulled up Kathy's chin and looked into her eyes.

"Let 'em laugh and let 'em talk. After Saturday they can say what they want, but they'll be calling me Sifu when they say it." Maggie winked and a shallow grin spread across her face.

The bus pulled up, and the doors opened loudly giving them both a start. Passengers began streaming out.

After a glance around them, Maggie leaned in and gave Kathy a quick kiss, softly, on the lips. Kathy touched her hand lightly on Maggie's cheek.

"Miss me?" Kathy asked, smiling, anticipating the answer.

"Always," she said, handing the nearly finished cigarette to Kathy and turning to board the waiting bus.

Maggie found a seat and watched out the window as Kathy stood where she left her. She saw her face make the effort of a yell but could only barely make out the words: *Kick some ass, Maggie,* as the bus lumbered loudly away. She watched Kathy take another drag of the cigarette they had been smoking, and then let it drop, casually, on the blackened sidewalk. She put it out, slowly, with the twist of her shoe.

As she lay in bed, Sifu Chang's words about fear ran through her mind. As preparation for the test, her teacher had been especially insistent that Maggie spar with one of his high-ranking students from his regular class.

The student he chose was big and he was good. He had warmed up with a series of impressive kicks and punches, each landed with a solid thud on the bulky pad held by another student. His punches were rapid-fired machine-gunned flurries. They landed on the focus mitts clean and hard. He had power. The student holding the pad registered the impact of each strike with a wince or a grimace when they hit. She could tell that the force of the strikes bled through the bag. *Don't get hit.*

It was difficult not to feel insecure watching his powerful display of technique. She walked slowly back toward Sifu Chang, who was busy sorting out the minimal protective gear that they would use: Gloves, mouthpiece, and headgear. Before the sparring session began, she turned her back toward her teacher to speak with him over her shoulder, without appearing too obvious to anyone who would be watching.

"Sifu, I'm a little afraid."

"Yeah?" He responded without looking up, "Well, if I were you, I'd be a lot afraid, that kid is good and he's a lot bigger than you, but it doesn't matter."

"It doesn't matter?"

"No. You will face him, and you will hold your ground, Maggie." The sifu said, not looking at Maggie, but across the school's improvised ring, at the opponent.

Maggie looked at Sifu Chang's face as he watched the bigger competitor continue his impressive preparation. The sifu appeared to be trying to mask his concern. Maggie gulped as she watched her rival continue his beatings on the bags and pads, each one landing with a thudding report.

"I get, uh, you know, butterflies in my stomach...sometimes."

"So do I, we all do. But the best move forward anyway. Okay? Even with the butterflies flapping in your stomach. You must say, 'Butterflies be damned!' And move forward."

Her sparring partner was staring at her and pumping his gloves together from across the makeshift ring.

Sifu Chang slapped her shoulder with a friendly tap, gave her a reassuring smile, and then shoved her into the ring with a stern nod signaling his belief in her ability to defeat the bigger opponent.

She had done better than she expected with the competitor. She moved in determined to keep her cool. He had power, but she was fast. He had to catch her to use it. She was evasive and it led him to miss and make mistakes. It had been difficult, and she picked up a cut from a glancing blow of his glove and a bruise to her ribs from a kick she didn't see coming. Still, she had managed to keep him off balance and give him some clean hits to remember her by. As she filed away the lesson, the message was clear: She had given him too much credit and herself not enough. After the experience, she learned a better way to deal with fear, but it didn't make it go away. Maybe it never did.

Test day. She awoke before her alarm clock. It had been hard to sleep. The electricity of anticipation ran through her body, and she popped up in bed, snapped back the covers, and threw her feet to the floor. Sitting on the edge of the bed, she closed her eyes, took a deep breath, and let it out slowly. It wasn't good to be so anxious. But it was hard not to be. She didn't know much about the test and didn't know what to expect, beyond the fact that today was important, and she needed to be at her best.

After she got dressed, she grabbed the blue and white duffel bag she borrowed from Kathy and put her things in it. She would wear her black uniform bottoms for the walk to the school, but she kept her formal uniform top, an extra undershirt, her notebook, along with a brown bag containing an apple, banana, and a thermos of cold water, in the duffle.

She swung the duffel bag over her shoulder, but before leaving, walked to her bedroom window and parted the faded peach curtains with her fingers as she gazed into the gray morning covering Chinatown. It was still early. Some of the lights from the restaurants and nightclubs were still twinkling through the rising light. It made the day seem special, magical. *Today's the day. Time to go.*

She stepped quietly through the silent apartment. As she put her hand on the doorknob, she noticed something on the small table next to the door. A bracelet made of braided thick red thread sat conspicuously upon a small white piece of paper. The note said, *"For luck."* Maggie put it on. The bracelet fit perfectly. She shut the door behind her and heard the lock click before she turned and walked down the hall.

The streets were virtually empty. The brightly lit signs of nightclubs and restaurants began to flicker off with the coming light of day. Maggie walked briskly toward Sifu Chang's school to meet him there, as he had instructed. As the time got closer, she felt a complex set of emotions well up within her. There was a mixture of happiness at the thought of completing the test, and fear of the test itself. She knew that it would be difficult to keep her feelings in check, but she recognized that anticipation of an important event was often worse than the event itself. *Calm down. Don't worry, breathe.* The mantra was repeated with each step she made toward the school. Still, as if her body knew better, or out of some biological defiance, she felt her stomach begin to get queasy.

She arrived at the school and went around to the back door announcing herself with a loud rap of her knuckles. She looked around the parking lot, as she waited and noticed the boxes and other debris piled up next to the dumpster. There were two cars in the parking lot. One with a flat tire and another with unusually fogged windows. She looked up, closed her eyes, and took in a breath. Just as her mind started to drift deeper into herself, the door opened. Sifu Chang answered in a clean white t-shirt and freshly pomaded hair.

"Good morning, Sifu."

"Good morning, Maggie. Come in," Sifu Chang motioned a wave of welcome with his hand, and let Maggie walk past him through the narrow doorway. He stuck his head outside and briefly looked around before he shut the door. She waited for him in the small hallway. *Was he nervous about something?* They walked back to his office. Two metal folding chairs stood diagonally facing his desk. She sat in the closest chair putting her backpack next to her feet. Her teacher plopped into his office chair, the chair squeaked loudly in response. He proceeded to look through the bottom drawer of his desk for something.

"You hungry? Did you eat anything?" He asked, without looking up as if speaking to some strange creature inhabiting the drawer.

"No."

"Did you eat something before you left home?" Sifu Chang looked up at her for a response.

"I wasn't hungry. I just don't seem hungry yet. I brought an apple and a banana for later."

"Butterflies?"

"Who's eating butterflies?"

"You know what I mean...smart-alec..." He said with a slight smile as he started writing something on a notepad that he had pulled from the drawer. It felt strange to be in Sifu Chang's office and to see him do something as mundane as office work. She had only been in the office a handful of times over the years, and it was usually just to retrieve something he had forgotten like a note, his glasses, or something from his, catastrophically, unorganized file cabinet. It always felt like trespassing though. The office had a large window that faced the training floor, so he could see what was happening while he was meeting with someone. Anytime she had to enter the office, she would shut the door, and look at the training area through the window. Sometimes picturing what went on during a regular day, and sometimes she remembered the first day she came in. That day was burned into her memory. Even though she had cobbled together some martial arts training on her own before then, Maggie thought of that day as the beginning for her. Even with Sifu Chang sitting opposite her, and on such an important day, it still felt like a place where she didn't belong.

As she waited, she surveyed the sifu's desk and the surrounding area. The place was a mess. Sifu's filing system, as he called it, seemed to lack any system at all. Stacks of papers were assembled in dubiously ordered piles, and between them were bits of wrappers from candy bars, paper cups, and assorted pens and pencils. Ceramic coffee mugs with varying measures of liquids were abandoned strategically around the room waiting for anyone that wanted an old, cold, cup of coffee. Numerous books littered his desk, and stacks of books were piled on the floor in quantities rivaling the papers. Sifu Chang read a great deal and the books were on a wide variety of topics from philosophy and mathematics to biographies of famous Hollywood icons. The subjects spoke to the deep inner workings of his mind. He was analytical, but with an odd sense of whimsy. He was interested in understanding complex subjects but also dying to know if Errol Flynn was romantically involved with Olivia De Havilland after all those movies together. Sitting high atop everything on the pile on his desk, in plain view, was a very official-looking certificate. It was printed on parchment complete with scrolling embellishment around the outside edges, and a detailed watermark of a dragon and tiger just like the one on the wall of the school in the training area. It was a promotion diploma. The date and name were left blank.

"Is that for me?" Maggie said through a crooked smile.

"I don't know, do you think I will need it? Sifu Chang responded stone-faced, "Maybe it's for Phil? His material has been looking pretty good lately. Maybe it's for someone else?" She watched him as he placed the certificate in a manila folder and carefully put it into his black duffle bag along with his black uniform top.

A loud knock came from the back door.

They looked at each other, and then Sifu Chang got up and put his finger to his lips, urging for quiet. He stepped quickly out of the office. She heard the door open and then the low murmur of voices. It sounded like directions. She heard the door close. The sifu came back into the office, looking like he meant business and like he was now in a hurry.

"All this damned cloak and dagger. Ok, the location has been set. The board will be waiting for us. We have to go to the Golden Dragon Club and meet in about thirty minutes," he turned his wrist to check his watch, "shouldn't take too long. It is just across the park and about a block past the big temple." Sifu Chang stopped, waited for a beat, and then put his hand on Maggie's shoulder, "You ready?"

"Yes, of course," She forced a smile, her stomach getting queasier by the minute. The Golden Dragon club was the home of the Gui Feng, The Ghost Phoenix Gang, the most notorious triad in Chinatown. They were often the subject of news reports, and police investigations, and they also unofficially regulated the martial arts in Chinatown through The Council. Officially, the club was a place where they met, played Mahjong, and had parties and other social events, but everyone knew that it was where decisions were made for their criminal enterprise. *Was this dangerous?* She trusted her sifu's judgment, but it didn't keep her from feeling a little anxious about going to a place that was home to a smorgasbord of crimes including gambling, extortion, drug dealing, and contract murder.

Sifu Chang grabbed the duffle bag and a waxwood staff from the corner of his office. He looked at Maggie and nodded toward the door. She started to follow him out of the office and was curious to notice that there was another certificate on his desk. She paused for a moment and then grabbed her backpack to follow him. The door to the school shut behind them. They walked together down the steps and across the parking lot.

The Golden Dragon club looked plain and unassuming from the street—a simple brick building with no distinctive features. It could easily be mistaken for any city agency. It wasn't even as distinctive as the restaurants that flanked the club on either side. Apart from a very small green placard written in white block letters hanging on the wall outside next to a slender door, there was nothing to indicate that the club even existed.

Sifu Chang opened the door, holding it so they could walk together into the small entryway. Once inside, the stark contrast between the plain exterior and the grand interior was staggering to Maggie.

The air was lightly perfumed with jasmine, and the aroma brought her senses to life. The white walls of the entryway were pearlescent, shimmering. She had to squint a bit at the brightness. By the door, a free-standing waterfall gurgled quietly amidst the lush foliage of a miniature garden. The soft sounds were soothing to the ear. In perpetual meditation nearby, a small golden Buddha statue sat peacefully. They exited the enchanting foyer, passing through a massive oak door, into the main hall.

Their footfalls broke the stark silence as they entered. Even though they both trod softly, their steps on the marble floor echoed back to them as if stomping. Maggie hesitated. Stopped in her tracks. After a moment of taking in the surroundings, she put down her bag beside her and took a deep breath. *It was going to happen soon, wasn't it?* Her heart quickened. Her teacher had proceeded forward. Noticing she wasn't close by, he looked back, and with a jerk of his head, indicated she was to follow. Maggie picked up her bag, nodded understanding, and began to follow him again. He didn't offer any words of encouragement or chastise her for taking a moment for herself. The message was clear: *the time is now, let's go.*

Their trek was like a trip through a museum. Traditional paintings and parchment scrolls adorned the walls, stately and evocative. Maggie studied their form and themes. Majestic mountains and lotus blossoms, flowing rivers, small villages, forests, and golden sunbeams.

Intricately detailed cherrywood sculptures of tigers locked together in mortal combat flanked their path. In a mural, a phoenix rose, and cranes danced.

Most prominent of all, was a pair of dragons that coiled around two columns marking the middle of the hall. They could have been a portal into another world. The dragons held their mouths agape, fearsome fangs exposed, their claws grasping for purchase on the slick white columns. Even from a distance the ridges of the individual scales and those relentlessly focused, lifelike eyes, lent the impression of reality to the fantastical sculpture. The gold dragon on the left was coiling upward to the ceiling. The green dragon on the right was coiling down toward the floor. The sifu stopped to point out the significance to her.

"The golden one is ambition; you follow your dreams upward." He spoke softly and pointed delicately as if telling a secret. "The green one is fortune, money. Opportunity is found on earth, right? That's how you make it happen, the green with the gold."

Maggie nodded.

He returned a quick nod as well and took the lead again.

Upon passing between the double dragon portal, the two started down a long hallway that extended deep into the building with doors on only one side. The corridor was lined with statues of cranes, tigers, dragons, and the Buddha.

Rising at the very end of the hallway was a dragon throne made of cherrywood, so well lacquered that it glistened as if wet. The head of the dragon hung over the top of the backrest. A pair of clawed feet at the bottom of the massive chair arrested Maggie's attention. Each five-toed foot grasped a great pearl.

Who would ever sit on such a throne? Was it just for show? Or was it maybe a shrine for the spirit of the dragon? Maggie felt that she had entered into another place in time, mystical and artful. A land of myth and legend. It was both intimidating and exhilarating for her.

They came to a stop at the end of the hall before a set of imposing wooden double doors. The archway above the doors was crowned with a gold-sculpted dragon that appeared to be taking flight in front of a mural of a blue, cloud-graced sky.

Two identically attired sentries stood on either side of the doorway. Each man wore a black leather jacket, a white silk shirt with the top three buttons undone, and a matching gold necklace with a dangling menagerie of charms, a few of which Maggie recognized: an Egyptian hieroglyph of Set, a pentagram, and King David's talisman. An Italian Corno, or devil's horn, was pinned to each man's jacket. The guards seemed out of place amidst such explicitly traditional Chinese imagery, but then Chinatown is a disparate mix of the ancient and the modern.

The guards stood as still as statues, until Sifu Chang gave them an upward nod of acknowledgment, and received a downward nod of acquiescence in return. Each sentry took one step back. Sifu Chang pulled open one of the large wooden doors, and then motioned with a sharp head tilt and expectantly raised eyebrows for Maggie to walk in before him.

She entered first and the sifu followed. Though it was dark, she could tell it was a ballroom. The only light came from a high window. The light poured down and pooled upon a long table draped with a white tablecloth, and set with a pitcher of water and three glasses. As they approached the table, Sifu Chang put down his bag and motioned for Maggie to do the same.

"Change into your uniform and stretch out a bit. I've got to let them know we're here." Her teacher disappeared through a door near a far corner of the room. At the soft thud of the door closing behind him, Maggie realized she was completely alone.

She felt ready for anything. All the nervous anticipation was behind her, and her body was energizing itself to meet the challenge before her.

As she slipped into a side room to change into her uniform, she tried imagining what a social gathering in that room would be like. It was probably used for weddings and events for the members of the club. It could hold at least as many people as had been at her cousin's wedding last summer. The room would probably be filled with Chinatown's elite, a cabal of bankers, slumlords, garment factory owners, and Council members, all dressed in black tie attire, dining on fine China and drinking from crystal flutes filled with Champagne. They would all be glad-handing each other and toasting their good fortune.

The Council was the most powerful force in Chinatown. However, their reach was from the shadows. Known, but rarely discussed in the open. Growing up in Chinatown, Maggie thought, you only really learned anything about The Council by a kind of osmosis. They were treated as if they were some demon that could be invoked when their name was spoken, and so people didn't speak of them unless it was necessary. But in the dark corners, where the city's neon lights could not reach, their presence was felt.

She went back out into the ballroom. She kept glancing at the door the sifu used to exit. *How long would he be? What is he doing? Is patience part of the test?* She tried to stretch out a bit by doing some relaxed snap kicks. After a while, her mouth began to get dry, and she felt like she had to use the restroom. *Would there be enough time to run out to a restroom and get back?* Not wanting to take the chance, she decided to wait. Surely it wouldn't be much longer.

She jumped in the air and landed softly on the balls of her feet a dozen times. Her landing was quiet even in the echoey room. Blood started pumping fast. She rotated her arms backward and forward a half dozen times and then stood quietly with her hands lightly resting on her abdomen. She breathed long and slow breaths, feeling her hands rise and fall with the rhythm. She closed her eyes and quieted her mind.

The door opened behind her.

She heard someone enter the room. She kept her eyes closed. They tread lightly with careful footsteps, but she still knew that they were there. *Was this part of the test?* She resisted the urge to immediately look behind herself and took three more breaths. Long and slow though they were, she still felt anxiety developing.

She opened her eyes and looked casually over her shoulder, trying to convey a lack of concern.

An Asian man stood a short distance away, just inside the door. He looked older than her, by five years or so. His face betrayed his life experience, with a faint scar on his right cheek, and a nose that looked like it had been broken more than once. His eyes expressed a firm grasp on reality and radiated a cool pragmatism. His long hairstyle, parted in the middle, was unusual for men in Chinatown. At first glance, she almost mistook him for a Native American. He was wearing a dark brown suede fringe jacket and blue denim pants which didn't fully camouflage his muscular body. *Was she going to have to spar against him?*

He looked formidable. *Menacing?* No. Not that. His stance was one of confidence and ability. She felt that he was very experienced in fighting and had trained a great deal in some kind of martial art. *More than one?* The energy that emanated from his presence made her feel sure that he was good at what he did.

He looked around the room giving a few nods of understanding and affirmation. *Who was he? What did he want?* When he looked at her, she turned her face away embarrassed to be caught staring at him. She tried to act like she didn't care that he was there, but she could feel her pulse running a little higher. To her surprise, the door softly closed as unexpectedly as it had opened, and without a word, like a ghost, he was gone.

The lights came on.

A moment later Sifu Chang returned. Two other men followed him. Maggie didn't realize it, but she had been holding her breath. She let it out and tried to get her focus back on the task at hand.

"Stand here, Miss Long." Her teacher pointed to a spot just a few feet from the front of the table.

Sifu Chang and the other men took their seats and situated themselves behind the table, adjusting their chairs and pouring themselves a glass of water. Her teacher sat in the middle. The other two men sat on either side of him. She had never seen them before.

The man on the left had a long mustache and beard. He looked to be in his seventies. He was wearing a traditional Chinese uniform that looked gray, but she suspected that it had likely been solid black before daily usage and hours in the sun took their toll. He was wearing a small circular hat and a pair of round, gold wire-rimmed glasses.

The other man appeared to be middle-aged, and his muscular frame was evident even under his clothes. Although he wore traditional uniform pants, gathered at the bottom, he had on a black silk shirt, open to his chest, with two gold medallions that were difficult to make out from the distance at which she stood. Still, she thought he looked like a movie star. His hair was combed back neatly and feathered on the sides, long enough to cover his ears. He had styled himself like a young man and was able to pull it off rather convincingly.

She didn't recall having ever seen either one of them before.

"These masters have agreed to help me with the test," Sifu Chang said, as he nodded toward each of the other men in turn.

He used his hands to gesture with more formality than she had ever seen him do before, letting them unfold in a very grand way as if pointing at exquisite artwork.

"To my right is Sifu Jun."

As his name was mentioned, the elderly sifu closed his eyes and lowered his head in a graceful nod. His movements were slow and deliberate, as though his entire body was engaged in a never-ending performance of Tai Chi. His eyes were alert and active, beaming with youthful energy.

"Sifu Jun is the head of the Internal Martial Arts Academy, and his lineage stretches back through the oldest times into one of the remotest villages south of the Yellow River."

Sifu Chang then motioned similarly, in his elegant way, to the man on the other side.

"This is Sifu Zhu. He is the highest-ranking teacher from the Northern Schools of Beast Arts: Dragon, Tiger, Crane, Leopard, Eagle, and Cobra."

The sifu sat with arms crossed and acknowledged the introduction with a single deliberate nod of his head. Even seated, he looked like a beast prepared to strike.

Maggie felt honored to stand before them. She saluted them all collectively with a fist meeting an open hand, the weapon, and the shield. She gave them a single nod as she slowly rolled her salute right to left, and back again, paying her respects to all three men.

They each returned her salute. She watched as Sifu Chang then shuffled a couple of typed pieces of paper before him. The energy and anticipation were building again. *This is it.* She knew that they could ask her to demonstrate anything and everything, and they likely would. They would want to see her spar with someone. At least one, and maybe more. It could be anyone, even one of the sifus or all of them. Anything could happen. She thought of Sifu Chang's running joke to expect anything, even someone dropping out of the ceiling. This was the last step of the journey that had brought her to this point, and the first step for everything that would come after. Rarely, do moments come that are instantly recognized for their significance. This was a rare time, indeed.

She took a long deep breath, and slowly let it out. Quickly, she tilted her head from side to side and produced two audible cracks. She shook her arms loosely at her sides and started shifting lightly from foot to foot. Another deep inhale followed by a loud exhale, and then she became still. Every fiber of her body was alive. Crackling energy seemed to emanate from her being. Her pulse pounded in her ears.

"Are you ready?" Sifu Chang questioned with a stone-faced expression.

"Yes."

"Begin!"

The doors exploded open. Maggie stumbled, breathless and completely exhausted, out into the hall. Gasping, she took faltering steps away from the ballroom. With her hands clasped over her head, she tried to regain her breath. Her legs were weak, they felt like they would give way at any moment. The cool air of the hall found every drop of her body's sweat and gave her a sudden chill.

She sensed a renegade bead of perspiration running down her cheek. A quick dart of her tongue intercepted it at the corner of her mouth. It wasn't sweat. A dab with the back of her hand revealed that it was blood. She doubled over, resting her hands on her thighs, as her body took big, slow, heaving breaths. The air didn't return quickly enough, no matter how big a breath she took. Until, after some time, finally, she began to breathe easier.

She looked back at the doors and thought about the test and wondered what the masters were saying to each other as they deliberated. They would be comparing notes. She imagined what they would be saying.

"Hmm, pretty good…for a woman, but not good enough."

Would Sifu Chang stand up for her, or would he cave? "Yeah, I knew she was no good, but what could I do? I've had her for a while and needed to make it look like she was worthy. Anyway, I got this other kid, Phil…"

She shook her head as if to shake away the negative thoughts from her mind. Her preoccupation only lasted for a few moments, and then she decided that it didn't matter. She had done her best. It was about as hard as she thought it would be. Many times, during the process she had found herself questioning how badly she wanted to go on. And that was precisely the point of such a long and difficult test. They wanted to see if she would quit.

Better to know now, than when she would face a difficult opponent and shame them all later. After all, that was what it was about. *Wasn't it?* They were going to be hanging their reputations on her success. From now on, if she passed, they would ultimately be responsible for her promotion. Bad enough she was a girl, they had to be sure she wasn't a quitter. They were risking a lot just acknowledging her, and she knew it.

Standing erect, hands on her hips, she leaned her head back and looked up at the hall's painted ceiling. She stood as if in communion with the unknown, awaiting some magical answer to some mystical question about the universe. She sensed someone watching her. Given the reputation of the environment, she thought it best to be cautious. Her eyes subtly and intuitively scanned the hall, only momentarily distracted by the artistic lure of tigers, cranes, and the ubiquitous dragons, and then she saw him.

Standing motionless next to a pillar was the same young man she saw earlier. He was standing so still that she almost didn't see him looking at her from the other end of the hallway. *How long had he been standing there?*

Feeling another droplet form, she wiped the blood from her mouth again with the back of her hand, as she looked at him. He gave her the traditional salute and a slight nod, but his face was expressionless.

She glanced down to look at the bloody line on the back of her hand. Tears and sweat were easily taken in stride, but blood, no matter the cause, always seemed to be a more serious matter. She looked up. He was gone. *Had he been out there the entire time, waiting for her to finish? Had she even seen him at all, or was it just some crazy delusion?*

The doors creaked open, and Sifu Chang came out into the hall.

"Come back in," he said, jerking his thumb toward the ballroom. She nodded to him and walked back into the room. For some reason, she thought that if she failed, her teacher would probably have said something when he came out to soften the blow. Still, she wasn't sure. She followed the first rule of dealing with the unknown and kept herself ready for anything.

She returned to the same spot where she had stood when the test began. Now it was a slippery slick of sweat and a few drops of diluted blood. Sifu Chang walked around the table and took his seat between the other two sifus. They briefly conferred with each other holding their sheets of notes and nodding to each other.

She was breathing slower but was still perspiring, and she could feel what was likely not the last drop of sweat start its journey down her face. The drop rolled forth and held its place, impressively, as if waiting for permission to fall from the end of her nose. She made a quick twitch and crinkle of her nose, and the drop fell into the small puddle that had begun to form on the floor between her feet.

"We have come to a decision," Sifu Chang announced, coolly. "We have found your skills satisfactory, and we proclaim you worthy of promotion to the rank of sifu."

Sifu Chang looked to either side of him and got the obligatory and necessary nods of agreement from each of the other sifus. Their heads only moved slightly. With the light of the afternoon sun blazing through the window behind them, it turned the sifus' faces into dark masks that were hard to make out. Only the occasional rising and falling of their cigarettes, and their glowing cherry embers, betrayed the fact that they were not phantoms.

She clasped her hands behind her back, stood a little straighter, and then removed the slight smile as soon as she felt it appear on her face. *Be humble.* Her body was rapidly cooling, she tried her best not to shiver. *Don't show weakness.* Her muscles twitched involuntarily, sweat fell, and the shivers came and went. She ignored it all.

As the first female sifu in Chinatown, she would be judged harshly, she knew that. She might even be challenged by some doubters of her abilities, or just people jealous of her ascent to such a high rank. It wasn't the end; it was just the beginning and she welcomed it.

"The sifus thought that your skills were impressive, and the entire board was very happy with your test." Sifu Chang stopped for a moment, a smile formed quickly and then disappeared. He paused the same way people do when they are about to say something they are unsure of. "That said, the board expects that you will assist me as the senior student for the next six months, and then you may stay on with me and become an assistant teacher."

"I will definitely do that, thank you," she said emphatically, wearing a big happy smile. "That will give me the experience I'll need to open my own school. You won't have to worry for a moment that I won't give back to this community, I certainly will. That is all I want to do, open a kung fu school and teach."

The Sifus shifted in their seats as if they'd become suddenly uncomfortable. They exchanged glances that seemed to carry more meaning and significance than they probably meant to show. The atmosphere had become very thick. Suddenly, all three sifus seemed to think that studying the pages of notes in front of them was more imperative than looking her in the eyes.

"Yes, well. You will, uh, remain an …assistant. Though the board recognizes your ability, without question, there are certain traditions that we have to…certain traditions, you see, that must be followed. You are not authorized to open your own school," Sifu Chang looked slightly down as he delivered the blow. He had suspected Maggie had planned to open a school, and in his meetings to arrange the test, and even in the deliberations after her exam that day, he had tried to sway them, but to no avail. The powers that controlled Chinatown were immovable in their age-old traditions.

Maggie felt her stomach sink and the elation that she had felt only moments ago quickly evaporated. *Control yourself.* She tried to reason with herself, but anxiety and panic were strangling her. She knew that one should never question the board evaluating a student, but protocol be damned! Her temperature began rising again, this time from anger rather than from physical exertion. She used all of her effort to control her words and not say something she would truly regret.

"But I passed, right? I mean I did everything...and you...how can it be that I—"

"We doubt neither your talent nor your abilities," Sifu Jun interrupted in his sing-song cadence. "We were all quite impressed by what we've seen here today. But we have certain traditions. They are very old traditions, and they must be honored. I'm sure you understand. It's the balance, you see, the correct relations of yin and yang. The proper order must be maintained—"

"Why?"

"Maggie," Sifu Chang urged. His voice tried desperately to keep things from getting out of control.

"Call me *Sifu*..." Her eyes were aflame. "I am a sifu, right? You said I am. I mean I earned it, right?"

Instinctively, her body had turned slightly to a fighting stance, and her fists clenched tightly as if she was getting ready for combat. Maybe she had said more than she should, but there was no going back.

"Very well, Sifu." Sifu Chang added with a slight nod of understanding, "Maybe you need to look at this situation through the filter of the old Chinese proverb which says—"

"Maybe I should look at this like the message in a fortune cookie!" Maggie spat her words of frustration with her eyes ablaze. Even in her anger, she knew she had crossed a line.

"Enough!"

Sifu Zhu's open palm slammed the table for emphasis, propelling him to his feet. The room fell silent. His bulky, muscular frame cut a formidable silhouette against the light from the window. "You will treat us ALL with respect!"

Maggie, instinctively, bowed her head. Memories of her father's anger over not being able to pay the rent, the price of food, or getting a "D" in Social Studies, all came to the surface.

"This is the way we do things. Do you understand? You will treat us with respect! This is an exception we will not make, for anyone!"

Maggie felt Sifu Zhu's anger from across the room and his eyes boring into her skull as he continued.

"I don't care who you are. Chinatown will not change for one girl, upset because she doesn't get to stand decades of tradition on their head." Sifu Zhu straightened his shirt, put his hand through his hair, and took a drink of water before continuing. "You will teach as an assistant to Sifu Chang. You will NOT open a school." His posture became aggressive and bestial as he added emphasis. "If you do, you will not have our blessing. You MUST have our blessing. You must have it. If you don't like it…" He paused, took a breath, his face red, eyes aflame, and the silence in the room became an unfillable void, "…then refuse your promotion and study somewhere else more in keeping with your new-found ways." He cocked his neck to the side and produced a large cracking sound as he lowered himself back to his seat.

The words hung in the air like invisible smoke, and it made it difficult for Maggie to breathe. Maggie looked up and the sunlight shining in through the window struck her eyes directly, nearly blinding her.

"Maggie...er, Sifu, please take this." Sifu Chang rose out of his chair and extended the certificate toward her. "You earned it, and we are all proud of you. It is a great accomplishment. I don't want that to get lost in this— Focus on what you have done here today."

Maggie felt her eyes start to well up, but she would rather die than look weak in front of them. She would not cry. She pushed her sweaty hair back with one hand, locking it behind her ear, and then acted as if the sweat had stung her eyes. She rubbed her hand across her face. Better to face hell than to show them the pain of the emotional blow.

She reached out and accepted the certificate with both hands, and then gave a slight bow and a handshake to each of the sifus in turn. She walked back to the center of the room where she had been standing and gave a final salute to them all. They returned the gesture, their faces indiscernible.

Taking a deep breath, Maggie retrieved her bag and walked out of the testing room. The doors closed behind her with a grim thud of finality. She wiped her eyes, and her face, and followed the long hallway to the door she had entered hours earlier with her teacher.

The decorations in the hall were no longer as impressive or distracting as they had been before, as she walked lost in the thoughts and disappointment of the moment. She stopped and took a deep breath and wiped her eyes before opening the door to the street. A moment of reflection was needed. It came and went with no change to how she felt.

With a strong push on the door, she exited The Golden Dragon and was suddenly and completely enveloped by the noise of the busy street and the blazing afternoon sun of Chinatown.

PART II

1979

"It's a beautiful morning! Rise and shine!" A loud rooster's crow punctuated the DJ's schtick of overly happy talk, entirely too excited and upbeat to sound like the voice of any normal person. "If you're in your car now, battling traffic on your way to work, well, then you already know how beautiful it is! Am I right? Oh yeah!" He concluded with a deep voice, apparently quite close to the microphone. "You betcha!"

The sound of an old car horn inexplicably interrupted the DJ's delivery.

"Yes sireee. Seventy-nine degreeeees, with light winds from the southwest, aaaand…not a cloud in the sky here at WXQM, 92.1 FM on your radio dial. It's 8:32 in the morning, and all I ask is that you don't bring me down."

The drum intro to E.L.O.'s *Don't Bring Me Down*, filled Maggie's black Pontiac Trans Am as she cruised along the freeway. It was indeed a bright, sunny day, and like the DJ said, not a cloud in the sky. Her mind had fallen into her commute mode, and her attention began slipping away toward the problems of the day.

Project running more than a week behind. The staff seems unmotivated. My fault? Am I too hard on them? Too easy? Ugh. Evaluations are coming up. Crap, I need to start writing those soon… Wendy's being bitchy. What the hell is with her? Dishes left in the sink—was that some kind of payback for coming home later than usual? Why can't she understand my work is not the kind I can bring home and fix in front of her? God! Her jealousy is ridiculous…Damn! It's Tuesday! The laundry guy! God, I completely forgot, missed him again…

She smoothly changed to the middle lane. Roadwork had been going on for weeks. The large orange signs with black lettering told her to expect delays. *Yeah, yeah, delay, delay, crap.* She had planned to leave the house extra early to compensate, but she never did.

As she got closer to the work area, traffic slowed to a parade of creeping vehicles past the scene. She looked to her right and saw workmen in hardhats and orange vests shoveling a black oily mix onto the road in the path of a giant roller operated by a man with sunglasses and a large belly. An unlit cigarette hung from his mouth.

"Who's the idiot who scheduled road work during morning rush hour anyway? When is that ever a good idea?" For some reason speaking her thoughts out loud always seemed to make her feel good, though they made no difference to the situation. "Maybe I should carpool, so someone has to hear all my ideas about the injustices of morning rush hour?" She looked ahead at the long, crawling, line of cars before her and then glanced in the rearview mirror at the line behind her. Lost in her thoughts, she stared a moment too long, released a heavy sigh, and looked ahead again to see cherry red brake lights flashing right in front of her. Reflexively, she hit her brakes and heard the chirp of her tires as the car came to a sudden jerking stop. She had narrowly missed the oxidized gray Buick Riviera in front of her.

Shit, that was close.

She let out a breath she didn't realize she had been holding and grabbed her pack of cigarettes from where they sat below the gearshift console. She brought the pack to her mouth and pulled out a cigarette with her lips.

"Eyes on the road," she whispered to herself. *Shouldn't tempt fate again.* She brought her lighter to the end of the cigarette and ignited it. Her left hand found the handle to the window and cranked it down. The air, polluted with the stench of exhaust and fresh asphalt, along with all the highway noise, rushed at her senses and filled the car.

Barely moving since the first sudden stop, she took a quick look at herself in her rearview mirror. With her middle finger, she adjusted her newly styled bangs over her forehead and her large black sunglasses. She was trying to make herself look like Sally Field, but her hair was too straight. Given those sunglasses, she looked more like Elton John. She accepted it with a sigh of resignation. *Can't always get what you want.*

She looked back into the rearview mirror and decided that she couldn't work any wonders with her hair, and then she noticed a patch of unblended foundation on her cheek. *Crap, how did I miss that this morning?* She tried to use her finger but then decided to grab a tissue from the box next to her cigarettes and blended it in with the rest of the makeup. *Better now.* She studied her profile, right and left, for any other gaps or misses in her appearance stemming from her rush to get out the door in plenty of time that morning.

As she was ready to pronounce the job done, a loud series of honks startled her from behind. The Buick that she had nearly rear-ended was already long gone and appeared small ahead of her.

"Don't get your panties in a bunch! I'm moving!" She threw the stained tissue on her passenger seat. With the cigarette dangling from her mouth, she put her car in gear, revved the engine loudly, and peeled out.

Get up early, go to work, go home, eat dinner, watch TV, go to bed, wake up in the middle of the night, take a pill, finally get to sleep, repeat until the weekend. Get up on Monday and start all over again. Nothing much changed. She knew she wasn't alone. Probably every driver on the road had the same schedule as she did.

Once she passed the roadwork, the traffic loosened up a bit. She shifted into third gear and then into fourth and then rolled smoothly under the expansive maze of shadows from the elaborate labyrinth of concrete freeway routes above her. Her exit was coming up, 2 ½ miles, exit 5B. Same old commute, just another day. She rolled up her window, turned up Donna Summer's *Bad Girls*, and took the exit into downtown Chinatown.

The Trans Am rolled through the familiar streets. She stared through the glare of the morning sun as it pierced the windshield, and remembered what a long trek it had seemed to her back then to walk from her family's apartment to Sifu Chang's school near the park. Now it looked to be a few short blocks. Everything seemed to have shrunk.

Once, after returning from a conference in Toronto a couple of years ago, she had driven by her family's old apartment building. Since it was still early, she parked on the street and walked up. The hallway was tiny, but otherwise, it looked the same. The paint was a slightly different shade of institutional green, but still an ill-advised choice. The hallway light that always seemed so high was now easily within an arm's reach. She approached the door and ran her fingers lightly over the number, *12*. Maggie could hear the typical morning stirrings of the people within, so she turned to tiptoe away. For a moment, she felt like she had been transformed back into a child, once again sneaking off, as she had done so many times before. She heard the door open.

"Ah, you there! What you want, huh?" An old Asian woman, hunched over, wearing a gray housecoat and amber-rimmed plastic spectacles shouted at her back.

"Sorry, I was just—" Maggie thought briefly of making up a story, but decided against it. The old woman probably wouldn't be easily fooled anyway. "I'm sorry. I used to live here. I was just curious to see it again."

"Oh, long ago, huh? I live here for a long while now."

"Well, it's been a while, yes."

"You want to see it?" The old woman pointed to the open door and tilted her head toward the apartment.

"Yes, could I?" Maggie gushed.

The old woman smiled, nodded, and stood back a bit to let her enter.

With one step inside, Maggie felt as though she had entered a time portal and was sent back to her childhood memories. Although the family had lived in more than one apartment over the years, this was the one she remembered most. They had been there when she was a very young girl becoming a young woman. The place was so small she couldn't imagine how four people had lived in it. Let alone how she ever had any privacy.

It occurred to her at that moment that her parents may have willingly overlooked more than she ever knew. Maybe she hadn't been as clever as she liked to believe. Perhaps they simply chose to let her have her space. There must have been phone conversations that were overheard and ignored, and incidents of her sneaking in and out of the apartment that were purposely unacknowledged, maybe even wisps of gossip about her secret life that reached their ears, but went no further. *How much did they know?* Probably a lot more than she realized. Well, of course, there was the bracelet on test day.

Although never acknowledged in the open, she knew that her mother had left it for her. They knew a lot.

Though they weren't a very close family, they did the best they could. Her father's heart attack had come like a strong wind and scattered them all. The work was hard, and he worked longer than he should have. The end came suddenly and without parley. Her mother, grief-stricken, went to live with Aunt Lily. Sam graduated early from school and left for California to join some friends and start a computer company. She left for college. Nobody wrote or called much. There was an occasional card at Christmas from one or both. Everybody was doing their best, but everyone was best on their own. After a moment to collect herself, she thanked the old woman, descended the stairs, and exited back to the street.

The Trans Am slowed and stopped before the upraised hand of an orange-vested, suntanned, construction worker. His blonde hair curled out from under his white safety helmet, and his eyes were hidden behind mirrored sunglasses. His expression was blank. He paused the traffic so a truck could deliver a trailer load of steel to a barren lot where the Peking Garden restaurant once stood.

All the new construction in Chinatown was part of an ongoing revitalization program. She had heard talk indicating that the changes were being greeted with mixed emotions by the community. While some saw it as creating new opportunities, others saw it as the beginning of the end, the death of decades of tradition. She wondered, a little cynically, if things were really changing at all, or if all the grand effort amounted to nothing more than a new coat of paint to cover what was immune and unyielding to progress.

The construction worker glanced at the truck, as it moved away, and then back at Maggie. He lowered his hand and then waved her through. He tipped his hat with a beige-gloved hand and gave her a toothy smile as she drove past. She smiled back, although she felt a little awkward about it. Her disinterest was sometimes misconstrued as being aloof.

Wendy would always say, "Smile, and don't say anything. Let them think what they want." Since Wendy was decidedly better at most social interactions, Maggie usually deferred to her advice. In their years together Wendy had been the one to show her the "right way" to do things. There was no doubt that in the relationship, Wendy was the grownup, and they both joked about Maggie being the rebellious daughter.

The light turned red. She rolled down the window as the car came to a stop. Lighting another cigarette, she held it aloft with the cherry end out the window. She waited patiently, surveying the neighborhood when a white banner with red letters caught her eye. It was hanging loosely from the awning of what used to be an imported furniture store, flapping in the breeze: SPACE FOR LEASE, the banner announced in big block letters. She tried to look through the large front window, but it was difficult to see clearly with the reflections of passing cars and the sun glinting off the dirty glass.

She took a drag, hit her turn signal, and pulled over into a vacant parking spot. From within her car, she peered inside at the large open space. An abandoned showroom. Lots of potential. She nodded to herself, put the car in gear, and pulled back into the flow of traffic.

Her heart rate quickened as certain familiar landmarks began to indicate she was getting close to Sifu Chang's school. She missed him. As a child, she had welcomed his clean and simple approach to life's problems. Now, as an adult, she had begun to appreciate his wisdom even more.

When she would get bogged down, thinking too much about one of life's dilemmas, he would sweep it away with an uncomplicated solution. "Sometimes you just have to act, Maggie. Thinking's overrated." He would say with a crooked grin

It was true. It was good advice. She had benefited more than once by acting, rather than standing still, and becoming paralyzed with fear, while relentlessly scrutinizing her options. She had often found that things worked out better for her when she just moved forward and went with her gut instinct.

She smiled at the thought of Sifu Chang standing in his folded-arms-stance, as she called it, dispensing instructions, reprimands, or advice. He could be two people. Often, alone he was the loveable instructor and friend, but when necessary, whether to get his point across or to show he wasn't a pushover, he morphed into the implacable Sifu Chang: tough, certain, and resolute. A leader known and respected for his ability and character. He always seemed to know the right time to be one rather than the other.

Off to her right, she observed as the familiar building came into view. The golden-yellow painted brick façade stood out between the red brick building on one side and the gray stucco on the other. She watched as she drove by and her car's reflection cruised across the large window. For a moment, the name *Chang's Kung Fu* was magically superimposed onto the side of her Trans Am. She noted that the color of the letters was the same as those of her car; black, and gold.

The school was empty, of course. It was early, so there weren't any classes going on. She wasn't sure what Sifu Chang did with his time anymore. He was getting older. He was likely slowing down as most did. If he kept up teaching, he would probably still be in good shape, but even that wouldn't last forever. Age is a force as unstoppable as the rotation of the Earth. You do what you can, she thought.

She stopped at the light and adjusted her rearview mirror. Reflected in it was the image of Chinatown. In the bright daylight it lost some of its mystery, but none of its appeal. It was still full of powerful memories for her. She glanced at her watch. It was time to get to work.

The parking garage was cool and a pleasant relief from the morning sun. She slowed as she pulled up to the attendant and held up her employee pass. With a smile and a wave, he raised the white barrier arm, and she drove through. Her eyes were having a harder time than usual adjusting to the dark of the garage until she realized she was still wearing her sunglasses. She took her glasses off as she pulled into her designated spot, number five. The placard for Tor Kem Labs covered each of the ten spaces allocated to the company in the garage. She put the car in park, shut off the engine and put a cigarette in her mouth as she reached into the backseat for her black blazer. With her cigarette dangling from her lips, she got out and used the driver's side window as her makeshift mirror and adjusted her white shirt collar over her blazer. Her collar up, and the cigarette dangling from her mouth, looked pretty good. As she was admiring her decidedly editorial look, she heard footsteps behind her.

"Hey there, foxy. You got a light?" a man questioned, with an unlit cigarette held in front of his face. He was stocky with more fat than muscle. He looked like he lifted heavy things, but not often enough to work off whatever he liked to eat. He needed a shower and a shave.

She hesitated for a moment unsure of how to respond. She didn't want to let him get too close, but she wasn't going to run away either.

"Here." She lit her smoke, tossed him the lighter, turned, and began walking away toward the pedestrian exit.

"Don't you want it back?"

"Keep it."

"Hey foxy, don't act like a bitch. Here, let me give it to you."

She could hear his echoing footsteps as he chuckled to himself.

She glanced with her peripheral vision and kept her ears attuned as she continued her trek out of the garage.

"Yeah, let me give it to you!" he repeated.

When she could hear that he was almost within arm's reach, she whirled around, furious, eyes blazing, and moved toward him aggressively. His laughter stopped. His smile fell. His eyes widened. He instinctively backed away as she took his space, closing the distance and leaving no doubt about what was going to happen next.

"You're about to get something, but I don't think you're going to like it." Her words were loud, clear, and emphatic. He continued moving backward and almost tripped over his own feet as she continued taking his ground.

"Okay, okay. I got it," he said, as he nodded in defensive agreement.

"Get the hell out of here. Now!" she shouted. Her words ricocheted and rebounded off the walls and ceiling throughout the garage like a spent bullet.

He turned and ran.

She watched until he was out of the parking garage. Almost to the exit, he looked back and flipped her his middle finger, without slowing down. She exited the garage and walked through the door into the hallway that led to the lobby of the Tor Kem Labs building.

"Asshole!" She was still fuming and walking with her head down, and didn't notice someone approaching her. She looked up at the man coming towards her in a white lab coat.

"Bad morning, Maggie?"

"Sorry Doug, I didn't mean you."

Doug smiled as he walked by.

She walked casually to the bank of elevators and slapped the button to go up. The lobby was quiet. Only the gentle sound of water falling from a waterfall in the lobby oasis, as it was called, could be heard. Her focus was inward. She stood listening to her heartbeat as she waited. The elevator doors opened. She got on and exhaled a long breath that she had been holding in as she watched the doors slowly close. Her heart rate started to fall as the elevator ascended. Once she got to her floor and entered the overly air-conditioned hallway, she could feel the cool wet spots where her sweat had collected on her body and clothes. She didn't have anything to change into. Still, she headed to the restroom to do what she could to freshen up.

She set her purse on the counter between the sinks and took off her blazer and undid the buttons on her shirt. Once off, both were laid on the counter.

In the mirror, she studied herself. She was wearing a black satin camisole. Without her professional clothes, she could see herself as she was years ago: Bare arms, hair hanging loosely. Her hands raised to guard position and squeezed into fists. Arms flexed, muscles taut, she saw someone else looking back. *Where did she go?*

The creak of the restroom door startled her. Quickly, she grabbed two paper towels and started to dry her underarms, neck, and the darkened wet areas on her shirt. Though she figured she wasn't the only one that posed in the mirror, she was still self-conscious about it. *Most women are probably checking their make-up, or their boardroom game face, not making fighting stances and clenched fists.*

An older woman walked in from the lab down the hall. Maggie could never remember her name. The woman was gently pushing doors open looking for an empty and suitable stall. They exchanged awkward smiles in the mirror as the woman found one and went in.

Maggie went back to drying herself and her shirt.

In a few moments, Maggie started to hear percussive biological sounds emanating from the stall and took it as a cue that the woman would be in the stall for longer than a minute.

Time to go. Maggie put on her shirt, and blazer quickly fixed her hair, grabbed her purse and coat, and went to her office.

The plate on the door read Lab 3. Most of the staff worked in Lab 2. Treasuring her solitude, Maggie did her work in Lab 3 with the reason of needing the special equipment there. She entered, hung up her blazer, and grabbed her white lab coat on her way to her station. Casually, she dragged the stool closest to her into position, opened a manila folder lying next to the microscope marked "Pre-trial tests," and readied herself to pick up where she had left off the day before.

She paused for a moment, looked up, and peered around the empty lab. The tables had the same number of stacks of reports as before. The other technicians' lab coats hung on hooks next to their names. The Muzak was playing the same lame version of The Beatles' *Yesterday* as it had…yesterday. Everything was the same as it had been before. No changes in the lab. No changes in her routine. No changes. She pulled the microscope closer, wrote the date on a blank sheet of paper, and started her work.

As she stared into the eyepiece, Maggie was lost in the microworld of bio-particles floating on her slide. Her hand held the focus knob more out of a need for reassurance than a need to fine-tune the image she was viewing. The tiny world in the microscope was a welcome relief from the office drama and problems that encircled her in the macroworld. She observed, then recorded her findings.

The lab door opened, and the hydraulic mechanism hissed as it worked to slowly control its close. A familiar stiletto-heeled pattern of footsteps made their rhythmic approach.

"Dr. Long?" questioned the young blonde intern.

Maggie, jotting down her findings, did not look up, nor did she speak, though she saw the intern in her peripheral vision.

The intern rocked, impatiently, from side to side, holding her clipboard tightly, close to her chest. It looked natural to her. Maggie assumed she once held her textbooks the same way in high school. She could picture the intern in a cheerleading outfit, blonde hair flowing over her shoulders, holding her books clutched tight to her bosom, batting her eyes, getting her way.

The blonde gently tapped her thumb on the clipboard as she waited for a response. Maggie continued with the task at hand.

"What do you need?" she asked the girl, without looking up.

"I need you to sign my form," the blonde intern said, extending her clipboard toward Maggie.

"What form?"

"Uh, the one that every intern must submit that confirms that I actually do work here, so I can get credit towards my major, you know?" Blondie made no effort to hide her sarcasm.

"Ah yes, that one. I know it well." Maggie acknowledged with her trademark deadpan tone.

Finally, she paused, rubbed her eyes, and pushed aside the Petri dishes and folders next to her to clear a space.

After removing her rubber gloves, she pulled a pen from the chest pocket of her white lab coat. With a lightning-quick click of her thumb, she scribbled her signature across the form.

She handed the clipboard back to the intern, without looking at her, and turned her attention back to her microscope.

"Watch your tone," Maggie stated before looking into the eyepiece.

"Yes, ma'am...thank you."

Blondie scurried away.

It was 5:45, well after quitting time. She removed her lab coat and hung it on the hook between two others. One was for the head of research, who was never in, and the other was for a coworker who had been fired a month ago and replaced by the intern.

Maggie knew why. Her ex-coworker was a pretty young lady, but she was not willing to "work late" with the boss. She was eventually fired for some ridiculous infraction and then replaced with blondie. Maggie figured blondie did what her boss wanted, so she would likely be around until he got tired of her and went on to get a new one that satisfied the same agenda.

In her current position, Maggie had only found security in the fact that she could do everything herself, running the entire lab complex. She knew it was the combination of her utility and the knowledge that her boss had no attraction to Asian women that kept her around. She became angered when she thought about it, so she tried not to.

She was usually the last one to leave, and today was no exception. The empty floor used to be a little spooky to her, but now she was accustomed to it. She had come to appreciate the quiet seclusion. It was comforting hearing her lone footsteps echo in the empty hall.

Not one for small talk, she came in earlier and left later than most. She was terrible at it anyway. She wasn't always comfortable speaking to her coworkers. Always professional, just not always familiar. Work was like high school, only she didn't have her one best friend. There was no Sifu Chang either. She was in a world that she had chosen, but not one that she wanted.

Rounding the corner toward the elevators, Maggie smiled and waved to the custodian as he mopped the hallway. He acknowledged Maggie's wave with a nod and a smile back as he continued making his silent serpentine pattern.

As she stood looking at the elevator's stainless-steel doors, she could see her distorted reflection looking back at her. She was always surprised to see herself in professional attire. It was with a little shock that she realized she looked like an adult. *When did that happen?*

She became lost in her thoughts and was transported to the day she became a sifu. Standing before the board. Cold sweat dripping from her body.

It's too late. You can't go back. You make your choice, and you move on. You move on.

Shutting the front door and with a heavy sigh, Maggie laid her keys down on the yellow-beige Formica countertop. With one serpent-like twirl of her torso, she created enough centrifugal force to swing her heavy purse in a sweeping arc and make it land softly next to her keys. *Ha! Still got it.*

She ran her right hand roughly through her hair twice, as if to loosen and let float away, the day's worries. Gently, she shook her head, and let her hair fall back into place, as she kicked off her shoes. The black pumps landed close to the kitchen table, next to another similar pair that had been there for a day or more.

She padded softly to the refrigerator and pulled out a bottle of Tab. The cool cola tasted good. The cold liquid running down into her stomach gave her a shiver. She pulled out a chair from the kitchen table and sat down.

The house was quiet. Wendy wasn't home yet. She always came home, put down her purse on the counter between the toaster and the fondue pot, and then put on a record. It used to be Peter Frampton's *Frampton Comes Alive* until she got into soul, and recently disco. They had gone to see *Saturday Night Fever* the year before, and ever since, it had been all disco all the time.

Not that Maggie minded Wendy's music, but she found it refreshing to come home to a quiet house occasionally. The silence cleared out her mind. It gave her a moment to reflect on the day. Wendy liked to call that her "big girl time".

"What the hell do you mean by a big girl time?" Maggie had asked, as they both were cutting a large block of cheese into little cubes at the kitchen table for the fondue dinner party later that night.

"You know, don't you? It's when you come home after work and brood over your soda about life as a big girl. Being an adult."

"I wouldn't say I'm brooding. I'm just deep in thought about my life for a moment."

Maggie continued cutting the bricks of orange, yellow, and white cheeses into one-inch cubes without looking up.

"Isn't that the definition of brooding?" Wendy said exasperated. "You know, it's okay to second guess your life choices. You just have to decide what happens next. What are you gonna do about it? You know?"

The kitchen table became very quiet with only the sounds of knives hitting the wooden cutting boards peppering the silence.

"I'm not second-guessing anything," Maggie said, as she studied her slices and cut them carefully. "I've made great life choices, haven't I? Sometimes, though, work just gets to me."

Wearing a glowering expression, Maggie grabbed a loaf of French bread and began cutting the bread into cubes roughly the same size as the cheese. "It gets to everybody eventually, I'm sure. The day-to-day grind, you know what I mean?"

"It *does*. Most people don't do what they want to do. That's why it's called work. If you enjoyed it... I guess they'd call it something else," Wendy shrugged her shoulders as she spoke.

Maggie took in what she said, and decided she had nothing to add, so she kept cutting. Their busy hands were on autopilot as they kept carefully and diligently cutting cubes of cheese and bread. When they finished, they pushed the cubes into separate piles. Huge piles. The cheese looked like a giant heap of deconstructed candy corn. Given their modest-sized fondue pot, they realized that they had enough cheese for at least four fondues.

"That's a lot of cheese," Maggie said succinctly.

"Yeah, it is. How many are coming, again?"

"Two. Two people."

They both sighed heavily, and then looked at each other, letting a moment pass, before sputtering out raspberries of disbelief that descended into a fit of laughter.

"Where is it?" Maggie yelled from the bedroom closet to Wendy in the family room. Her voice was barely audible over the Isley Brothers, *"Fight the Power"* on the turntable of the quadraphonic stereo system.

"I told you it's on the top shelf!" Wendy's disembodied voice reverberated through the house and landed at Maggie's feet, as she stood on tiptoe atop a three-step ladder, teetering on the highest step. She was pushing aside boxes of mementos, clothes, shoes, and papers looking for the Apollo 11 photograph, signed by all three astronauts, that Wendy simply had to have at this exact moment.

"Where?" Maggie yelled again, exasperated by the mess.

"Top shelf!"

Maggie realized that she had extended herself too far as she reached toward the very back of the closet's top shelf. Unsteady, she knew she was about to fall. As if in slow motion, she felt her body fall from the ladder and land on the stack of pillows that she had placed there for just such an emergency.

The large brown box she had been trying to push aside landed with a tumbling thud just beside her. The contents spilled out onto the floor. She sat there, irritated at having fallen, and feeling rather undignified at landing so clumsily.

"Did you fall? It sounded like you fell."

"Yes, but— Everything's all right."

Where the hell was her old kung fu reflexes?

She was happy to be unharmed though. She propped herself up on her elbows and, for a moment, tried to think of some good reason not to just stay on the ground and relax when she noticed—

"Did you get it?" Wendy's voice asked from the other room.

"Yeah! I got it!" Maggie said, as she stared at the box's contents scattered on the beige carpeting.

"Oh good! I don't need it now, but you know...I like to know where it is..."

"Yeah. Uh-huh,"

She stared transfixed at two of the items that had spilled from the box. The rest of the assorted junk held little meaning for her—the broken ballet dancer atop a white music box, loose papers, and a half dozen eight-track tapes. She pushed it all to the side.

117

Carefully, she picked up the mementos that called to her, a brown document mailer tube, and an old flier for Sifu Chang's school, and laid them on the bed. She handled the items like precious relics from a time capsule. The tube was labeled with the address of her old apartment building, with no return address. She knew what was in the tube, and opened it gingerly as if handling a sharp object. Her fingers gripped the paper and slid it out, careful not to rip it.

The scroll was unrolled with difficulty from being in the tube for so long. She gave only a glance to the beautifully drawn dragon and the long strokes of hand-lettered calligraphy. Then, as if it were some forbidden treasure, she rolled the masterpiece quickly back up. It took her a few twists, but eventually, it fit back into the tube that had held it for so long.

She flopped herself onto the bed and laid back as she studied the flier from Sifu Chang's school. On the front was the dragon and tiger image with text over the top in large yellow letters urging the reader to "Sign Up Today!" She flipped it over and read the handwriting on the back.

That was the one time that her teacher had tried to contact her after the test. She never responded. Maggie was slightly disappointed that he didn't send something more formal than just a note on the back of a flier advertising his summer program. Even though Sifu Chang had, undoubtedly, guessed that Maggie wouldn't tell her parents what had happened, and thought the flier would be a way for her to receive correspondence without attracting attention, it still annoyed her. The whole situation was devastating at the time, but upon reflection, with the passage of years, it was now just something she had learned to live with. At least that was what she told herself.

She read again what the sifu had written in his scrawl across the back of the flier:

Maggie,

I am sorry that you were not happy with the details regarding your promotion to the rank

of Sifu, but I hope that in time you will come back and help me teach at the school.

You are my best student. I would hate to lose you.

S. Chang

"What are you doing in there, girl? Did you hurt yourself when you fell? Get knocked out? Did you fall asleep?"

"If I was knocked out— Never mind, I'm fine."

"Then come out! *Dallas* is on!"

Maggie took a breath and put both items back in the box. With quick-moving hands, she gathered up the other items, deposited them as well, and threw the box on the floor in the back of the closet. She slid the large, mirrored closet door shut and looked at herself for a moment before turning to leave the bedroom.

"I'm coming! Tell me what I missed!" Maggie yelled as she tried to ignore how she felt.

The Muzak at the grocery store was the same as the Muzak at the lab, and it drove her crazy. She tried to tune it out by quietly humming *"More than a Woman"* to herself, but that was difficult. She picked out large tomatoes and put them into a clear plastic bag. She weighed them, and then placed the bag in the shopping cart. Next, was the green bell peppers as Maggie worked her way down the list of ingredients for one of Wendy's secret recipes that seemed suspiciously like plain-old spaghetti sauce. Wendy had handed Maggie the list, and

119

with a peck on the cheek told her, "Get only the best that they have."

Maggie feigned more interest than she felt since she didn't consider herself a connoisseur of gourmet cooking. Wendy had a passion for cooking and food that Maggie just didn't have. She didn't care what Wendy made to eat, as long as it was edible, and it didn't make too much of a mess. She pushed her cart to the avocados and examined the selection carefully.

Just as she was about to drop the produce into her cart, her eyes locked on a striking Asian woman carefully selecting oranges across from her.

The woman had styled her hair like Kate Jackson, and she wore a dark blue jumpsuit that she filled out nicely. Maggie gazed at her, surreptitiously. Her eyes moved from the avocados to the woman and back again. She was attractive. She was fascinating. She was— familiar. Maggie frowned a little trying to recall. Finally, she realized it was Kathy. Maggie hadn't seen her in years, but she knew it was her. She was beautiful and had grown into a stunning woman. In addition to her physical looks, she had a certain presence, and quiet confidence, as if she knew exactly who she was, and was comfortable with it. She was different from the girl she knew all those years ago. *Do I say something to her? Would it be strange to do that?* Kathy was walking toward her.

"Hey, tough girl, can I bum a smoke?" Kathy gushed, smiling big.

"Kathy?"

"Give me a hug, tough girl!" Kathy pulled her close. Maggie knew as soon as they embraced, that things were different. It was the hug of an old friend, not a long-lost love.

"Fancy meeting you here, huh?" Maggie was wearing her best awkward smile.

"I know. I'm not usually here, but I'm in town because my husband's gone on a business trip to San Diego, and I figured I'd see my mom while he's away."

"You got married?" Her eyes blinked her surprise.

"Yes...Yes, I did." The pregnant silence was filled with the sounds of the bustling supermarket produce aisle. "I guess it happens." Kathy shrugged her shoulders and wore a blithe expression.

"Well, I'm sure he's great." Maggie nodded while she reorganized all of the items in her basket for no reason whatsoever.

"He is. He's the best. And you?"

"I'm with someone...Not like you though." Maggie smiled a knowing smile.

"I know." Kathy nodded. "And you are a kick-ass sifu now?" She emphasized her statement with overly theatrical hand gestures. It was an odd phenomenon that most people seemed to feel obligated to act out mock techniques when they spoke about martial arts. Kathy added a kick that made her jumpsuit look like it was in danger of splitting down her backside.

"No, I'm a scientist, a lab tech, really," Maggie added what she hoped was a convincing smile.

"A lab tech?" Maggie Long? The only girl to be a sifu in Chinatown, is a lab tech?" Kathy looked slack-jawed.

"Well, choices...Ya know? Life choices. You want different things, sometimes. You should *obviously* understand that, right?" Maggie tried not to sound defensive as she looked away from Kathy and put two apples she didn't want or need into a bag and dropped them into her cart.

"So, you just changed your mind about it? I thought you really wanted it. I guess, I just never thought you would quit." Kathy crossed her arms and looked quizzically at Maggie.

"It's not like that...I never quit. When I left Chinatown, I studied Judo in college, and I still train now, I —"

"Are you happy, Maggie?" Kathy interrupted with a searching look.

"Yes, I'm happy." Maggie pushed her cart back and forth, nervously, "I changed my mind about it all, ya know? Things are what they are now. You grow up. You just have to grow up." She stared into the cart watching it move as she spoke.

Kathy put her hand on Maggie's.

"Well, a wise person told me, you can fool everyone, but yourself, tough girl. Remember who it was?"

Maggie's words rang in her head as she watched Kathy shift her purse to her other shoulder.

"Look, it's not my place to tell you how to live your life, especially in the produce section. For that, I have to be by the wine," Kathy's smile was big and her eyes showed compassion.

They both chuckled and Kathy's hand gently touched Maggie's face. She let her knuckles lightly brush down her cheek.

"It was good to see you."

"You too." Maggie forced a smile until Kathy turned and walked away.

She stalled and adjusted the items in her cart again. She didn't want to watch her walk away, fearing Kathy would turn and look back. She put two grapefruits, a head of lettuce, and three plantains into her cart. She didn't want any of them. With her eyes moist and her vision blurry, she pushed her cart away from the produce section toward the next aisle and went looking for milk.

The night was warm, and Maggie had rolled down her window to catch the subtle night breezes as she watched Sifu

Chang teach his class through the front window of the school. She leaned with her elbow out the window as the radio quietly played. She kept a bottle of Tab between her legs, occasionally taking a sip. Initially, she had planned to just walk into the school, but on further thought, she decided to time her entrance so that Sifu Chang would have an opportunity to speak to her after class without interruption. At least, that's what she told herself.

She knew full well that she was delaying going in because she was just plain scared. So much time had passed. So much had been said and left unsaid. *Will it all be water under the bridge? Or will it be a stagnant lake of resentment?* She gulped her Tab.

Maggie enjoyed the silent instruction and watched as the students stood in a semi-circle around Sifu Chang and another student. He was demonstrating a tiger striking technique. With no sound, it looked like an elaborate pantomime. The sifu and the student stood in a fighting stance, facing each other. The sifu's hands were flying quickly in strikes and counterstrikes as he instructed. He had his students' full attention.

Sifu's face was expressive, full of energy, and intent. He didn't look much different than before, despite the years that have passed. He looked like he always did when he taught, happy. Maggie couldn't help but feel envious of the students learning from her old teacher. She missed training and she missed having a mentor. And most of all, she missed him. It was time to go in.

Not wanting to disturb the class, Maggie entered the school as stealthily as she could. The street sounds faded with the soft closing of the door behind her. The first steps transported her back like a time machine to the first time she had walked into that place when she was just a girl. Not much had changed.

The same pictures were on the wall, though now faded from the sun. Same rickety folding chairs that squeaked when you sat on them. The same smell of bleach from the bathroom. It was nice to be someplace familiar. It was like pulling out a nugget of memory and studying it with old eyes.

She took a deep breath, closed her eyes, and let it out. Her palms became clammy. Sifu Chang was still teaching the class. She moved close to the metal folding chairs along the wall and took a seat as quietly and inconspicuously as possible, although the squeaking report was hard to avoid.

Next to her, an old woman sat reading a book. Maybe it was a good one; the reader never looked up when Maggie sat down. Or maybe, she imagined, she had been so catlike that the woman didn't even know she was there. Then she reminded herself, *this is Chinatown, and people tend to mind their own business. Not all of the old traditions are bad ones.*

The class was loud. The energy could be heard and felt with thuds and whacks on pads as the students dutifully worked on power drills, speed drills, and applications of their skills. After a few moments, the class paired off, and the students began sparring. They were blocking, kicking, and using their most recent instruction to try to overcome their opponent's defenses and position. Sifu Chang moved strategically around the room giving his corrections and commentary. Some of it was gentle, some of it was harsh, and some of it was comical. All of it was necessary.

A master of the art of teaching, he tailored his approach to what was needed for each student to be able to understand and make the appropriate changes. Some students needed the carrot, and some needed the stick. Some needed a bigger stick.

Maggie overheard him using some of the same old expressions that he used when he taught her. She watched as he rolled his eyes at one of the boys who had half-heartedly struck at his opponent with a roundhouse kick, failing to attack with any power, because he was leaning away to avoid getting hit. She already knew what was coming for the boy.

"Is that how you kick? You know, I would say you kick like a little girl, but that would be insulting to little girls!" The boy struck again, but this time he committed himself and kicked with greater force. Connecting with a heavy thud, the blow made the receiver wince, then he grinned, and gave the kicker a thumbs up.

Sifu smiled broadly, "That's better," he said. "Now you're hitting more like a *big* girl!" He and the two students chuckled. "Keep at it, eventually you'll hit like a tiger!" he said, as he walked away to help another pair of students.

Two boys sparred close to the door where Maggie was seated. Sifu Chang was watching them closely. One boy was bigger than the other, but the smaller one was using his size as an advantage. He stayed close to his opponent, slipping out of everything thrown at him. He dodged punches and ducked kicks. The big guy could never seem to get a hold of his smaller challenger. Maggie knew what the student was doing wrong, and that the sifu would point it out.

"No! Bend your legs! You have to use your power, and you have to blend with him. You look like you're trying to swat a fly and the fly is winning!" the teacher said, admonishing the bigger student.

When the sifu turned away from the boys, his eyes locked onto Maggie. She saw that he was looking directly at her, but he registered no reaction. She panicked for a moment. Had time done so much damage to the memories of her that he didn't recognize her? Or had his feelings about her changed over life's angry years?

A big, warm smile stretched across his face, and his wrinkles deepened.

"Everyone, hold it! Stop for a moment."

Maggie took a deep breath. *What was he going to do?*

Sifu Chang raised his arms to command their attention, and the class grew silent. He looked around to make sure he had everyone's attention.

"Turn and give the sifu a salute," he said, still smiling.

The students looked confused. Some of them gave half-hearted salutes, looking here, there, and everywhere. Others searched the room more carefully for whomever they were supposed to be saluting, but they didn't see anyone. Maggie knew that they were looking for a man. They saw nothing but two women in the lobby waiting for the students to finish the class.

She rose from her chair. This time the woman beside her looked over.

"I think he means me."

The students saluted her, and Maggie returned the salute to the stunned class.

"Have a seat," Sifu Chang gestured to the chair in front of his desk with an outstretched hand. He couldn't quit smiling as Maggie sat down. He saw her eyes surveying the mess that was perpetually atop his desk. He knew he should straighten it up, but there is always tomorrow. They hadn't been in this room together since the day of the test. *Seemed like yesterday.*

Their eyes met and he gave her a wink as he settled into the battered, worn, and heavily padded office chair. The chair protested with a modest squeak.

"So, Maggie, how are you doing these days?" he said, reclining back in his chair.

"No sparring gear for the students, huh? Still doing it the old way?" Her eyes scanned the walls as if searching for something important.

"This is Chinatown." He lifted his palms and shrugged his shoulders. "We only have old ways."

He searched her face for a reaction but found none.

"That's why I'm here…I want to see about opening a school, on my own." Maggie dropped her bombshell and then avoided his gaze. He watched her eyes as they surveyed the desk and then the walls before settling on studying her shoes for a time. Finally, her eyes fell on the small rosewood dragon sculpture on his desk.

Sifu Chang tempered his initial reaction of surprise at her announcement as he watched her and took in her transformation into an adult. The Maggie sitting before him was now a grown woman. It made him feel old. He could still remember her as that tough little girl that first came into the school that fateful afternoon all those years ago.

He watched her as she continued to stare at the small dragon sculpture near the edge of his desk. Her eyes were so concentrated it was as if she was waiting for it to move, or at least for him to say something. He let out a heavy sigh and waited until her eyes found his.

"Nothing has changed, Maggie. You know that, right?" The sifu spoke softly, a far cry from his booming voice on the mat. The students didn't know how carefully he had cultivated the persona of the confident teacher. And though it was effective, he was more at home as the mild-mannered guy in the office, though he seldom let that side be seen.

In this circumstance, he knew that a gentle word from a friend would have more influence on her than merely parroting the edicts already rejected. He watched Maggie go back to observing her feet, so he craned his neck and tried to look under her gaze.

"I know, nothing ever changes, but still, I want to do it." She didn't sound entirely confident. He watched her body language closely, looking for clues as to what was going on inside her head. She looked scared, wounded, and determined. Not the best combination to have.

"It could be dangerous for you. Once you put out your shingle with your name on it, I can't help you." Sifu Chang moved the dragon to the side of his desk and leaned forward making Maggie look at his face. "Even if I give you my blessing, they will still come."

"Blessing? I just want to know that you won't try and stop me," Maggie said, finally looking into his eyes.

"Me? I would never try to stop you. What could I do anyway? I'm an old man." He smiled and watched Maggie chuckle. "Look, I think this edict in Chinatown is a silly relic of the past, and the time will soon come when it goes away, but until then, I know they will defend it with everything they have." He landed with a firm tone. "No, I won't try and stop you, there will be enough people doing that already."

The sifu leaned back and reached for a mug of black coffee that he knew was hours old. He didn't care. He took a big drink of the cold bitter liquid and put the mug on the corner of his desk, wiping his mouth with the back of his hand, "They will be lining up to take a swing at you. They won't want to just stop you; they'll want to make an *example* of you. Are you prepared for that?"

"Yes." She was resolute and her eyes bored into his. "Would they come after you?"

"I'm not sure what they'd do to me. Not sure at all." His eyes squinted as he contemplated the question. "They may take into consideration my past association with you and decide to make an example of me too, but I don't think so."

He shrugged his shoulders, "Would it even matter?"

Sifu Chang stood up and walked partway around his desk. After pushing aside a stack of books and papers, with some hitting the floor unnoticed, he sat on the corner.

"You were my best student, Maggie, and it crushed me when you left, but I understood. I respected your choice. Now, I am asking that you take your next step very carefully."

He studied Maggie's face. Her expression indicated that she was steadfast in her decision.

"From what I understand, you have a good job and a home. You have someone special too, right? Someone that loves you?"

Her head nodded in agreement.

"Do you want to give it all up for *this*?" Sifu Chang held up his hands gesturing to his messy little office. "Really, *this?*"

He stood and leaned on the filing cabinet near the window where they could both see some students still lingering on the mat. He let a beat of time pass. "Do you have some score you want to settle? Why now?"

Maggie sighed and gently shook her head before she spoke, "No scores. I just want to do it. I always have. Now's the time, that's all."

"Do you think all students are like you? They aren't. Most are quitters and there is no loyalty from them." Moving from the file cabinet to the seat next to her, he held her hand. "The reason why you were so unique, why you were so special, is because you were loyal. I knew my time wouldn't be wasted with you. Only one in a hundred are like you. Maybe it's one in a thousand now, as life gets easier, and people complain more about how hard it is."

Maggie looked into his eyes, but he didn't know if the words were getting through. He hoped she was listening and not just hearing him. He could feel his pulse quicken and his heart start to pound. The subject always made him get excited. Too excited. He needed to get a hold of himself.

"Now, running a school? Do you really want to run a kung fu school? Are you sure? Please, think hard. The pay is low. The hours are terrible, and there is no retirement. I've been married three times!" He held up three fingers in front of her eyes.

She shifted in her seat.

"For you, it will be even worse: A woman running a martial art school in Chinatown? First, there will be laughter and then there will be tears. Your tears!" He pointed at her with an incriminating finger. "They will feel threatened. *Everyone* will feel threatened by you for upsetting the status quo, trying to change things. Nobody likes change, Maggie. They will make fun of you. Then when they see how good you are? They will come after you and try to destroy you."

The sifu rose and worked his way back around to his desk. He sat down and folded his hands.

"They will not treat you fairly, Maggie."

Sifu Chang looked at her face, studied her expression, and wondered what she was thinking of as she scanned the office floor.

"Why don't you go back to your life now and forget all about this crazy idea while you still can, okay? Don't do something you will regret. You can train here with me and help teach. The students will salute you. I will teach you. You can still have everything that you have now." He sat back, took a deep breath, let it out, and leaned across his desk toward Maggie looking, waiting, and hoping for agreement.

It was clear that she had listened intently, and he could see her processing his words through her mind as her gaze shifted and wandered from his eyes to the ceiling, to her shoes, and finally back to him. *Would she listen?* He knew that it was the same offer she had turned down years ago. He knew that it was a tough sell. In his heart, he didn't think that she would come back just to fall in line. He knew Maggie. She wasn't just determined, she was indomitable.

From the time she was a little girl, she had been one that made decisions and stuck to them. He heard Maggie take a breath and let it out.

"You taught me to accept all possible outcomes but to pursue the one I want. That is what I will do." She adjusted herself in her chair.

He nodded his head at the expert use of his own words against him before he spoke.

"Okay, well, if you're looking for a spot for your school my ex-brother-in-law is a commercial realtor, he can — "

Maggie interrupted, "I already have a spot in mind. I am going to open in a couple of months," she stated confidently and stood up extending her hand with a practiced technique.

Sifu Chang nodded. "So formal now, huh?"

"I don't know that I've ever said it before, but thank you for being my teacher," she declared, shaking her teacher's hand with both of hers, and smiling, her eyes glassy.

Sifu Chang could tell she was trying her best to fight back tears, and it made him remember when she had come to the funeral. She became special to him that day. He knew that she had used all her skills to find him and come to the ceremony. When he looked down and saw her standing next to him, she earned a special place in his life. As he saw it all in his memories, his emotions stirred, and a tear was threatening to come forth and run triumphantly down his cheek. He fought it back.

"You don't have to say it. I am proud to be your teacher, and friend," He put his other hand on her arm, "and that will never change." He stepped around the desk to hug Maggie.

"You know, I am glad that after all those times you drove past the school, that you finally came in."

Maggie's eyes registered surprise.

"They had so many pretty ones, why the black one?" Wendy asked, holding the ladder steady while Maggie stood on the highest rung. Maggie was hanging a black dragon's head, from a dragon dancing costume, in front of the school. She was putting the last nail in the mounting bracket and was concentrating intensely as she did it, to ignore the question.

Normally, dragon dancing costumes are colorful and shiny, and the heads are as well. Maggie had asked the owner of the shop for a black one, and she had nodded, knowingly. She then grabbed the least decorated white head, removed all of the extraneous glitter and other decorations, and then let Maggie know it would take two days for the dying process: one day to dye it black and another for it to completely dry. Maggie had agreed and paid her. When she left, she caught the reflection of the shop owner in the shoplifting mirror positioned high in the corner of the store and watched as the woman leaned over to another woman working behind the counter. The shop owner whispered something to the other woman that made her shake her head. They both stared at Maggie with concern as they watched her walk out the door.

After a few heavy swings of the hammer, Maggie secured the dragon's head in place. She hopped down from the ladder and landed next to Wendy. They both looked up, using their hands as shields from the brilliant glare, and studied the new decoration. The black dragon's head was an ominous silhouette against the marbled sky of blue and white. The dragon's dark visage stared down menacingly at the street below. With its large, fanged mouth hanging agape, it

132

appeared to be ready to attack and consume whatever came near it.

"Why the black one?" Wendy repeated with her arms crossed as she looked up, waiting for a response from Maggie.

"It's a symbol," Maggie said, evasively, as she started folding the ladder, never looking up at the ominous totem above her.

"What kind of symbol?" Wendy continued with her hand shielding her squinting gaze.

"It's a symbol that tells everyone that I have a new school, and I am opening up, you know, to the...community." Maggie shrugged her shoulders dismissively, as she tried to evade the entire line of questioning and move inside.

"And? It sounds like there is more to it than that." Wendy stood now adopting the standard posture of disapproval with one hand on her hip, and her head tilted, awaiting the truth.

"*And*, it means I am open to any... or...all challengers...I accept all challenges," Maggie finished quickly, slightly exasperated and trying to minimize what she had just said, acting as if it took tremendous concentration to fold and carry the ladder through the doorway.

"What? You're asking for a fight? Are you nuts?" Incredulous, Wendy followed Maggie into the school while Maggie appeared to search for a perfect location to store the ladder in the back room.

"It is a tradition, you know? All the new schools do it. You have to do it if you want to be respected," Maggie leaned the ladder against the wall and tossed the hammer into an open toolbox, where it landed with a heavy metallic bang.

"Says who? My cousin opened a school, and he didn't do this!"

"He opened a school in Des Moines, it's different. This is Chinatown, and some traditions I plan to follow. I figure it will show that I am not asking for exceptions, just a chance." Maggie continued putting the rest of the tools back in the large beat-up gray metal toolbox that she had borrowed from the handyman, Mr. Liu, next door.

The space she had leased for the school was old. The building was built in the early 1920s and everything creaked. The wooden floors dipped slightly toward the back. Maggie had taken a ball bearing and placed it on the floor to see how bad it was. The ball bearing started rolling almost as soon as she let go of it. It coasted quickly and then slowed slightly, before running into the back wall. She made a mental note of the floor and would keep it in mind when training students.

There was no central heating, merely a radiator instead. It was an old coil affair like they have in cartoons. She hadn't seen one since she went to her grandmother's apartment when she was a small child and touched it, despite her parents' urging her not to. That's when she found out that sometimes rules were there for a reason.

The building's window frames, walls, and doorframes had been painted over so many times that nothing shut or sealed correctly. It also had a damp musty smell that seemed to hit you right in the nose when the door was opened. It either became less pungent as you walked to the back, or you just got used to it. She hoped airing it out and the new carpet would help freshen the place up a bit. Maggie was brought back to the moment and the issue at hand by the stern tone of Wendy's continued discussion of the black dragon head.

"If I would have known about this, black-dragon-head-thing, I never would have gone along with it," Wendy said, following Maggie into the back room of the newly carpeted school, where Maggie had her uniforms hanging next to her small office nook, which consisted of a desk, a file cabinet, and two chairs. She had started her improvements in her office. It was newly painted. The new carpet made the old space seem like a breath of new life had been breathed into it.

"That's why I didn't tell you," Maggie was putting on her kung fu uniform with the newly embroidered *Sifu* on the left side over her heart. "Thanks for this, by the way, it looks nice. I love the embroidery."

"You're welcome!" Wendy said, curtly.

Maggie continued to admire the uniform top as she picked a few unseen specs of lint, and then brushed the rest aside hoping that her distraction would derail the conversation back to mundane topics but knowing that it wouldn't.

"What else haven't you told me?" Wendy leaned against the office doorway, arms folded and looking at Maggie with an unyielding expression.

"Look, this is something that I have to do. I know you don't understand, sometimes, but I have to do it," Maggie declared, but did not move closer to Wendy. She looked at the space between them and thought that maybe it was greater than it appeared. Since embarking on this endeavor, she felt that there was a growing chasm between them that was in danger of becoming a void.

"So, is this dangerous then? Opening this...school?" Wendy's tone lingered on the last word as if she was having trouble getting it out.

"It could be."

"I thought you talked to your teacher, and he said it was fine?" Wendy leaned forward as if she thought she would have trouble hearing the answer.

"He did, but he isn't in charge of Chinatown, he's my old teacher, he runs a school. I really just wanted to make sure he knew I was back, and what I was doing, that's all." Maggie folded her arms and waited for the next volley of questions.

"Look, I'm not sure I understand all the subtle nuances of kung fu masters in Chinatown, but I know this: Don't keep things from me. I deserve to know the truth. I'm in this too, ya know?" Wendy picked up a box of nails from the floor and placed them purposefully on Maggie's desk with a sudden thudding emphasis, before turning and walking out of the school.

Maggie watched her leave, as she silently crossed the carpet. There wasn't anything Maggie could say to make Wendy understand a world that she wasn't a part of. At some point, Wendy would leave her. She didn't want it to happen, but she felt it was inevitable. Maggie had tried to bury her passion deep, but now it was loose, and it was burning up the old life they had together with an all-consuming fire. Maggie thought of Sifu Chang and his failed marriages. *Inevitable.* Though she was close to Wendy, and they said that they loved each other, a dark thought arrived. Maggie thought that perhaps she couldn't love anyone, at least not as much as they needed.

Wendy would probably never understand that people like Maggie and Sifu Chang were different. Sifu Chang would always train and study kung fu because it was a part of him. It was as necessary as food and breath. Maggie was the same way. Those that didn't study, couldn't understand, and never would. Maggie felt like she had cocooned herself in the chrysalis of the nine-to-five world of ordinary life for a long time, and now she had to break loose and spread her wings. She was ready to give up everything she had. It both scared and exhilarated her. She was on the precipice of chaos, and as she had read in Sun Tzu: "In the midst of chaos, there is also opportunity." Maggie thought about all these things as she rubbed her fingers over the raised stitching on her uniform, before being startled by the bell on the door announcing someone's entrance into the silent school.

"Hello, anyone here?"

It was a woman's voice. Maggie was a little surprised at having a visitor since she wasn't open yet, and she had only just a few moments before hung up the black dragon's head. *Surely, a challenger wouldn't show up that quickly, would they? And a woman?*

"What can I do for you?" Maggie walked toward the small lobby at the entrance of the school. A cute Asian woman was walking toward her carrying a bouquet. She was shorter than Maggie and a few years younger. She looked like a doll with a short bob haircut and the biggest smile she had ever seen. Her smile beamed as if it was powered by a massive flow of energy. It lit up the room. Maggie found that she couldn't look away from her.

"I wanted to welcome you to the neighborhood. I'm Emily. I have the flower shop two doors down," she said with a smile, extending the bouquet of purple orchids, white gardenias, and one lone daisy toward Maggie. She received them and promptly brought the flowers close to her nose and inhaled deeply, savoring the perfumed air.

"They're supposed to be good luck, but they smell nice too," Emily added.

"How thoughtful. Thank you," Maggie said, with a smile. "Yes, they do smell lovely." A beat of awkward silence held the space before Maggie realized that their gazes were locked on each other. "I've seen it...your shop, I mean," Maggie stated, breaking her vision away with a quick shake of her head to look at the bouquet and then back at Emily. *What to say?* "I meant to come by and say hello. I've just been so busy, you know, with everything."

137

Maggie looked around and gestured with the bouquet to the paint buckets and tools lying around, testifying to the work that had been keeping her busy for the previous couple of weeks. "Wow, thank you again, they're really beautiful." Not knowing what else to say, she said the same thing, again, "Thank you."

Again, Maggie brought the flowers to her nose and breathed in deeply. Once more enjoying the pleasant aroma, not realizing that she was staring at Emily as she did it.

"Martial arts? Kung fu? Who's the teacher?" Emily asked innocently, as she looked around.

"Me, I am. I'm the teacher."

"Oh, I'm sorry, I thought it would be your husband or — "

"No, there's no *husband*. I, uh…There is no husband, and I'm the teacher, and there is no, uh, husband…at all."

Maggie, looking for something to occupy her hands, patted the wrinkles from her uniform purposefully and nervously with one hand as she spoke.

Emily nodded, acknowledging that she completely understood everything said and unsaid. "The black dragon head out front. Do you have witnesses in case of challenges?"

Maggie was surprised that she knew about the symbolism of the black dragon head and then felt slight irritation at the question from the cute flower girl. "Witnesses? I don't need any help, or witnesses, actually, I can —"

Emily smiled bigger. "Don't take it the wrong way. I'm sure you're great. I hope you *do* have witnesses, so they can't say you didn't beat them when you win, you know? And then try to take back their loss?"

"I'm sure…I'll be fine."

Emily kept a big smile on her face as she reached into the bouquet in Maggie's hand and pulled out one flower, the daisy. Maggie watched as Emily looked around for a moment and then spied a half-full cup of water sitting on the shelf, put the daisy in the cup, and placed it on the entry table by the front door.

"You should always keep a flower by the front door for luck. Daisies are best."

Emily stood still for a moment, and they both looked at each other and then around the room, sharing the same awkwardness that had visited them earlier. "Okay, well, I'll see you around, I bet. Time to go back to work." Emily winked and then turned and left.

Maggie watched Emily walk out of the door. She turned and waved as the door shut behind her. Maggie stood alone in the quiet of the empty school holding the bouquet, and then she heard herself, "Damn."

Despite the back door being open to the cool alley, the air in the school was warm and still. Maggie had her small, black transistor radio resting on the pail shelf of the ladder, speaker side up. She was enjoying the steady rhythm of K.C. and the Sunshine Band's *Boogie Shoes* as she did her best to eyeball the most appropriate location for the nail on which to hang her long dragon scroll. The scroll was given to her after she was promoted to Sifu.

"Given" was the wrong word though. It had shown up one day in the mail when she was still in high school. The scroll was a long parchment paper with an ink drawing and classic Chinese calligraphy that said: "To the dragon, long life."

Maggie had always assumed that Sifu Chang had sent it, but she didn't know. Maybe it was one of the other sifus at the test or some random admirer. She thought about the man she saw that day. He was so mysterious. She always wondered if it could have been him. Not likely, but it was someone that knew she had been promoted to Sifu.

She had spent a few days pondering the identity of the sender before finally hanging it behind the door in her room. There it hung never being seen by anyone but her. She figured her parents wouldn't ask about it if they didn't see it and she was right. Until it fell out of the box in the closet that evening months ago, she hadn't thought about it.

Lost in thought about where to hang the dragon scroll on the wall, she had barely noticed the sound of the bell on the front door letting her know that someone had entered.

"I will be with you in a minute," Maggie yelled to the unknown caller as she started to climb down the ladder.

From the corner of her eye, she caught an outline of a man. She tried not to look too startled as she realized that he was wearing a black belt over his white Karate Gi. He was standing in a square horse stance with his arms flexed at his side and his fists clenched.

He looked like he could've been an extra on break from filming a Karate movie, she thought. With his blonde hair, he seemed like a discount version of Chuck Norris. He appeared formidable. She tried to tell herself that maybe he was just inquiring about lessons, but in her heart, she knew that wasn't the case. He was going to be trouble. She felt the butterflies in her stomach starting to take flight as she realized that this would be the first of many times, she would face danger.

As she stepped off the ladder, she questioned him innocently, "Hello, can I help you?"

"Yeah, I want to leave a message for the teacher," the Karate man said in a gravelly voice.

The two ends of his black belt were hanging slightly unevenly between his legs. He grabbed both ends and tugged at them horizontally making the ends snap and even up into a tight knot. Maggie could see the white speckles and streaks in the belt showing that the belt was worn and weathered; He had been training for a while. She knew he was a challenger, and since he had entered her school in such a threatening way, whether he knew it or not, he had given up all pretense of decorum. This was her school. She just had to win.

"Okay, what's the message?" Maggie said, as she wiped her hands with a towel that she grabbed hanging from the ladder.

"Tell him, whoever he is, I'll be back to kick his ass!"

"Oh, that sounds important! Let me get a pen."

Maggie, still with a surprised expression, put down the towel and acted as though she was looking for something to write with. After miming looking to and fro, she reached for the pen that was sitting on the pail shelf of the ladder, and acted annoyed, rolling her eyes, and shrugging her shoulders, upon noticing that it was right in front of her.

She then tried her best to make it look like she accidentally dropped the pen on the floor. The pen fell very close to the feet of the imitation Chuck Norris, who took a short, accommodating step back. Maggie smiled and winked at "Chuck," and then lowered her body in a crouching stance to pick up the pen in front of the blonde Karate man.

Once she was down on one knee, she exploded with a punch into the genitals of the challenger. He doubled over sucking air loudly and made an audible gasp. She grabbed around both of his legs and drove her head into his solar plexus for a double-leg takedown. The Karate man flipped backward, and landed with a dull thud, the back of his head snapping back and hitting the floor hard like a bowling ball dropped on concrete.

Maggie kept hold of his legs when he fell backward. She was standing over him and holding the Karate man's ankles forming a "V" with his legs. She drove up her knee high into the air, and then stomped hard on the black belt's groin. His

141

scream of pain was at first loud, but gradually became quieter and then mutated into a soft whimper as his body tried to process all the varieties of pains simultaneously.

When she let go of his legs, "Chuck" withdrew his limbs to his body like a frightened turtle. He rolled to his side in pain and confusion. The whole incident had taken only seconds.

Maggie reached down, and as the Karate man writhed in agony clutching his groin, she untied his belt. After pulling it free, she threw it back over her shoulder toward the toolbox.

"You can leave now, but you don't get to keep the belt. It's mine. I earned it."

She waited for the realization to register on his face that he had been beaten.

"Tell your school to leave me alone, and I will leave them alone. I am going to stay in Chinatown. No one can make me leave. Got it?"

The challenger got up slowly, staggering a bit, looking at the door, and then looking back at where his belt landed. His face gave away that he was thinking of attempting to get the belt back.

"Don't even think about it." Maggie threatened through gritted teeth and eyes aflame with fury.

The Karate man hesitated a moment and then nodded in agreement. Maggie, in a flash of mercy, tilted her head toward the back door, letting him save face by not leaving through the front in his injured and beaten condition. She was hoping he would appreciate her gesture of mercy, and that he would spread the word of her ability as well as her generosity. But she wasn't counting on it.

That was the first challenge, and it was easy since no one knew her. Once the word got out that a woman had opened the new school in Chinatown it would escalate. They would come for her in any way they could think of. Honor was reserved for men. She was a woman, and most men would not think that she was worthy of honor, fairness, or respect. Hard lessons would be taught.

She would have to be better than all of them, more cunning, resourceful, and creative. She was prepared to use all her skills to establish herself as a more than worthy opponent for any man. She was determined to triumph.

After a few moments, her adrenaline dissipated, and she caught her breath. She picked up the belt from the floor and tied it neatly in the traditional square knot and hung it on a long nail above the training mirror that she had reserved for just that purpose.

She studied the unfinished school. Buckets of paint squatted on drop cloths, and pieces of lumber for shelves lay uneven next to resting tools. Shiny swords, traditional weapons, and pictures of tigers, dragons, and cranes leaned against half-painted walls. She was consumed with thoughts of all that needed to be done, as well as how she would handle the next challenger. But there was another wrinkle. Still, though she tried not to, she couldn't stop thinking about Emily.

"Yes, I know she has returned."

Sifu Chang spoke in a sober tone to the person on the other end of the phone. He rocked back in his squeaky office chair and looked up at the broken-framed and faded picture of General Yue Fei that he kept above his certificates, awards, and competition medals. As he spoke, his eyes studied the image of the general standing in full armor with his sword ready, his hand held up in a powerful fist.

"No, I warned her, but as I told you the last time when I was summoned on the *other* matter, I won't participate in this…endeavor. I can't. Yes, to me, she is family."

Sifu Chang picked up the miniature dragon statue from the side of his desk and placed it in the very center. As he listened to the person speaking to him, he slowly turned the dragon statue upside down.

Most people thought that the dragon was a trivial paperweight, just one of many of the innumerable objects that littered his desk. Many similar ones could be found in any merchant's shop up and down Chinatown's main street, but this one was different. It was an old shamanic artifact used in *Wu*, Chinese magic, to bring clarity and stability from chaos.

The dragon stood perfectly stable, though upside down, as it was designed to be used in either position. The dragon upright reflected the time of order and good luck. When times of trouble or misfortune arrived, the dragon was turned upside down, so it could release its magic properties to bring about the return of prosperity and good fortune. Sifu Chang stared at the dragon with focused intent as he continued his call.

"I am not surprised. I believe that they will all end up the same way. She is probably the best, not just in Chinatown, but in the League as well, if she ever fought there. She has a power that even she doesn't realize. She is...different. You should turn away from this one and leave her alone."

Sifu Chang again rocked back in his noisy chair and looked at the dirty ceiling tiles above him. "Yes, well I told you I would like to avoid the whole episode, but I understand."

He hung up the phone and leaned forward on his desk, distressed, looking at the dragon. He pulled out his incense holder, and two incense sticks, and lit them, slipping a picture of Maggie under the dragon.

Closing his eyes, he placed both of his hands on either side of the makeshift altar and visualized the outcome he wanted. He focused on putting all his Qi, all his power, into the simple magic spell. If there was any way that he could bend the forces of nature toward Maggie's favor, then he would do it. It was the least he could do.

Emily arranged a bouquet. As she worked, moving this flower there, placing one back, adding some baby's breath, she cultivated a quiet thoughtful mindset amidst the perfumed air. The work was meditative. It was soothing. It gave her time to reflect inward even as she busied herself outward.

Her hands moved as her mind stilled. She enjoyed these moments, and they were the reason that she decided to become a florist. Ever since she was a little girl, she had loved flowers. She loved their scents, their brilliant colors, and their diverse shapes.

More than anything, though, she loved what flowers meant. They expressed feelings. They made things special, and they didn't last. Their presence was temporary. Like people we care about, feelings we have, and events that transpire. They are here, and then they're gone. They are transitory like life.

When she was a child, she always presented her bad report card to her mother with a small bouquet of red tulips or yellow Chrysanthemums. She would pick them on the way home from school from the front of the Water Department Administration Building. She used cellophane from the lunchroom to wrap them and tied them with a bow made from braided yarn from the teacher's utility room.

The bouquet made it easier for her mother to sign the card, and just give a stern warning, rather than a brutal beating. Flowers had a soft power—

Her thoughts were interrupted by the delicate ringing of the bell on her door announcing a visitor.

Emily craned her neck around her arrangement. The kung fu teacher, Maggie, walked into the shop. Her black kung fu pants and white sleeveless blouse made her stand out amongst the color and light of the store. Her long hair was in a ponytail, and she wore only some light makeup, mascara, and lip gloss.

Maggie wasn't wearing makeup when she met her for the first time, which seemed an interesting change. She was pretty, but she often had a pensive expression. Maybe that was something that she had to do to be taken seriously by her peers. *Not many women in kung fu, are there?*

Maggie paused at the entrance as the door shut behind her. Emily followed her gaze as it found the light from the high windows and then traveled down to the displays of arrangements and bouquets. Her eyes bounced from shelf to shelf of all the various floral varieties.

It was always interesting for Emily to watch the effect of the bright shop, with its stunning array of colors and powerful scents, on the unfamiliar observer. When Emily had to leave the shop for a week to take care of her mother, the return to work was almost overwhelming, as the powerful perfumed air from all the different varieties of flowers vied for her attention all at once. It was a soft and pleasant assault on her vision and olfactory senses, and one that she happily adjusted to. It was a welcome divergence from the harsh polluted air of the street just beyond her door.

Emily watched silently as Maggie snaked through the aisles of displays of cut flowers and prepared arrangements, and eventually made her way closer to the counter. Maggie grabbed a half bouquet of sunflowers and tucked them gently under her arm as she continued to look around the shop.

Emily could hear her feet lightly scuff across the cement floor as she got nearer but acted like she was too engrossed in her work to notice. She decided to say something, but just then the bell on the door rang again. The soft awkward silence was broken as an elderly woman entered and walked straight to the counter.

"Emily, I need to order those mums for my grandson's wedding—you remember the ones we talked about?"

"Of course!" Emily put the arrangement she had been working on aside and gave her full attention to the woman. She leaned her forearms on the counter, locked her fingers, and looked straight at the woman as she spoke. "How is Albert? Have you met the bride?"

"Oh yes, many times. Nice girl. From Tai Pei. Beautiful girl. Her father is a banker. The mother owns a restaurant supply company."

"Wow, that's a pretty busy family. I'm sure Albert will be happy. She sounds like—"

"Maybe not 'mums, huh? What about gardenias?" The old woman interrupted, changing the subject as she turned her attention to the buckets of white gardenias next to the counter. She reached toward the flowers and gently moved them around as if looking to select some.

"Okay, but I already ordered the 'mums, so..."

Emily's voice trailed off as she reached under the counter for her prop clipboard, which had a paper with printed boxes and numbers that she used whenever she needed to make a point with a customer, but didn't have anything readily available to back up her argument. It looked official enough.

"Yeah, I see they were ordered, so..." She said with a series of slow nods, a squinty thinking face, and a few taps of the pen for emphasis.

"Oh, okay No gardenias. We'll keep the mums."

The old woman rejected the idea with a big nod, a crinkled nose, and a dismissive wave of her hand.

Emily watched Maggie secretly, as she spoke to her customer. Maggie was on the far side of the shop and appeared to be studying the dwarf banana tree intently. She noticed Maggie was looking under the leaves, feeling them with her fingers, and checking the soil. It looked like her attention was riveted on the large plant. *Was she looking for a banana to pop out?*

"You know Chiu's?" The old woman questioned with an innocent expression, as she pointed out the window and down the street.

"Chiu's Flowers?" Emily feigned ignorance at the well-known location of her largest competitor, with a faux expression of bewilderment. "The ones by the seafood restaurant? Yeah, I think I know them."

"They have a good price on the mums. You know? Veerrry good price," the old woman nodded slowly with her eyes wide.

"I'm sure they have lovely flowers, but this is for Albert's wedding, right?" Emily gave a questioning tilt of her head.

"And I know everyone, especially you, wants the best they can get for the very best price. That is what I can give you. I'm not really sure that Chiu's knows Albert, do they?" Emily looked casually at the ceiling, and then at the old woman with her questioning gaze before she reached for the old woman's hand, gave it a light pat, beaming a soothing smile at her, and seized the silence as agreement.

"So, it's all settled then, right? The mums are on the way, everything's taken care of, and Albert will live happily ever after, like in a storybook, right?" Emily smiled a big toothy grin.

A smile broke across the old woman's face.

"Oh, thank you, Emily! I'll see you on the big day, huh? See you."

The old woman put on her dark sunglasses, grabbed her purse, and turned to leave. Emily came from behind the counter, put her arm around her, and walked her to the door.

"I wouldn't miss it for anything!" Emily announced as she opened the door, and the bell rang again, announcing the old woman's exit.

She stood for a moment watching through the window to see if she went up the street toward her apartment, or down the street to Chiu's. The old woman crossed with the light and made a gentle arc up the street toward her apartment.

Emily let out a sigh of relief.

In the quiet shop, Emily could hear the light footsteps of Maggie walking around the miniature fruit trees. *Maybe she wants to put one in her school like an organic vending machine?* She seemed deep in thought about something, but Emily had never known a woman that owned a kung fu school. *Maybe it was stressful?* She walked over to her.

"Fancy, meeting you here," Emily announced, acting surprised, smiling big, with her arms akimbo and her head tilted for the look her mother called, maximum cuteness.

"Yes, well. It's Tuesday, so I needed these sunflowers," Maggie said with playful sarcasm and a slight smile.

"Well, you have a good eye. I think that those sunflowers are great, especially on a Tuesday. You need anything else?"

"Oh, I suppose not. I just wanted to come by since…you know, you came by."

"You don't owe me anything, you know? I was just welcoming you to the neighborhood."

Emily took the sunflowers from Maggie and started toward the counter. Maggie followed.

"Yes, I know. I mean, I didn't come out of obligation or anything. I just wanted to see what it was like to be in a shop with flowers all day. It must be pretty groovy, or cool?" Maggie questioned, amusingly.

"I still say groovy, don't you?" Emily asked as she prepared the flowers to be wrapped. Maggie looked nervous about something, but Emily didn't know what she had to be nervous about.

"So, working in a flower shop...must be..."

"Well, as you can tell, it's bright, smells incredible, and looks beautiful. I guess it's a little different than what you're used to, huh? Where is your school moving from, by the way?"

"You mean, where was it before?" Maggie answered with a blinking expression.

"Yeah, aren't you moving your school from somewhere else?"

"No, this is a new thing for me. A career change, as they say. Follow your dream..." Maggie nodded as she spoke.

"Really? Did you go to E.S.T. or something?" Emily asked intrigued.

"No, nothing like that. It's just been something that I've wanted to do for a long time."

"Yeah, I don't see many women doing it, ya know? Running a kung fu school in Chinatown?

"No, you don't see any kung fu schools run by women. Not in Chinatown. None. I'm the only one, so far." Maggie's tone and expression became gravely serious.

Emily could see the conviction on her face as she spoke. It sounded like an ominous pronouncement. She hoped she hadn't hit a nerve with the pretty kung fu teacher.

"What did you do before?" Emily began to busy her hands with the bouquet and clipped the odds and ends of the flower stems with meticulous precision.

"I was a scientist, well a lab tech, really." Maggie looked down as she spoke. Emily followed her gaze and saw it end at her shoes.

Was it difficult for her to talk about it?

"Well, you seem like you chose something you wanted to do, and I'm sure you'll be happy and successful. I think doing what you like to do is important."

Emily finished wrapping up the bouquet of sunflowers in green cellophane, and carefully handed it to Maggie with an enhanced version of her standard smile.

"How much is it?" Maggie asked.

"One lesson."

"You want to learn martial arts?"

"Yeah, well, I never tried it before. I thought it was something boys did, I guess. I never knew a girl who did kung fu before either or even knew of a school run by a woman. That's probably a big deal here in Chinatown, isn't it?" Emily asked innocently, thinking back to the point she made earlier and confirming that Maggie was starting more than a new business venture.

"You have no idea."

"Okay, well when you're open, I'll come down for my lesson. Just don't expect too much from a little Chinese girl who sells flowers. Okay?"

Emily crinkled her nose as she put her hands in the pockets of her overalls and rocked back and forth onto the balls of her feet and heels. She felt that there was an unmistakably consequential moment that passed between them, though no words were said, their eyes locked—

The bell rang again to announce another customer to the shop.

A Chinese woman entered. She was about the same age as both she and Maggie. She looked like she just got off work at a bank or something. She was wearing a charcoal gray jacket, slacks, and a white blouse. The blouse was unbuttoned so that the thin gold chain she wore caught the light as she walked.

She was beautiful, but her eyes were too made up with blue eyeshadow and black eyeliner. Her expression looked intense, and she strode into the shop determined as if she was looking for something.

"Hi, may I help you?" Emily turned to the woman and greeted her with a wide smile.

"I actually just came for this one here," the woman said, putting her arm around Maggie's shoulder with a playful tug. "Although I have been meaning to come in here and get some flowers. You always have such lovely ones here."

The woman picked up an orange lily and smelled it slowly while she looked at Emily and then at Maggie with a wary gaze and a crooked grin.

"Whenever I walk by the shop going to my car," she continued, "the smell always seems to grab me for a few moments. It must be heaven working in here all day."

"We were just discussing that," Emily said, still smiling, as she looked awkwardly between the two women. *What is going on?* But she followed her rule for dealing with all of the unexpected circumstances of life: When in doubt, smile.

"Yes, it is, I think," Maggie whispered. Her smile looked forced.

The woman looked intently at Maggie and then raised her eyebrows with an expectant gaze.

A few beats of abundant quiet created an uncomfortable silence until, with a smile, the woman reached for Maggie's sunflowers.

"I'll take these flowers back to the school and put them in the lobby. They should help to brighten up the place." The woman extended her hand to Emily. "It was nice to meet you...?" She asked, letting the question hang in the air as she glanced at Maggie.

"I'm Emily," she said, as she pointed to herself, wide-eyed and blameless as if to not only identify herself but to fully disclose that she didn't understand if there was a problem between the two ladies. She shook the woman's hand with a big smile as she began to suspect who and what she was to Maggie. *Trouble.*

The air felt heavy. Tense anxiety was sitting like a large obstacle between them all. Though it remained unspoken, there was no mistaking its effect and that it was taking up all the available oxygen between them.

"Wendy," the woman announced her name a little louder than necessary, as she was still shaking Emily's hand and clutching the flowers in the other. "Let me pay you for these." She handed Emily a single five-dollar bill. "Well, I should be getting back to the school, and then home to start dinner for Maggie and myself. We're having scampi tonight." Wendy said directly to Emily through a smile with unmistakable intent: hands-off.

"Yes, I should go too," Maggie said, taking some of Emily's business cards from the counter. "I'll keep these in the lobby, and hopefully send some business your way—as we discussed."

Emily nodded, nervously.

Maggie looked as if she had just stolen something precious that she didn't plan to return.

"Thank you!" Emily smiled and waved to them both, as she sauntered back behind the counter to the register and her neglected arrangement. She put the five-dollar bill in the drawer and watched as Wendy and Maggie walked awkwardly toward the door. Wendy exited quickly. Maggie stopped at the door for a moment. She paused holding the handle, she looked as if she was going to turn and say something, and then looked like she changed her mind and left. The bell rang after her.

Emily tried to act like she hadn't noticed anything as she watched Maggie walk by the window, but she knew that more had happened than meeting someone and just selling them some flowers. She hadn't felt it for a while. A long while. She stood alone behind the counter of the empty flower shop. Even though she was directly in the rays of the bright sunlight as they filtered through the window, her mind felt foggy and unfocused, unsettled. She started to pick at the arrangement but couldn't concentrate. She pushed it aside. When she thought of Maggie, her feelings stirred. She leaned onto the counter, and then let her head fall back to seek life's answers from the ceiling.

The sun poured in steadily from the high window. The light's delicate touch warmed her as if in an embrace. For a moment, she closed her eyes, and breathed in the multi-layered floral scent of the store, as she enjoyed the sun's pleasant caress on her face and body.

Though both women had left a few moments before, she found it difficult to stop thinking about Maggie. She breathed in deeper, and realizing that her heart had quickened, she smiled a little. She enjoyed the splendid sensation of the moment as much as she could, realizing right then exactly what it was.

It was late. Chinatown appeared deserted. Even the moon hid behind the clouds. Traffic had evaporated, and the streets were all but empty, except for the odd pedestrian walking purposefully to some unknown destination, and the occasional taxi searching for fares.

Maggie locked the door of the school, her mind full of the myriad of tasks she needed to complete for the approaching grand opening. *Hang the grand opening banner and get some sidewalk signs. What about fliers?* So much to do to get the school ready for the event. She was concerned that she had already spent too much on the school itself. Given how much she spent on repairs, wall-sized mirrors, and the new special flooring, there just wasn't much left for an advertising budget. She chalked it up as one of the many lessons learned by a new business owner.

Thinking of the grand opening, made it all real. *It's happening.* She tried not to be nervous about it. Better to just do the best you can and trust that it will all work out. Her mind shifted immediately to her biggest fear: *What if no one shows up?*

The concern was persistent, and the image of her standing alone in an empty newly renovated school with people walking by, and occasionally looking in at the new Chinatown oddity, was clear. She had to accept it as a real possibility. Would it be like the countless birthdays where no one came, and her family acted like they didn't notice? She never had many friends, and the scars of those times left their mark. She tried to right herself. *Can't get bogged down in a bunch of fear and hurt feelings. This is business.*

As she walked, she could hear, only faintly, her footsteps on the sidewalk. It was a reminder that even amid a vibrant city full of people, Chinatown could be a lonely place. Walking past the darkened windows of the shops and stores, she let the colorful glow of the neon lights illuminate her way. The sidewalk light show was punctured periodically by the occasional dark alley and empty storefront. Their stark emptiness stood out like a black hole in space.

She kept walking and thinking about how the local shopkeepers were either dismissive of her or acted oblivious to the school entirely. Maggie had heard talk around town, whether in whispers in the grocery line, or discussions in the restaurants, about the crazy young woman that called herself a sifu and was opening a kung fu school in Chinatown. More than once she had put her items on the conveyor belt of the check stand, acting like she was making sure there were only ten, and listened to the women in front of her.

"I hear she was kicked out of a finishing school up north, got a job as a stripper, and now she thinks she's some kind of kung fu master. Can you believe it? The woman's eyes were wide with the thought of such audacity.

"Well, my Nathan said he heard she is trying to set up some kind of front for a drug operation in there. I just hope someone does something about it, and quick." The woman paid her bill, politely nodded to Maggie, and the two women pushed their carts toward the parking lot.

There had been a couple of challenges since that first one with "Chuck." Each one bested, and each one left out the back door minus his rank. Of course, that gave rise to the rumor of a bodyguard working at the school. No one believed a woman could be beating these challengers. He was said to be a fighter from the League. Sent from Hong Kong. He was described as big and fierce, although no one could say that they had seen him. The idea that such an absurd tale would seem logical to them made Maggie's head shake, but still, the rumors persisted.

Are those footsteps?

She stopped to listen and then started walking slower hoping to gauge the distance and speed by their sound. It was hard to hear. She looked over her shoulder, barely turning her head, using her peripheral vision. Then she turned around quickly but spotted nothing except a collection of shadows. The sounds of footsteps had stopped.

It wasn't much further to her car. She just had to walk to the corner and cross to the parking lot across the street. Even with all her training, she had to admit that the streets at night were creepy.

She walked on. Her mind obsessively picked up where it left off. Once the school was open, she knew that either the community would continue to completely ignore her, or they would attack her relentlessly. *There wasn't a third way, was there?* Being accepted was out of the question for the time being.

Given the choice, being attacked wasn't as bad as being ignored. Being ignored scared her the most. An all-out assault would be the easiest thing to confront. It would be combat. She was prepared for that. She would take on whoever came at her.

And if ignored? She would then take the challenge to the leaders of the biggest schools in Chinatown. It would be the only choice. It was going to be fire or ice.

What was that?

A clinking sound, like a bottle being kicked and skipping across the pavement, arrested the silence. The sudden impact of the shattering of glass was loud in the otherwise quiet street. Standing still as a statue, her eyes quickly scanned the area.

Where did it come from? All she could see were shadows, no movement in the night. It was tempting to see what wasn't there, as her mind created moving phantoms. Even though it was late, it was Thursday, a weeknight. Not much happening.

Quit being jumpy! She shook it off. As she continued up the street toward the corner, her mind was still swimming in thoughts of the school, although it had shifted to an assortment of other problems, new worries, and unrelenting concerns. *Need to make a schedule...Keeping up with training is important…Emily and Wendy, what to do?… What if this whole thing is a mistake? What if Sifu Chang was right?*

Then, everything, all worries, evaporated at once, when a strange sight grabbed her attention.

What the hell is that?

As she was walking past an alley, from the corner of her eye, she caught something moving in the darkness. At least, she thought she did. *Was she seeing what she wanted to see?* She stopped. Her eyes squinted into the dark as her blood pulsed faster through her veins.

No, it was not her imagination. She looked closely, seeing a dark figure emerge from next to the shadow of the dumpster in the alley. She stayed still and her eyes alternately studied the open street and the alley entrance looking for anything else moving.

Was it time to run? Running was always an option. She had nothing to prove on a lonely street alone at night. She heard footsteps, saw a shadow grow long near the edge of the dumpster, and watched as it stretched out into the street. Someone was coming.

She stood still, put down her purse on the sidewalk, and stepped instinctively into a fighting stance. She was ready. Her hands repeatedly pulsed into fists, as she stared and awaited the entrance of the dark figure.

What happened to running? Crap, too late.

She watched, waiting, and then it came: a drunk staggered into the light. He was a patron from the Jaded Lady, a bar on the other side of the alley, a place for middle managers to get sauced on their way home and try to forget their troubles, and their unquenchable desire for a buck. He looked unsteady like he could barely stand. His fine light-colored suit was filthy and stained, especially on the knees. He had fallen in the dirty alley a few times.

She breathed a sigh of relief and let him stumble on his way. She picked up her purse and continued on her way too. *Relax, for god's sake.*

She stood at the corner ready to cross the street to the parking lot. Even though the street was empty she waited for the signal to cross. Old habits. *Mom would be proud.*

It took no time at all for her thoughts to swarm her consciousness again. She thought of Wendy and Emily. She had a strategy for just about everything in her life, except for her feelings. It wasn't like training to punch or kick, no matter how long she did it, she didn't feel like she was any better at it.

She had been with Wendy since college, longer than she had been with anyone else. They were practically married. She loved her, but she didn't know if she was *in love* with her anymore. She had always followed Wendy's lead, but it appeared that now that she was asserting herself more, they were in a power struggle. The stresses of this new life had thrown a wrench into their finances, plans, routines, and relationship, but she felt awakened by the new energy and the thrill of finally doing what she wanted to do.

The urgency of the moment overtook her, as she saw two men walking toward the corner on the other side of the street. She hadn't seen them before. Given their pace, they would arrive at the corner at the same time she did. They were about her height, stocky, and wearing dark clothes. They looked too old to be students and too young to be hanging out at the Jaded Lady.

One looked at her and then said something to the other as he glanced over at the parking lot. Her mind started analyzing, theorizing, and putting it all together. They must have been following her as soon as she left the school. They probably had been hanging back watching her for some time and knew that she parked in the lot across the street. They must have been the reason for the sounds she heard earlier. *What else could it be? Get ready.*

The light turned green, and she left the corner quickly, headed for the fated rendezvous with the two men. She realized that she needed to be ready once she arrived at the corner. *This is it. Give it everything you got.* Her hands were pulsing into fists again. Her heartbeat quickened. *Butterflies.* She was getting close. She saw that one man had a hand in his pocket, probably a knife or a gun. Her thoughts screamed: *control the weapon!* She was steps away. They were looking at her as they both walked toward the corner. They would both be there at the same time. *Closing in.* Once she was within arm's reach of them, she quickly dropped back with her hands ready and her feet in a deep fighting stance. She let out an audible hissing breath with eyes blazing.

They stopped and stepped back. They just looked at her, smiled, and kept moving. They crossed to the other side of the street. She could hear the two men giggle to themselves as they walked on, keeping a rapid pace before they disappeared up the street.

Crap.

Feeling completely ridiculous, she commanded herself to relax and quit worrying. *How many false alarms do you need, girl?* Maybe she had taken Chinatown's reputation too far. It was starting to impact her normally good judgment.

Arriving at her car in the parking lot, she breathed a heavy sigh as she fished in her purse for her car key. The lot was nearly empty. Just two other cars, a blue Buick and a green Pontiac. A single flood light shined on Maggie's car. She put her key in the door.

From behind, she felt a strong hand holding a wet rag over her mouth and nose. She felt herself being pulled back as arms encircled and restrained her. The sweet medicinal smell and taste of chloroform filled her nose and mouth. She knew that she didn't have long before she would lose consciousness.

Looking up at the night sky, she saw the light of the parking lot start to roll and tumble in her field of vision. Soon the clouded moon started to tilt, and she felt herself getting weaker. As she hit the ground, she looked up to see two shadowy faces over her. Everything seemed to go silent before it all finally went black.

Jesus...ugh...what the hell happened?

It was as though she were coming out of a dark, misty, void, into consciousness. The faint voices of two men could be heard, but she couldn't hear what they were saying. They were not too far from her although she couldn't see them. She couldn't see anything. Everything was black. The voices of the two men came through a muffled filter. She could tell by the coarse fabric lightly touching her cheek that a burlap sack was covering her head. A big one. The kind rice came in for restaurants. Her mouth was taped shut.

She could feel that her body was sitting upright in a chair. Her hands and ankles were restrained. When she tried to move anything, any part of her body except her head, she was unable to. She tried again with great effort, grunting a bit as she did, but to no avail. Nothing budged. She was at the mercy of whatever forces had brought her here, and though she suspected, she didn't know who they were or where *here* was.

After a few moments, though it could've been longer, she suddenly remembered the last thing that had happened to her.

She never saw them. There must have been two though. She chalked up her strange and disoriented feelings to the lingering effects of the chloroform. As she awoke, and her adrenaline started to flow, her body responded letting her know that she had not been resting. She had been forcibly put under and restrained. Taken against her will.

Odd pains became noticeable. Her neck hurt. Probably from her head hanging down, limp, like a rock, for an unknown measure of time. Her legs were cramped, and her hands felt slightly numb. A feeling of numbness in her extremities became more prominent as she awakened. *How long was I out?*

Fear started to enter her slowly at first and then quickly, like a boulder rolling downhill. A hot wave of anxiety broke over her body, leaving small pools of sweat in its wake. *Don't panic. Be Calm.*

Her anxiety increased despite her best efforts to quell it.

Her heart was pounding harder as the full weight of her situation became reality.

Helpless.

Her breathing became shallow. Her mind was processing the situation. Like a jog to a sprint, her thoughts raced, weighing all the unknowns, thinking of options, and her body all the while trying to move and get her out of there, but it couldn't.

Breathing through her nose wasn't getting enough air into her lungs. They were noisy, sniffly, shallow breaths. The thoughts kept coming back: She was afraid. She needed to get a hold of herself. *Control your thoughts. Control the breath. Slow breaths, as if to drink in the air. Remain calm.* Soon the breaths were coming slower, longer, and deeper.

First things first. What can I do?

She flexed her hands and fingers slowly testing the rope that was restricting them, but the knots were tied tightly. Unless she had a latent superpower, she wasn't going to be able to pull her hands free. She tried shifting her weight to see if she could rock the chair over, but it was too sturdy. Listening very carefully, she judged that the voices were still very close to her. Not wanting to draw the attention of her captors to her awakened state, she made only slow deliberate movements in her claustrophobic cocoon. Hopefully, they would keep talking, move closer, and she would be able to overhear what they were saying.

Straining her ears to hear, she didn't hear anything she could recognize. They were speaking softly, and she figured, due to their proximity, that they probably knew she was awake now.

A beat of time came and went and then she heard light footsteps grow louder and walk quickly past her. A few seconds later there was a loud click followed by a long creak as if a door was unlatched and then squeakily opened. The quick rush of air against her body made her feel that the door led to a larger room. She heard two people walk by her, and then three others followed. One of them was walking slower than the other two.

Breathe deep.

As she tried to reach out with her other senses and listen more intently to her surroundings for any clues of where she was, a presence arrived and was suddenly looming above her. She could feel it. It was ominous. Intuitively, she knew that it was a man. There was palpable masculine energy surrounding the space. His weight caused the floor to creak. He was close.

She held her breath as she struggled to sense a picture of him. Her sightless head tilted toward the space above her, and though she tried to see with all the psychic energy she could muster, he remained a phantom.

As she strained to study the blackness, a sudden squeak and heavy footfalls were indicating his retreat. He had not been there long, and he left quickly.

Maggie thought over the incident with the unknown presence, and then, after a few moments, she sensed the walls that surrounded her, move. It was as if the room around her dissolved. There was a sudden light breeze. She knew that she was in an open area, alone.

Still blinded by the cover over her head, she tried to visualize where people would be standing, based on where she last heard their footsteps. Outnumbered. If she had to jump up and fight from her chair, she would need to be as efficient as possible. However, that was only a wish, with her ankles tied to the legs of the chair. As she assessed the situation further, and though she hated to admit it, she knew she had to be realistic. *What could she do?* Her hands were tied. Ankles bound. Mouth taped. She had a bag over her head. Her thoughts returned to the same place where she had started when she came to: She was completely helpless.

The bag was tugged from her head. The rough scratchy material grazed across her nose and cheeks. She had to squint as the sudden assault of light overwhelmed her. Her peripheral vision was drawn to the movement of a figure walking away from her. He must have been the one that removed the bag. He returned to what she assumed was his post behind her to her right.

In a fraction of a second, she saw her environment as a still picture. The visual information streamed into her eager eyes all at once. It took a moment to focus and get her first look at where she was.

It was an old theater. A movie palace from long ago. One of those extraordinary theaters that used to play movies or feature live performances. Men would take their wives to see a grand performance of *Othello* or take their mistresses to see *Casablanca*.

Rows of red and gold flowed over the spaces low and high. The seats were a deep red velvet, faded and worn from decades of use, with gold armrests, their luster diminished by time. A large balcony hung miraculously over the house seats, with no visible means of support. Like many of the grand movie palaces of the era, the decorative theme was exotic. While some chose Egyptian, Japanese, or the popular Art Deco decor, this theater was decorated in a distinctly Chinese style. Broad columns hosted golden dragons swimming upward and downward through the air. The ceiling portrayed a gold phoenix in flight against a red sky.

Despite the theme of the decorations, Maggie knew that she wasn't in Chinatown. The theater looked more like something that would be in Old Town, the downtown of Terre Promise.

With everything now revealed, Maggie felt a little better about her situation. Her vantage point was a chair facing the stage in the middle aisle of the old theater. She was still restrained, but she could see what was going on around her. If something was going to happen, she would see it first, and she took some comfort in that.

On the stage were three Asian men sitting on magnificently sculpted rosewood thrones. Though she had never met them or seen them, she had deduced that she was looking at the members of The Council, the shadowy governing body that ostensibly ran Chinatown and controlled the martial arts schools. Although all the thrones were large, the one in the middle was the grandest of them all.

By observing the thrones, Maggie sensed the hierarchy. The man on the right had the smallest throne, but it was still ornately decorated, and detailed with a tiger's head, bearing fangs, over the headrest. The feet of the throne were fashioned into fierce tiger claws. The man that sat on the tiger throne was an Asian man that looked to be about 45 years old. He had a muscular build and deep-set eyes. His expression was menacing. He had a detached sense of rage about him. She had the impression that he could kill you, and then calmly order Chow Fun. He looked like an enforcer for one of the triads, or he had been one.

The throne on the left of the stage was a crane-themed visage. Crane wings served as the armrests, and the serpentine neck of the crane had been fashioned into a noble "S" above the headrest. The man sitting on the throne had a long scar vertically across his left eye and down his cheek. He looked about ten years older than the man that sat on the tiger throne. Although he was thinner, he still appeared formidable. His presence implied that he had had some harrowing experiences in his life, and his face and body told the tale. The man's gnarled fingers gripped the armrest like talons ready to seize prey. There were scars on his forearms, which betrayed a life of violence whether as an enforcer or a competitor. It was hard for Maggie not to believe that most high-level martial artists, and certainly any on The Council, had not paid their dues in underground matches, or as enforcers, for any number of the triads whose reach extended from Hong Kong to Chinatown and beyond. He had a face she would not soon forget. Of the three, he seemed like the one to be most feared.

In the center was a stately throne. Although Maggie had never met him, she was certain that the old man who occupied it was DaSifu Dao, the head of The Council. He was wearing a silk uniform. The uniform top was half black and gold. A swirling dragon was embroidered in black on the gold side. He had a cigarette smoldering idly in his right hand. She watched the smoke rise from it, and then her gaze moved to the throne. It was the most elaborate of the three. It was constructed as a scene of a dragon twisting and swirling around the chair in an awe-inspiring display. The five-toed, clawed feet of the throne were holding the elusive pearls prized and pursued by dragons. Winding high above the headrest was the fearsome fanged dragon's head. The mouth was agape to dispense wisdom, fury, or devour whatever came in its path.

Next to the DaSifu's right hand was a courtly silver cobra ashtray standing submissive to its dragon master. Maggie wasn't sure who the other two men were or where they fit in, but she was certain that the man in the middle, on the dragon throne, was in charge.

The DaSifu brought his cigarette slowly to his lips, as he gazed down directly at Maggie. His eyes began to squint as he slowly inhaled, and the cigarette's tip grew bright red. The arm holding the cigarette moved meditatively back to its original position. The motion was as purposeful as a Qigong exercise. The three men each looked down at Maggie from their lofty perch with indefatigable stares. The only thing that moved was the smoke from the dragon's hand. Their observation of her was made more threatening by the unearthly quiet of the theater

"Remove the tape and untie her, please," said DaSifu, breaking the thick silence with his soft, confident voice. Immediately, a man came from behind her and cut her restraints. She was relieved to finally be free. The same man then removed the tape from Maggie's mouth which allowed her, for the first time, to take a deep breath. She could still feel the lingering sensations of the rope around her wrists, ankles, and the adhesive around her mouth. She took deep breaths through her mouth and massaged her wrists briskly, feeling the pins and needles of blood returning to her extremities.

She stood up and looked around. She was a little stiff and unsteady, but she felt better being unrestrained and standing. She felt less helpless, though, in reality, she knew her situation hadn't changed. Far behind her, she noticed two men in the darkness, by the door. There had to be more men around, likely standing quiet and still in the shadows. Possibly, they were standing in all the darkened nooks and coves of the old building, ready to materialize if the need arose. It was a world of unknowns. *Be cautious, not afraid.*

"Do you know who we are, Maggie?" DaSifu asked, His soft voice seemed to grow heavier and thicker as it approached her ears and reverberated off the walls of the large open space. He sat with a hint of a smile and an air of complete confidence, taking a slow drag of his cigarette while he awaited her answer.

"You are The Council," Maggie said, still rubbing her wrists and looking at each man in turn. "I know that you are DaSifu Dao," she said, with a slight nod of acknowledgment, "I apologize that I don't know the others."

"No apology is necessary, this is SiGung Hen," DaSifu said, as he gestured casually with an upturned hand toward his right, to the man seated on the crane throne. SiGung Hen gave a slow nod of acknowledgment. "This is Sifu Shou," DaSifu said, gesturing with another open hand to his left, toward the man sitting on the tiger throne. Sifu Shou gave a quick nod in recognition.

DaSifu Dao crossed one leg over the other and took yet another long slow drag from his cigarette. Maggie concluded that he did it for dramatic effect. With these men, everything had a reason and a purpose. *Be patient.*

"So, you must have deduced why you are here, correct?"

"No," Maggie said, trying to sound surprised, but knowing that they wouldn't believe her.

"You are here because you did not heed our policy regarding opening a school in Chinatown, and so we have decided that…maybe…you needed to hear from us directly,"

DaSifu Dao took another slow draw from his cigarette, his eyes disappearing behind the red ember, and then softly materializing again, as smoke meandered from the corner of his mouth twisting like the dragons on the columns in the theater.

DaSifu Dao nodded an acquiescence toward his right indicating that he was giving the floor to SiGung Hen perched on the Crane throne. DaSifu made the recognition grander by adding a sweep of his hand toward the SiGung.

"DaSifu has spoken about our policies toward new schools often enough with all of the guild's members that you should have known not to open a school. Your Sifu informed you of this, yes?" He looked down at Maggie, with his scar commanding her attention while she felt his gaze scan her face for lies. Like a prosecutor, his relentless stare announced to her that he was asking a question that he already knew the answer to.

"Yes…but," Maggie was hesitant to answer. *What would happen to Sifu Chang if this line of questioning didn't go well?* She labored over how she could implicate only herself in her situation and leave him out of it. There was an expectant silence that filled the theater before the next person spoke.

"You should have followed his instructions. You should have honored his advice, which we know he gave you. You can teach at his school or someone else's school, but no woman has ever, or *will ever* be the head of a school in Chinatown, and that is the way things are." SiGung Hen declared emphatically, and then sat back confidently, having restated the edict that had been in Chinatown, observed, acknowledged, and unchallenged, for so long that it might as well have been chiseled onto the decorative imitation jade stones on the Chinatown gate.

169

"Why?" Maggie asked, a little louder than she meant to. It was a blatant questioning of their tradition. *Too late. Can't take it back.*

Sifu Shou rose to his feet as if being pulled up by some mysterious force. His stocky muscular build was imposing. His posture was like a beast on two legs, and she saw the look of anger on his face. She could admit to herself that he was imposing, if not downright scary.

"You question us?" Sifu Shou stood aggressively with his arms flexed and hands formed into rock-like fists flared at his sides. "It is not your right to question us. YOU NEED TO LEARN YOUR PLACE!" Sifu Shou yelled. His words ricocheted from the mezzanine to the orchestra pit, as he pointed an accusing finger at Maggie.

The DaSifu, with his face expressionless, softly waved his hand toward Sifu Shou and gently gestured for the sifu to sit down. To Maggie, it appeared that Sifu Shou had broken some protocol.

The sifu's expression was unchanged as he sat back down on his throne, grabbing the armrests aggressively, fingers clutching, and his mouth twisted into a snarl.

Waiting for a moment, DaSifu Dao let the harsh energy dissipate from the air. He put out his cigarette with a long, methodical twist of his hand, into the free-standing cobra ashtray.

"You can see how passionate we all are about this tradition...this law if you will. If this law were to be broken, perhaps others would think to question our other laws as well, and then Chinatown will cease to be the special place that it is for all of us." DaSifu Dao used the sweep of his hand to include the empty theater as the symbolic Chinatown in his proclamation. Everyone nodded in agreement, except for Maggie. She was neither surprised nor converted.

"We have thought deeply about it, and we would like to help you and help your teacher. He has been a fine teacher in Chinatown, I'm sure you agree?"

Maggie nodded in agreement.

"We would like you to help Sifu Chang grow his school, and in so doing, help yourself. You can merge your location with his, and become part of his family by putting his chop on your door. This way you will have protection, the challenges will cease, and everyone will get what they want." DaSifu let rise a warm smile of reasonable understanding. "You will teach at a school, *basically* of your own."

The word "basically" stood out as it was intended. Its meaning conveyed the inequity she was expected to agree to. Maggie remained stone-faced as DaSifu Dao continued.

"Sifu Chang will expand his business, you will teach, and the law will still be the law." The DaSifu wore a friendly smile as he looked to accept nods from his right and left. SiGung Hen and Sifu Shou nodded their agreement and only then did DaSifu Dao sit back, still wearing a convincingly pleasant expression aimed at Maggie. The rest of The Council didn't mask their feelings or expressions and stared at her as if trying to crush her with their gazes. She thought that they might.

"So, I must be under Sifu Chang?" Maggie looked at each member of The Council in turn and watched as they all nodded their heads but said nothing.

"Go back to your school tomorrow and remove the black dragon head. Replace your chop with Sifu Chang's chop on the front door. Once a month Sifu Chang will check on you and make sure all is well," SiGung Hen stated, unequivocally.

"What if I don't want to do this? What if I want to go on my own?" Maggie questioned, shifting from foot to foot out of anxious frustration. She strained to conceal the irritation, injustice, and incredulity in her voice.

"Then you will want to open a school in Des Moines," DaSifu Dao said, as he folded his hands. At first, Maggie was caught off guard, but then she was hit with what felt like an electric shock of revelation when she understood the reference and its significance. She felt a deep sense of betrayal. Anger welled up in her. It could have only come from Wendy. *How the hell had she talked to them? How did she know them?*

"You will go back, and within ninety days you will begin to follow our agreement. Also, on your opening day, you will have fifty new students as our gesture of goodwill," DaSifu added with both his palms facing up as if presenting Maggie with a gift. "I know you won't disappoint us."

All of The Council members nodded to each other before turning their commanding presence and attention toward Maggie.

The deal was done.

The Council members gave her the traditional fist and shield salute signaling that the meeting was over. Maggie thought to return the salute but was suddenly stunned by the feeling of a sharp pinching pain in her neck. She realized that she was about to lose consciousness again. The golden light of the theater and the image of the three mythic thrones began to fade. Soon darkness enveloped her.

She awakened groggy and disoriented. There was a consistent thumping and pounding in her head. It took a few moments to realize that the pounding she was hearing was not just the throbbing of blood making its way through the capillaries of her brain, but from a firm palm hitting her car window.

Maggie's eyes adjusted reluctantly to the bright morning light. As she moved to avoid the sun, she became aware of her body's pains from lying in an awkward position, curled up on the front seat. *How long has it been?* She figured a few hours at least. The nerve strike to her neck had dropped her almost immediately. It must have been from one of The Council's soldiers standing behind her. They were good. She never saw it coming.

Squinting at the light coming through the dirt-streaked car window, she saw that Wendy was the one doing the pounding. Her bug-eyed expression and exaggerated body movement were an exact contrast to the muffled voice that was barely audible through the glass. Maggie peeked through the slivers of her eyes to see where she was. Through the smudged windshield, she saw that she was in the parking lot across from the school. Back where she started.

The pounding continued, until, finally, and with a great deal of effort, she rolled down the window.

Wendy's voice filled the car with a volume and power that overwhelmed Maggie's current condition.

"My God, where have you been? Why did you sleep out here last night? I was worried sick! I drove everywhere looking for you, and when I came back you were here! Were you drunk? Why didn't you wake up?"

Maggie made no effort to stop or answer the rapid-fire interrogation. She brought her gaze to the headliner above her, studying its intricate and suddenly interesting pattern of wear, as the questioning ricocheted off of the windows and leather interior. She closed her eyes, let her head lean on the headrest, and sat stoically, waiting for Wendy to calm down and stop her unending quiz. There was a beat of silence, and then Wendy took a breath.

"I was knocked out," Maggie stated dispassionately, rubbing her eyes.

"You mean you got in a fight, and someone knocked you out?"

"No, I was knocked out by someone from The Council. Look, it's a long story and I'm just not in the mood to talk about it right now. I feel, uh, terrible." Maggie put her arm across her closed eyes to shield them from the sun's merciless rays.

"The Council? Why did you go see them?" Wendy questioned.

"It was their idea. Trust me, I would've preferred to stay home."

"What did they do? Drag you there? Is that it?"

"Yeah, that's about it." Maggie shielded her eyes from the light. She peeked through her fingers to get a good look at Wendy's reaction and saw that Wendy was shaking her head in disbelief.

"Why did they take you to The Council? Is it the school?"

"Yeah, the school. It was a warning…or an offer. Depends on how you look at it, I guess. If it was a warning, I am not heeding it, by the way. I didn't start this thing to be stopped by…threats. I won't let anyone stop me, anyone." Maggie made the declaration aloud as much to herself as to Wendy, as she rubbed her head. She remembered DaSifu Dao's words, *then you'll want to open a school in Des Moines*… She paused. She looked at Wendy and thought hard about how she would take the next thing that she asked her.

"What're you looking at me like that for? I'm behind you one hundred percent." Wendy enunciated each word carefully, but unconvincingly. Maggie's body threw off the groggy cloak that had covered her and became energized with anger at the thought of Wendy's betrayal. She got out of the car and slammed the door shut as she put on her sunglasses. They brought only the briefest sense of relief as she started questioning Wendy.

"Are you? Are you on my side? Maybe I should go to Des Moines?" Maggie accused.

"What does that mean?"

"I think you, of all goddamn people, know exactly what the hell that means! The DaSifu said something last night that could've only come from you. You said something to them, and that's why they came after me. You did, didn't you?" Maggie knew that though her eyes were hidden behind the sunglasses, they couldn't hide her intent.

"No…Well…" Wendy looked up and down the street as if waiting for a bus or a convenient distraction. Maggie studied her demeanor and watched her as she took a deep breath and then let it out.

"I thought that they could talk you into reconsidering this crazy freaking idea! Opening a school in Chinatown? Are you fucking nuts? You had a great job! We had a future! You blew your whole fucking IRA on this thing! What are you going to do when you run out of money? Fight the bankers? Bill collectors? What the hell are you doing? Quit trying to right some wrong from your youth and move on." Wendy's pleading hands contradicted her accusing stare.

"You take it so lightly like it's no big deal, but what if you get hurt, huh? What if some stupid-ass macho chump, that's a grand poobah in hoof-and-mouth-style, or tiger-gout-fu, or whatever other stupid shit these people give their allegiance to, comes down and caves in your skull with a tire iron! You're just a —"

"I'm a what? Say it." Maggie folded her arms. Enmity pierced her dark glasses.

The silence between them was long and crackling with the emotions and unsteady feelings that only come from speaking the truth out loud. Only the sound of the busy street reminded them that they were not alone in the world. Maggie leaned back against her car and watched Wendy do the same as they both sensed a stalemate.

"Who's this flower broad by the way, huh?" Wendy questioned accusingly as she crossed her arms. "Where the hell did she come from all of the sudden?"

"Finally, I thought you'd never get to the real point. I won't explain myself anymore. This is the path I've chosen. It *is* dangerous, and it just got more dangerous." Maggie let the words escape like steam from a boiling kettle. "Your friends on The Council, I don't know what they told you, but they don't discuss, they threaten, and I won't back down. Not to them or anyone else...even you." Maggie's expression was sullen. She was glad her eyes were hidden behind the sunglasses, as she felt them begin to tear. *Don't let it out now. Don't let her see it.*

A beat of silence came and went before Maggie realized that she was shaking, despite her best attempts to hide it. Wendy reached out to her and put her hand on Maggie's shoulder, rubbing it in tiny circles as Maggie stared through the black plastic, intensely, at the ground. She watched as pools of liquid gathered in her lenses distorting her view of the crumbling gray asphalt, the faded white stripe, and small glittering bits of broken glass.

She felt Wendy's hand leave her shoulder, forever changed. She listened as Wendy's footsteps walked away from her.

The car door opened and shut.

The ignition came quick, and the engine started up strong.

Maggie could feel her stare through the car window.

"Go to hell," Maggie whispered, without looking up. She heard the tires crush the loose asphalt as the car drove out of the parking lot and quietly moved into traffic.

It wasn't until she knew Wendy's car was far down the boulevard that Maggie looked up and watched as it disappeared into the city street.

Getting back into her car, Maggie carefully slid into the driver's seat, feeling the tight muscles and aches in her back, legs, and body. From the driver's seat, she looked at the front of the school and Emily's flower shop across the street.

She turned the key and listened to the engine come to life. After revving the engine with a few powerful pumps on the gas, she abruptly shut it off. A stunning realization hit her. It was a beautiful day, and everything she wanted was before her. There wasn't any place to go.

The three Council members sat at a Mahjong table in a secluded room at the top of the Golden Dragon club. The room was full of tables lined in orderly rows, folding chairs, and assorted strong boxes. Later in the evening, the tables would be full of gamblers smoking, drinking, and wagering what they couldn't afford to lose against what they knew they would never win.

The men appeared relaxed in their undershirts and khakis, with half-full ashtrays and tumblers of scotch before them. A glass of Glenfiddich in the middle of the day was a luxury that The Council members enjoyed often.

DaSifu Dao watched stealthily, from the corner of his eye, as the other two men smoked their cigarettes and sipped their scotch in near silence. They showed subtle signs of worry, especially SiGung Hen. Though he tried his best to hide it, the normally focused SiGung, was now more often seen staring off into space or his glass, with a glazed expression.

Sifu Shou also fidgeted in his seat more than usual. He appeared unable to ever get comfortable. DaSifu Dao kept his observations to himself, but he knew the source of their distraction. They were concerned about the situation with the woman. He knew that he had to address it and keep them on board with the plan.

"Gentlemen, I don't think we have anything to worry about, and I told One-Eye as much," DaSifu stated confidently. He took a dainty sip of the whiskey and set it down on the green felt as carefully as if it were nitroglycerin.

"You told him?" Sifu Shou asked, surprised, and in a tone and volume more aggressive than he should have used.

"Yes, I told him." The Council Chairman shot an imposing stare at Sifu Shou. The sifu, realizing he had inadvertently questioned the DaSifu's authority, immediately relented and dropped his gaze giving a quick nod of quiet acquiescence.

A pregnant silence hung in the room.

SiGung Hen showed his disapproval to Sifu Shou with a silent look from behind his cigarette's twisting smoke.

DaSifu Dao's stare harvested the quiet by sucking the energy from the sifu's eyes as if to store it up for later. Petty squabbles would be settled after, they had to deal with the situation at hand.

"There is no point in trying to hide anything from One-Eye, he sees all. The best course when presenting a problem is to tell him what you plan to do about it. He respects solutions." DaSifu Dao drained his glass smoothly, set it on the table, and wiped his lips with a finger.

"One-Eye doesn't care about our edict. He only cares that someone is making him lose face. And that, he will not accept. If we are to maintain control, we must end it soon," SiGung Hen said plainly, and then lit another cigarette from the end of the one he had been smoking. He leaned back in his chair producing a minor squeak.

"Will she accept our offer?" Sifu Shou asked meekly, leaning forward for the answer.

The DaSifu squinted as his cigarette smoke flowed from the corner of his mouth and he looked for an answer on the wall in front of him.

"I heard from our informer on the street that she is determined to challenge us. She won't come to heel, not willingly anyway. Even if she wins this confrontation, we must find a way to declare victory," SiGung Hen said, as he leaned forward and looked to DaSifu Dao.

DaSifu Dao stood, rising smoothly like a mystical force, and looked out the window down onto the busy street. The stream of cars and people was the blood of Chinatown. Though the other members could not see what he was viewing through the window, he was transfixed as he watched the hypnotic flight of a hawk darting between the buildings looking for prey. The quick dive of the bird toward a small roof rat kept the DaSifu's attention. He watched the hawk as it missed its target and skidded off the roof into the afternoon sky. The DaSifu brought his cigarette to his lips, took in the smoke deep into his lungs, and then blew it dramatically into the air.

"Gentlemen, things are changing."

Maggie pulled up next to the old-fashioned mailbox in front of the house, put her car in park, and shut off the engine. Her hands ran around the steering wheel, and she shifted in her seat a few times as she postponed her exit. *You have to go in.* It had only been weeks, but it felt longer since she had been to the house that she and Wendy had shared.

From the car, she studied the pewter finish of the mailbox and stand that had been stained dark to appear weathered and old in some places. Wendy had described it as stylish, though Maggie always thought that it looked pretentious. The usually well-manicured lawn looked a little overgrown. It needed to be cut and hadn't been edged since Maggie had done it herself months ago.

The silver garbage cans were tucked away on the side of the garage, as usual, but the lid of one was trying to cover, unsuccessfully, a couple of large pizza boxes. It wasn't like Wendy to eat out much. Things had changed.

Maggie had spent a lot of time doing the usual homeowner jobs like painting, yard work, and general upkeep, but she didn't see much of herself reflected in it. The constellation-silver paint color, looked like a drab gray now that it had aged, just like she'd said it would. Wendy said she had to have it and so she went along with it. The house was all Wendy, not her. The quiet street with people having barbecues, and kids having sleepovers, wasn't a place where she ever felt comfortable. Now that so much had happened, it was like traveling to some distant universe compared to the lights and danger of Chinatown.

She got out of the car.

The walk up the driveway was steeper than she remembered. She put her key in the lock and gripped the door handle tightly so she could give it a push. The door always stuck a bit, but it opened, nonetheless.

The familiar scent of jasmine hit her as soon as she entered. The back windows were always open a crack so that the vines in the backyard could send their perfumed bouquet into the house. It was pleasant and sometimes magical, but now it held no power. It was just familiar.

After walking the few steps from the entryway to the kitchen, Maggie put her keys down and spied the small note conspicuously placed on the counter for her to find. It was a piece of white binder paper with blue lines, folded neatly one time. Maggie's name was written purposefully on the side facing up, and it had been playfully scripted with an open circle used to dot the eye.

She picked it up and held it for a moment, but then put it back down on the counter unread. There was no point in reading it. She had already let it all go.

Shedding her old life was the cost of her new one. It was natural. Still, it hurt. It didn't matter though; she was moving on. She couldn't retrace her steps, and even if she could, it wouldn't take her back to where she had been. They had been lost in the shifting sands of anger and sorrow. Her course was now set.

In the bedroom closet, she found the few things that were hers and put them in a box. She could use some of them, like the camping stove and the pillows, but she would donate others. The box of new crystal champagne flutes would go to a shelter so that they could sell them and put the money to good use. A smile crossed her face as she thought of doing what she had always joked about with Wendy.

"You want to send these to a shelter? They can't drink there." Wendy declared, holding up one of the clear glasses.

"Yeah, I know, but if it was me? I would love for someone to send me these lovely flutes and a bottle of champagne to share. If I got nothing, I'm gonna love having a glass of champagne and living the high life, even if it's just for a few minutes." Maggie reasoned.

"Yeah, well, you can't donate alcohol, so come up with a plan B," Wendy said as she put the glass back in the box.

The memories made her smile. She put the box of flutes in a bag and covered the image on the box with a sweater and a pair of shorts. The main task at hand was to keep a clear mind, and not fall into the romantic memories of the past. *Just pack and go.*

Years ago, when they moved in together, Maggie had shown up with all her things, which fit easily in one large backpack.

"Is that all you have?" Wendy questioned, pointing at the bag sitting on the floor of the bedroom.

"It's all I need; besides, I have enough baggage up here." Maggie tapped her head lightly with her index finger. She broke a smile. Together, they laughed as they hugged, and beamed at each other and the thoughts of a bright future together.

"Click." "Snap." "Creak."

Her memory was immediately interrupted by the sound of the door to the garage opening. The clicking of the knob followed by the creaking sound meant that the door was already open, and someone was coming in. Maggie's pulse surged, and her senses became more aware and attuned, as she hard-shifted from her quixotic thoughts of the past to her fighter-mode. Wendy wouldn't be home for hours. *Who could it be?*

She moved into the hallway and stayed close to the wall. Stepping silently, she peeked around the corner. The garage door entrance was at the other end of the kitchen and the door opened into the house, so the advantage was hers for a surprise attack, if she could get close enough.

Staring intently at the open door, she held her breath. It creaked a bit and then looked like it was about to close. Whoever had opened the door was not standing behind it. Was it a ruse to get her to attack? If the intruder was just within the doorway, then they would have the advantage if she attacked prematurely.

She stepped past the corner of the hall and was walking silently through the dining room toward the door. In a few steps, she would be there. Her ears picked up nothing for now, as they were only hearing her heartbeat rapidly in her head.

The door opened slowly again. Maggie would be inches from the assailant, and they would never expect it. She had the element of surprise. *Strike them hard in the eyes, and then finish them off.*

Depending on how many assailants were after her, if she was overrun, she could exit out the back window, hop the fence, and get back to her car later. That was the plan, and it all sounded good, but first, she had to focus on this one, the closest threat. *Time to kick this guy's ass.*

One. Two. Three…

The door opened wider, and a person's head moved past.

Just as Maggie was about to smash her fist into the opponent's temple, she stopped.

"Mrs. Donner!"

"Oh, I hope I didn't scare you, Maggie," Mrs. Donner, the next-door neighbor, said, appearing startled and standing frozen in the doorway holding a pristine white casserole dish.

Though she insisted on being called by her first name, Abbie-Ann, neither Wendy nor Maggie could ever bring themselves to use it. It just didn't seem right. The relationship was based on her proximity, and so she became part mother, semi-friend, and known purveyor of neighborhood gossip. It was always assumed that since Mrs. Donner would tell Maggie and Wendy about everyone else's business, theirs was being told as well. Lucky for them, their biggest secret was that they weren't just housemates, but after all these years it was an open secret in the neighborhood.

Mrs. Donner was a good fifteen years older than both Wendy and Maggie and looked every inch the part of a suburban housewife from central casting: stretch pants, floral apron or occasional housecoat, flats, big hairdo, and coral pink lipstick. The running joke between Wendy and Maggie, since moving in years ago, had been that one day one or both of them, would turn into Mrs. Donner. When the transformation was complete their only desire would be the secret to a great meatloaf.

"Well, Maggie, didn't expect to see you here?"

"Well, I live…used to…live here…anyway, I was –"

"Wendy told me you were moving out. Sort of unexpected, huh hon?" Her risen eyebrows implied surprise and an invitation to tell her more.

Maggie kept quiet and acted oblivious to her intention.

"I hope I didn't scare you. I came to return this dish, used the side door in the garage." Mrs. Donner handed Maggie the white casserole dish, "I'm so sorry to hear about you moving. Bill and I really have enjoyed living next to you two," She smiled her practiced insincere smile big and wide.

"Yes, well, I'm sure Wendy'll get another housemate and you'll probably like her just as well." Holding the empty casserole dish, a dubious expression appeared on her face.

"I don't know, but I suppose you're right. Ya know, I used to enjoy watching you do that fancy stuff in the backyard with the…what did you call it, again?" Mrs. Donner questioned squinting one eye and touching her index finger to her lips.

"The staff?"

"Right, the staff…all that swirlin' that stick around was really neat. I hope you didn't mind me watchin'?"

"No, of course not."

Maggie, her smile turning to a smirk, put the dish on the nearby dining table.

"I heard you opened that school in Chinatown and can't make the rent, is that right?"

"Part of it."

Maggie was stunned by the directness of her question. It was more direct than usual and that's saying something when talking about Mrs. Donner.

"What happened to your job at the lab? You made good money there, didn't you?"

"Yes, but…Well, there's more to it than that, you know? More than just the money." Maggie leaned against the open garage door, as she mused about how much easier this all would have been if it had just been a simple assault.

"Well, I hope you make some money swirlin' that stick around."

"Staff."

"Right. Staff."

Mrs. Donner folded her arms and slipped into her posture of shifting onto one leg, which usually accompanied long unending tales. "Ya know, I always wanted to be a writer. Did you know that?"

"No, I –"

"Sure, I did." Mrs. Donner interrupted, "I wrote all through school, even into college. But, when I married Bill, he said it's me or *it*, ya know? So, I had to stop...which is fine...he's happier that way, Bill is..." Mrs. Donner looked to the ceiling as she spoke the words. Maggie questioned whether she believed them.

"What about you though, are you happy?" Maggie asked, and for the first time in her life wanted to hear her answer.

"Well, you can't just go and do what you want? Can you?" Mrs. Donner questioned rhetorically, "You have to make sacrifices, and, and, and, you know, grow up, right? I mean, Bill's happier this way, so you know...that's fine." Mrs. Donner's posture had changed when she finished speaking. She had slumped forward, and her folded arms seemed to be supporting her body as she looked at the floor. Maggie said nothing as she stared at the top of her neighbor's beehive coiffure.

The jasmine wafted through the open window and the wind chimes in the backyard tinkled a short melody during the silence.

"I'm gonna miss you, Mrs. Donner. Maybe I can read something you wrote someday, huh?"

Mrs. Donner cackled loudly. "That's so funny, no that's done there Maggie, ya gotta grow up, ya know... make the sacrifice and all...no, the time for that has passed...Bill is happier though...OK...so...that's fine." Mrs. Donner's eyes appeared to look everywhere and nowhere before she turned and walked back through the door.

Maggie listened as Mrs. Donner's voice trailed off into the garage and then beyond as she walked out the side door and into the world she chose, where dreams go to die for Bill's happiness.

Maggie closed the garage door, locked it, and walked back toward the front. She stopped for a moment and looked around the kitchen. She took a quick inventory remembering the life they had had together. It felt comfortable and it would be easy to go back to. Very easy.

As she walked out, Maggie grabbed her keys from the counter and pulled the door shut. The door locked behind her and she put her key under the doormat. As she walked down the driveway, she never looked back. She got in her car and drove away.

With all the drama occurring around the opening of the school, Maggie hadn't thought much about the August street festival scheduled for the following day. The festival was an excuse for shop owners to put their stock on display in the warm summer sun, and for restaurant and food vendors to offer one-day specials. Martial arts students, lion dancers, and Chinese opera performers would put on a dramatic show for the throng of tourists and locals. Firecrackers would fill the streets and red confetti would float through the air like crimson snow.

Though she wanted to be excited about the festival, which she always enjoyed as a child, she was still smarting from the grand opening of the school, which had been somewhat less than grand. With the words repeating themselves in her mind, *it will get better*, she tried to shake off the fear of failure that seemed to always come as a nightmarish vision of Wendy's disapproving stare. She had waited expectantly, in her neatly pressed uniform, behind her spartanly decorated table with fliers, business cards, and a jar with a daisy. Ready for a stream of students, she greeted only a few people that came in to inquire about the school, who she was, and the classes that she offered. She kept up the mantra internally, that it would get better. It had to.

She looked out the front window of her school and saw people blocking off the streets with white wooden barricades borrowed from the 12th police precinct. People on ladders were hanging bright decorations on lampposts. Long streamers of red, yellow, and pink fluttered everywhere.

The street would soon be full of music, the aroma of delicious food, and all the pleasant chaos that accompanies the festival. The jubilant atmosphere would attract people from Terre Promise, The Point, and even Argent Hills. Everyone seeking to evade their everyday troubles would come to have a day of fun. Chinatown would rise like a phoenix, at least for the day.

It had been almost a month since The Council had formally addressed Maggie with the ultimatum of running her school under her old teacher. She had not changed her mind. The door still displayed her chop, her name in a red square of script characters, rather than her teachers'. She was openly defying The Council and she knew what that meant.

They would send more challengers. Since they were the most powerful force in Chinatown, they would use their influence in the city to pressure her as well. She could look forward to intermittent interruptions of utilities and city services. Some things had already happened and some she knew were soon to come, such as electricity being shut off, though the bill was paid. Garbage would inexplicably fall off the truck in front of her school and not be cleaned up. Vandalism had become more prevalent on her street, especially in her building. Her car may be ticketed and occasionally impounded. Harassment would be a powerful way for The Council to assert who was in charge.

With Wendy gone, her thoughts turned more often to Emily. It was strange but she still felt guilty when she thought of her. The power of conditioning, she told herself. In the same way, Mrs. Donner would never dream of doing anything to displease Bill, she had been guilty of suppressing her thoughts, dreams, and feelings. It was like she had been asleep. *Wake up! What do I want?*

It was easy to answer if she was honest with herself. She was attracted to Emily. It was more than that though, she liked her and enjoyed being around her. She felt relaxed talking to her and found her sunny disposition infectious. When they talked though, Maggie felt her eyes lingering as they studied her round cheeks and sparkling eyes.

More than once, as Maggie crossed the street, her gaze had been drawn to the picture window of Emily's shop as she watched Emily working, only to be awakened from her somnambulist trek by a blaring car horn and shaking fist of an angry motorist that just missed hitting her in the crosswalk.

It was too much to think about for now, but it made her realize that she felt something. And at the very least, there was nothing wrong with going into Emily's flower shop, and visiting her, if she wanted to.

"Hello?" Maggie called into the empty shop, and after waiting for a beat, stepped into the small lobby still hearing the tinkling from the bells tied to the handle that announced her arrival. The shop was bright and cheerful with shelves full of flowers and plants everywhere she looked. The sounds of feet shuffling and other activity from the back room let her know that someone was there.

"Hello? Emily?"

Emily emerged from between the white drapes that divided the front and back of the shop, holding a small plant. She walked in measured steps and approached Maggie with her head down, looking oblivious to the world. With an almost religious reverence, she gave the plant a light kiss on one of its leaves, and then carefully placed it on the shelf. She brought her hands together in a praying fashion, bowed her head, and then when the ritual was over, returned to the world.

"Oh, Maggie, I'm sorry, I didn't know you were here," She wore an untroubled smile.

"I just came in. You didn't hear me?"

"No, I'm sorry, I kind of space out when I am working, sometimes, ya know?" Emily, still smiling, started humming as she faced the plant again and turned it so that the full leafy side was facing the customer's view, and then walked behind the counter. On folded arms, she leaned on the counter and looked up with dollish eyes, "What can I do for you?"

"I was wondering, are you going to set up something for the festival?" Maggie asked convincingly, as she struggled to find a reason to be in the shop.

"Yes, of course. Do you want to set up a table next to me? You could put up a sign and give away a free flower for every new student that signs up. What do you think?"

Maggie was deep in thought and suddenly overcome with emotions. Her body became cold and clammy as she became awash in guilt and fear at the idea of Emily being at the table next to her.

"Are you okay?" Emily's face revealed her concern.

"Yes, I just…Well, Wendy and I have…are not…The school is having some problems…and she…well, you know…so…I wondered if you would like to get something to eat?" Maggie looked at the floor, and then at the ceiling, and anywhere else but at Emily's face, unsure, and afraid of what her response would be. She could feel sweat start to form in the small of her back.

"Sure, let me get my purse." Emily dashed through the white curtain to the back of the store, and then returned moments later with a big smile and her small white purse under her left arm. "Pork buns?"

Maggie giggled and felt her smile break from ear to ear.

The couple walked up the street together and Maggie let Emily choose a small table for two near the edge of the sidewalk in the bistro-style seating at The Delicious Food Company restaurant.

"I always thought their name was such a Chinatown name," Maggie stated, as she sat down and adjusted her orange plastic tray with its pork bun, chow mein, and Tab cola so that it would fit better on the small wobbly table without knocking off Emily's tray with a pork bun, congee, and a Coke.

"You mean because it's proud and sorta in your face? Well, you don't get too far without tooting your own horn, especially in Chinatown, right?" Emily took a big bite of her pork bun, perhaps bigger than she intended and Maggie tried not to watch as she chewed it with some difficulty. Emily's eyes darted from the table to the street, as she chewed the mouthful of bread in large rolling motions of her jaw.

Maggie held back a smile as she watched Emily work indelicately on her mouthful of bread and candied meat.

190

"So, have you always been a florist?" Maggie asked before she took a decidedly small bite of her pork bun.

"Well, I've always loved flowers. They're just my thing, ya know? Have you heard of that new seminar people are going to where they discover their *thing*? What they want to do, or be? What makes 'em happy?"

"E.S.T.?"

Emily nodded, took a spoonful of her porridge, and continued.

"Yeah, well, I guess my thing is flowers. Lucky for me, I knew it early. I saved the $40 I would've had to pay for the weekend seminar to find it out." Emily took a drink of her Coke and sat back in her chair. "I guess your thing is kung fu, right?"

"Yeah, but I didn't always do it. I stopped for a while. I'm getting back into it now."

"Why'd you stop?"

"Well, that is a long story. And it is not all that pleasant. I'm not sure you'd want to hear it." Taking a moment, she realized that she was being more serious than she meant to be. She wanted to tell Emily about everything that had happened, but she was worried it was too much at once. "In life, I guess most people settle, don't they?" Maggie questioned herself, nervously. "I've always wanted to have my own school. It's forbidden in Chinatown, which you may or may not know. I've always loved kung fu though, all martial arts, really. And I was always good at them too, ya know? I could beat boys twice my size. It wasn't easy. I still had to work hard, but that didn't bother me. For a while, I did things that I didn't want to do, trying to hide my feelings about my *thing*." She nodded acknowledgment to Emily and then continued. "I tried to be someone I'm not, just to fit in. Just to get by. But now, well anyway, like Popeye, I am what I am." Maggie chuckled, awkwardly.

"Ya know, the past is usually unpleasant, isn't it? It's what makes you who you are though, right? You have to go through dark times to get to the light," Maggie was impressed as Emily revealed her sage observation, and then took a small bite of the pork bun.

"Sounds like some ancient wisdom. Something your mom told you growing up?" Maggie asked, as she sat back, comfortable for the first time in a while, and took a sip of Tab.

"No, just a conclusion I came to when I was in high school. After something happened to me." Emily put down her pork bun and stared into her congee as if it would reveal some hidden truth. She shifted in her seat, scratched her head, and adjusted her napkin in her lap. "I think we all have had unpleasant things happen to us." She leaned forward, took a drink, a small bite of her pork bun, and for the first time appeared disturbed. Uneasy. She looked like she was consumed with a dark thought.

"Hey, I didn't mean to make you feel uncomfortable. We don't need to talk about the past." Maggie reached across the tray and for the first time, touched Emily with a reassuring caress of her hand. She was surprised to feel that Emily's hand was rough. Cutting and twisting plants into living art and digging in damp earth over the years had made them coarse. It made sense to Maggie although it didn't seem to fit her personality. Though Emily was sprightly and cute, she wasn't dainty. She worked hard. Her hands were small, but they were strong. They were hands that worked with the elements, with life. They had power. Even from the slightest touch, Emily's energy was palpable, shimmering. It felt good to touch her.

Maggie left her hand on Emily's, and with her index finger, gently drew little circles as the traffic, breeze, and moments floated by their wobbly table.

"I was just thinking of something that happened a long time ago. I don't want to get too heavy, but I like you, Maggie. And I think you like me a little, right?"

Maggie nodded and continued to gently stroke Emily's hand.

"I wasn't sure if I should talk about this, but when I was in high school. I really liked a girl…"

Mr. Deming's lecture about the "alphabet soup" programs started by FDR during the depression, was causing Emily extreme drowsiness. Fifth-period history was never festive, but today it was excruciating. Her gaze began to drift over to Charlene, the shapely cheerleader that looked remarkably like Elizabeth Taylor: Porcelain skin, blue eyes, and raven hair styled in a soft bouffant with a white headband. She sat one row back and two desks over. For Emily, it was an easy tilt of the head and a slight sideways roll of the eyes to see her in a casual way that wouldn't draw attention. She could be simply looking at the clock on the wall, or the massive wall poster explaining the history of the Soviet Union, or any other reason that could be easily explained in the subtle, non-verbal language of distracted high school students.

Every boy in school was in love with Charlene. Occasionally, she dropped things from her desk, a pencil, eraser, anything, and the rush of hands to pick it up and hand it back to her was numerous and impressive. She was the head cheerleader and had her pick of the boys in school, but she was not going steady with any of them. At least not formally, anyway. She had been seen with plenty, but no one seemed to be able to get her out on a date besides a game or a dance. To

193

the frustration of many of her suitors, wherever they took her, there were always a lot of people around.

Emily, at first, would only look secretly at Charlene, but over time, she became increasingly comfortable and bold. Today, with the itemized list of the benefits of the New Deal, and specifically the WPA still in her ears, she feared that her eyes had lingered too long.

When her gaze locked with Charlene's, Emily smiled not knowing what else to do, and was ecstatic when Charlene returned a slight smile to her. Emily smiled bigger still, and then chuckled a little, not realizing how loud she had been.

"Emily, is there something funny about the New Deal to you?" Mr. Deming asked loudly, a few feet from her desk.

"No, I'm sorry, I just thought of something…that seemed funny…It doesn't seem funny anymore though, not really."

When Mr. Deming walked back to the front of the class, Emily looked around at the other students and saw more than one roll their eyes, before looking back at Charlene in her not-so-secretive fashion. Charlene was not looking at her anymore though, but instead was studying the notes on the blackboard.

Had she ever been looking at me?

Emily began to wonder if she had imagined the whole thing, though in her memory she could still see Charlene looking at her and smiling. She wasn't sure now if the whole thing had been a fantasy. It wouldn't be the first time. She knew that she had a vivid imagination, and often saw things how she wanted them to be rather than how they were. As she pondered the question, the bell rang.

Emily's locker was jam-packed with books, stacked in no discernable order. Scattered throughout were loose papers, stray pencils, erasers, extra gym socks, tampons, an autographed picture of Bobby Sherman, an *Abba-Zaba* candy bar, and a beaker from the science lab that she used as a tiny vase for a yellow dandelion picked from the front lawn of the school.

Focused on the comforting and familiar chaos of her locker, Emily ignored the herd-like flow of human traffic deftly navigating by her in the hall. The multitude of conversations created an impenetrable din that masked any sound not louder than a sonic boom. She didn't hear someone come up behind her.

"Did you take notes for Deming's class?"

Emily turned, and though she recognized the voice, was still shocked to see Charlene standing behind her. She didn't think Charlene even knew where her locker was. Inversely, Emily knew exactly where Charlene's locker was located, and her mind immediately raced to the other side of the wing. She pictured the top locker with the black and yellow smiley face sticker by the latch and the worn steel plate, number 263.

They never ran into each other when they were changing classes.

Why would they?

Charlene's presence before her was a complete surprise. Emily tried to breathe but found no air. She had to collect herself, and most of all, not freak out.

Don't freak out!

As she stood staring, dumbstruck, at Charlene, she couldn't help but notice that Charlene's long dark hair seemed to be even shinier up close. It was like a lustrous dark halo around her ivory-skinned face. With her so close, the height difference between them became more obvious. Charlene was a few inches taller than she realized. Everything became more pronounced. Charlene's clothes were pressed neatly and looked brand new. Her white miniskirt was pleated with razor-sharp ironed creases. Her orange ruffled blouse looked like a row of carnations lightly starched. She wore calf-high white boots.

Emily was immediately self-conscious of her powder blue top that had a small hole at the elbow and her frayed blue jeans with their botched embroidery of a rose on the right hip pocket. Her jeans still had dirt stains on the knees from planting in the garden that morning.

What did she ask about? The notes for Deming, right?

"Yes, I think I did… I think I do…I mean, the notes are good, I think, and, uh…" Emily stammered and sputtered out her response trying not to appear as smitten with Charlene as she was.

Charlene scrunched up her nose and flashed her perfect million-dollar smile.

"Maybe you can come with us to study today, you know, with my friends and me? We could all use some help in Deming's class. Bring your notes."

"Yeah, sure! That sounds great. I just love *the New Deal*," Emily cringed, internally as the words left her mouth.

Who enjoyed talking about the New Deal besides FDR?

Emily decided that it was best to play it cool from here on out. "Where are you going to study?" She said, wearing the most unemotional expression she could muster.

"We go to our own little place. How about you meet us in the parking lot after school?" Charlene asked, moving her hair behind her ear with her finger.

"Sure."

"Groovy, after sixth period, meet us by Mary's Mustang," Charlene paused and gave a puzzled expression, "You know Mary? Mary McDougall, don't you?"

"Yeah, of course, I mean I know who she is…Who doesn't? I'll meet you then. Mary's Mustang." Emily confirmed with a quick nod of assent.

"Groooovy," Charlene said, in a sing-song voice as she tilted her head and gazed at Emily intently before scrunching her nose again and finishing with a wink.

Almost overcome with excitement, Emily had to look away.

"Yep, I'll be there. See ya soon..." Emily was speaking, though Charlene had already turned and was far out of earshot. As she pretended to remove and then replace her chemistry book from the locker, she turned just enough to watch the white boots walk away into the throng of students.

Emily looked back into the random stack of books and materials in her locker and saw a kind of magic in it, as she looked past what was before her, and in the chaos, she pictured Charlene looking back at her.

BRRRNNG!

The bell rang. Class was starting soon. The hallway started emptying quickly. She had to rush to get to her next class. She grabbed her Trig book, slammed her locker shut, and took off. She couldn't help but wear a smile on her face on the way to class.

The window was rolled down and the cool wind blew through Emily's hair whipping it into a never-ending series of serpentine dances. The afternoon sun lay lightly on her skin. It was a sublime combination, made better only by being in the car with Charlene.

She didn't know the other two girls very well although she had seen them with Charlene before. The three of them seemed to hang out a lot. She knew that Mary, who drove the white Mustang, usually drove Charlene and other girls off campus for lunch. Emily was envious at the times when they returned with soft-serve ice cream.

Charlene said they usually all hung out after school at the quarry, where they could smoke and talk. It was like their hangout, she said.

As the Mustang sprinted through the lightly traveled country roads to the quarry, Mary and Charlene sat like royalty in the front seat. Emily shared the backseat with Laurie.

Laurie came across as awkward and cold. Emily had tried to make some small talk when they got in the car, but Laurie didn't seem interested. She appeared distant and a little anxious about something.

Occasionally, Laurie would glance over at Emily, and when their eyes met, she would quickly look away. *Had she made her mad or offended her in some way?* It was the strained and awkward silence in the back seat that made Emily decide to roll down the window and enjoy the wind and sun as they drove out of town toward the quarry.

The gravel quarry was where a lot of kids went after school and on weekends. It had once been a thriving business, but a few years ago it shut down. Now it was just a deserted shell of its former self.

She had been there once last semester on a field trip for her anthropology class. The machines still stood, though unmanned. The buildings were locked and empty. Through the dirty windows, intricate machinery could be seen sitting idle as if waiting for the workers to return from some interminable break and start again.

Some kids had broken into a few of the buildings; broken windows and graffiti randomly appeared throughout. Most kids likely became bored with their unrestricted vandalism and went back to drinking beer, smoking, or trying to have their first awkward sexual encounter. The evidence of their activity, beer cans, cigarette butts, and used prophylactics, was often laying in the small corners of the structures.

As the Mustang got closer, Emily could see the dark outline of the buildings and the mechanical equipment getting bigger. The cranes and conveyors created an ominous industrial skyline. The car turned quickly and pulled onto the gravel and dirt road. Moments later it passed the chain link fence that held the perpetually unheeded admonishment to "KEEP OUT."

Emily looked out the back window of the Mustang and watched as the dirt from the road left a cloudy trail that hung opaque for a few moments, and then dissolved magically back to the earth.

The Mustang ran toward the first building and then came to an abrupt stop in front of a row of buildings that looked like they held offices and barracks.

The engine turned off and everyone got out of the car.

The doors shut.

The four girls were all looking in different directions.

Emily looked around and was struck by the ominous quiet and seclusion. They were still close to town, but it felt like they were a million miles away. The ambient sounds of life died all around with nothing to reflect them: No walls, hills, or trees. Just the wind in her ears, and the naked sun above. Desolate.

With her senses still adjusting to the wide-open environment, Emily didn't hear the soft crunching of gravel as footsteps approached behind her.

Suddenly, she felt the dull percussive thud of a strike to the back of her head. The impact sent her reeling, disoriented, to the ground. Her body landed hard, and her breath left her. Shooting pains registered from all points of impact.

She struggled to turn over.

The sun was in her eyes.

Above her, the dark silhouettes of two heads looked down on her.

As the two heads got closer, she could make out the faces of Mary and Charlene standing over her with glaring eyes and crooked grins. Their faces could be seen enjoying their deed with evil satisfaction.

What the hell is happening?

Mary kicked Emily hard in the stomach as Charlene reached down and grabbed Emily by her hair, snapping back her head and her face toward the sky. With her hand holding Emily's hair firmly, Charlene pulled Emily up to her feet, and then grabbed her arms from behind and held her tightly.

Can't move.

Mary stood in front of her menacingly, pacing slightly as if taking in the moment. She slapped Emily hard across the face. Relishing the power, she slapped her again across the cheek, making Emily's head snap hard toward her shoulder, and then she slapped her across the mouth.

Her lips went numb.

As Emily got free and sought to move away from the assault, Mary slapped her indiscriminately across the ear and back of the head, and any other available target, as Emily tried to look away. Unexpectedly, Mary delivered a hard punch to Emily's stomach, and Emily's knees buckled as she fell awkwardly to the dirt.

From the ground, she watched a pair of boots approach her.

"Quit looking at me in class you little chink dyke!" Charlene spat the words out.

Emily looked up at her, grateful to only see one black shape against the bright sky. She heard Mary giggle a bit, and then the car door opened, and she got in.

As Charlene moved away, Emily got a better look at her and saw her smug satisfied look as she walked to the passenger side of the car. The door opened and closed quickly.

Emily looked at the dirt and then back at the sky and felt the sun on her face as the wind blew through her hair. She thought of how only minutes ago it had felt comforting and magical, and now it was crushing and all too familiar.

The white Mustang peeled out in the soft dirt kicking up rocks and debris that sailed through the air and stung her face. Emily watched the back of the car as it drove away. She saw Laurie looking out the back window. She was wearing the same sad expression she had earlier. As the car got smaller down the road, the face disappeared.

Emily sat up and rested in the dirt for what felt like a very long time. She looked up at the sky and then her eyes returned to earth. Her face and her stomach hurt. The sting of the slaps and the pain of the blows lingered. All at once, emotion overcame her, and she watched her tears fall and become dark circles in the dust.

Her eyes were red and glassy, and on her face hung a somber expression. It was as if she had just re-lived the entire event over again when she told the story.

Maggie gently squeezed her hand.

"It's sometimes hard for me to get close, ya know? I just want you to know that, okay?" Emily pulled back her hand from Maggie's grasp and took a drink.

The sounds of the busy street nearby filled the hushed pause. Maggie watched Emily study her tray.

"I had a friend in college that was attacked by some sorority girls. They just did it for fun. Bastards. I've known men with stories like yours too. I think there are a lot of people with stories like that. It can happen to anyone. A lot of people have

201

been hurt," Maggie said, as she pushed her tray away. "All we can do is hope that someday things will change...BUT, until then, I can teach you how to kick their asses!" Maggie said with a smile.

Emily, who after looking down at her half-eaten entrees, looked up and smiled back. Her eyes were still wet, but Maggie knew that the warmth between them would soon dry them up.

"Let's head back. I can't eat any more pork buns, or I won't be able to do any kicks higher than my ankles." Maggie smiled at Emily who chuckled at the thought.

They both got up, pushed their chairs in, and started heading back down the street toward their businesses.

"Yeah, I need to get back to the shop. I got orders to prepare. There is a wedding Saturday, and I also need to make a special bouquet for a guy that's a bank president. He's in the doghouse, as he calls it because he cheated on his wife."

"He told you that?"

"Sure, he wants to know the best flowers to get him out of the jam," Emily shrugged her shoulders and continued. "I'm like a doctor, only I prescribe flowers for your problems, ya know?" Emily stated confidently.

"What gets you out of that kind of a...jam?"

"Well, it doesn't have to be Saffron Crocus, they're about $500 per flower, by the way." Emily winked knowingly, "but it will definitely be something along the lines of my luxury bouquet, as I like to call it. It's the most expensive one I have."

"$500 a flower?" Maggie asked, dumbfounded by the amount.

"Yeah, $500 at least." Emily shrugged her shoulders again acknowledging that it was a lot of money, but as Maggie knew, all things were relative.

They both entered Emily's shop.

"I don't think he needs to worry too much about the flowers though. He dropped off a sapphire ring for me to put in a special box at the bottom of the clear crystal vase." Emily wore a knowing grin.

"You think she'll forgive him?"

"He's a regular. I know she will." Emily put on her apron and walked behind the counter. "She must have a heck of a jewelry collection by now."

Maggie noticed that Emily's expression had suddenly changed. She was looking at something behind her. Her expression became inquisitive.

"You may want to speak to those guys that just walked past the shop. It looks like they're headed down to your school. Maybe they want to sign up?"

"How many?"

"I saw two of them. Would you discount their tuition if they sign up together?" Emily asked.

Two men. Get ready.

It was as if everything had dissolved, as Maggie felt a rush of heat roll over her body, knowing full well that it was likely not prospective students, not at this time of day. Students would come closer to the evening when classes were held. The only people that come during the day are repairmen and challengers, and she wasn't expecting any repairmen. She thought for a moment and realized that surprise would be her advantage.

Think fast.

"Can I borrow that big bouquet of assorted carnations?"

"The big one? Sure, but that's the summer sampler celebration bouquet. I only have one left, so–" Emily exclaimed, slightly alarmed, as Maggie grabbed the entire bouquet with a swipe of her hand and then reached into her pants pocket.

"Here!" Maggie slammed down $10.00 on the counter and ran out the door with the flowers.

"Hey, but it's $12.50!" Emily yelled after Maggie as the door closed behind her.

The two men that had passed the shop were not on the street.

They must already be inside the school.

Maggie stayed close to the wall outside and peeked around the corner to look through the window. As she peered into the school, she saw that the two men were standing in the red-carpeted training area.

Both men were white and looked to be around 25 years old. They were wearing standard white Karate uniforms with black belts.

More Karate guys?

One of the men had dark hair and big shoulders. He looked like a wrestler. His uniform had cut-off sleeves to show off his muscular arms and accentuate his stocky build.

The other one was thinner and had a large dark afro that reminded Maggie of the Juan Epstein character from *Welcome Back Kotter.* A show that Maggie loved, and Wendy had only tolerated.

The Wrestler stood in a stance that projected confidence and to Maggie, he looked like he was the one in charge. She figured that "Juan" was just along as backup.

They were likely from a Karate school in the suburbs past Argent Hills. They may have come as far as Blackland or Orland Springs. The Council was using a different tactic with Maggie than expected. They must not want it to look like there is internal strife in Chinatown, or that they aren't in complete control, so they've brought in people from the outside.

She entered quietly and walked into the lobby behind the two men holding the bouquet of carnations in front of her. She grabbed a receipt from the hardware store lying on the shelf next to her and a pen from the desk by the front window. The bouquet would slightly obscure her face in case they knew what she looked like. She extended her hand holding the pen and receipt.

"Please sign for delivery."

Both men turned toward her with puzzled expressions.

The wrestler was the closest.

"We don't work here, dumb bitch!" The wrestler slapped away the receipt and pen from Maggie's hand. Juan laughed. The wrestler laughed.

Maggie yelled as she exploded into action, "AAHHHRRGGHH!"

She kicked the wrestler hard under the jaw. The crunch of broken bones echoed in the empty space and confirmed a broken mandible. The wrestler's head snapped back from the force exposing his muscled abdomen. Maggie fired a steely kick to his gut and felt his torso collapse and fold around her iron-like foot.

The wrestler slumped forward. She grabbed his hair and jerked his head back with enough force to produce a loud cracking sound. He was helpless, gazing at the ceiling when Maggie wind-milled her arm over her head and dropped the bottom of her fist like a hammer onto his perfect suburban nose. The nose exploded like a rotten tomato, and shot a red mist, with large red particles, into all corners of the room.

Juan had been shocked and left standing idly by. He likely assumed an easy win, but now looked stunned to see things suddenly go badly for his partner. He came running at Maggie in his blood-speckled uniform.

He ran at her fast and yelled loudly with a fierce Kiai, his face was formed into a mask of rage. As he approached, Juan leaped into the air and his body transformed into a deadly missile as he threw a flying side kick at Maggie.

Get out of the way!

Maggie ducked and slid like she was stealing second base dropping low, well below the kick. As Juan passed over her, she parried the kick overhead, and with the other hand, punched his groin in mid-flight. Unable to control his landing from the pain, he careened toward a wall of glass.

Juan's body exploded through the center of the window with shattering glass projectiles shooting in all directions. His body thumped onto the sidewalk as deadly shards rained down all around him.

It took only moments for the passersby to start to gather and form a small crowd around the bloody man in the center of the glassy debris field.

Maggie decided to take full advantage of the opportunity and walked confidently through the shattered window dragging the wrestler behind her. The crowd of onlookers stood staring in disbelief.

She dragged the wrestler's body by his ankle through the frame of the broken window, across the piles of broken glass, and dramatically placed him next to the bloodied Juan on the sidewalk for everyone to see.

Free advertising.

Maggie stood in a confident pose letting the crowd get a good look at her before speaking.

"Don't come back, or it will be worse." Maggie kicked the wrestler with a quick shot to the ribs as he lay next to Juan. He let out a small moan of objection and with his bloody hands, grabbed his stricken side.

Maggie stole the moment and gave a slow dramatic look around to the people gathered on the street as if to invite another opponent. She knew that no one would approach her. Instead, they would gossip to their friends and neighbors throughout Chinatown, and tell everyone they knew about the woman, with the new school, that had beaten two large challengers. The story would spread

Juan and the wrestler lay still at Maggie's feet as the crowd looked on. She looked down at the two opponents, and then at the crowd before she walked back with a confident swagger through the broken space where the window had been.

She felt electric.

Once inside though, she had to admit to herself that even though the whole event had been very dramatic, there was no denying the real danger that she had faced. It could have been a disaster for her, and she knew that she had been lucky. Her only regret was the expense of repairing that damned window.

The night was unseasonably warm, and a welcome breeze blew through the alley. Maggie and Emily were outside the school of White Crane Kung Fu prepping for the new plan to thwart surprise challenges: take the fight to them.

"Why White Crane?" Emily asked, "Is there something special about the school or something?"

"Why not?" Maggie answered by shrugging her shoulders.

They waited outside sequestered in the alley and listened to the loud spirited yells, and the thudding of hands and feet hitting pads, as the students performed various striking drills. The class was in full swing.

They had staked out the alley behind the school to avoid drawing too much attention to themselves as Maggie prepared herself to enter. She needed the time and space to change her clothes and get into character. One was easier than the other. The whole idea was a risk, and she knew it.

Emily was leaning backward on the front fender of Maggie's Trans Am with her hands in the pockets of her faded denim overalls. She was watching the street life and traffic flow by the alley entrance, and the glow of Chinatown's neon splendor. She glanced back periodically at Maggie, checking on her progress, as she struggled to put on her uniform in the cramped front seat of her car.

Maggie was adjusting her clothes with some difficulty in the awkward space, but eventually got situated. She finished dressing and then began checking her make-up in the passenger's vanity mirror, as she prepared to go in. A few quick dabs of foundation and then she got out of the car.

"You could probably just change out here couldn't ya? I mean it's dark enough," Emily suggested, as she continued to check the entrance to the alley periodically.

"I suppose I could, but I don't wanna take the chance of some kid seeing me in my underwear; kinda destroys the whole image I'm goin' for, doesn't it?" Maggie said, as she tugged and patted at her clothes, adjusting the fit.

"Hmm, probably depends on the kid." Emily folded her arms and then listened intently to the sounds of the class as they drifted into the alley. "There's a lot of them in there, huh?" she said, as she handed Maggie a hair tie, "I don't know much about this stuff. Do you think it will work?"

Maggie took the hair tie and pulled her hair into a snug ponytail before answering.

"It worked for Bruce Lee in *the Chinese Connection*," Maggie stated, as she worked as quickly as she could adjusting her hair and getting it to look just right.

"Really? You think Bruce Lee had trouble with his ponytail too?" Emily quipped and followed with a wry smile.

"Funny. Look, I don't have a choice. They are going to keep coming at me unless I can slow them down or make them stop somehow. The last two challenges were scary. That jerk that came through the bathroom window while I was trying to fix the toilet last week, almost caught me, literally, with my pants down. And that asshole that ate everything in my fridge while he was waiting for me to get back from the store, really pissed me off. At least this way I can choose the time and place and hopefully, catch them off guard."

"How many do you think there are in there?" Emily tilted her head toward the sounds of the school and was trying not to sound too concerned.

"Well, White Crane is one of the oldest and most established schools in Chinatown, so they have a healthy number of students. I won't have to fight them all though. Once I start, they will thin out, most will stand and watch, trust me." Maggie continued to adjust her uniform more out of distraction than necessity. "Look, just do me a favor, and stick around no matter what you hear in there, okay? Leave the passenger window down, and I will dive in if I have to, then you can get us out of here."

"Just like in the movies, huh?" Emily smiled. "Getaway car?"

"Yeah, just like in the movies, only it'll be me, with smaller tits than Sonny Chiba, coming through the passenger window like *The Dukes of Hazzard*."

Emily chuckled as she watched Maggie go through a series of physical actions that she assumed were some type of pre-fight ritual. Maggie took a deep breath, closed her eyes, and slapped her face a few times as if to wake herself up. She shook out her hands vigorously and then jumped up and down on the concrete like she was a child testing out a bed. She walked around in a circle a few times and then stood perfectly still.

With her hands on her stomach, she closed her eyes, took in a long deep breath, and then let it out slowly.

Maggie's eyes opened and Emily knew it was time.

"Well, this is it, I'm going in. Better put on my game face."

"You scared?" Emily asked, concerned, but trying her best to sound supportive.

"Are you kidding? I'm petrified."

Over the last few weeks, Emily had started spending more time with Maggie, and though Maggie was her polar opposite, Emily was feeling a growing fondness for her, even if she was scared about the situations Maggie seemed to keep getting herself into with the opening of her school. Emily had joked more than once that if she had to fight people to open her flower shop, she would probably open a restaurant instead.

With the moment at hand, Maggie smiled at Emily and gave a playful wink, before she turned away, and headed at a quick pace toward the front door of the school. Emily followed behind to watch her enter. Maggie looked focused as she put her hand on the door handle. It was as if she had transformed into someone else during the last few steps.

All heads turned in unison and all the action stopped when Maggie walked in. The students stood motionless with slack-jawed expressions as she strolled confidently through the lobby. Using the moment most efficiently, she took a quick headcount of the room. There were thirty of them: Twenty-eight students, one instructor, and an assistant instructor. She figured about half of them wouldn't want to fight or get involved at all. The head instructor wouldn't want to fight either, he had too much to lose. He would stay out of it and let his assistant, his second in command, handle her because he wouldn't want to risk losing face. He would only fight if he had to, however, this was combat and there were always exceptions and surprises.

To lose a challenge would be bad enough but losing to a woman would be a catastrophe. As much of a risk as it was for Maggie, she knew that they had more to lose than she did, and they knew it too. Maggie had so much more to gain.

Be fearless.

Presence. Her walk, her posture, and the look in her eyes, all exuded confidence. It radiated from her like heat from the sun. It served a dual purpose. She knew that her bold demeanor would really piss everyone off, making them incredibly angry, and hopefully inviting mistakes during combat. Also, she told herself that this was who she was. This was her moment. Like a tape in her mind, it played over and over.

Be fearless. Be strong. Be powerful.

She had rehearsed her new character in front of her wall of mirrors at her school. She was taking the stage like a hammy vaudeville performer, oozing confidence, a little arrogance, and some devilish charm. Maggie watched as the young men's eyes darted up and down her form. She knew that her new appearance was distracting too.

She had adopted a new look, eschewing the unisex uniform that was traditionally worn for something more dramatic and visually provocative. She was wearing a tailored black, satin, kung fu uniform top, with gold frog buttons, and black satin bottoms that were tight at the hips, but loose in the legs, and flared at the ankles. They showed her form but were still practical for fighting. She was wearing spiked high heels purely for theatrics. She couldn't fight in them and didn't intend to. Her eyes looked witchy with wings drawn in black eyeliner. Her ponytailed hair had been enhanced with subtle blonde streaks. She was determined to use everything she had and embrace her feminine attributes. When she beat them, they would remember it, and it would sting.

In the shops and on the street, she had heard people call her "dragon lady." They usually said it when they thought that she was out of earshot. When she passed the laundry or the local seafood restaurant, she heard the phrase in low whispers followed by giggles. One of the challengers from the week before had said it to her face. He said it dismissively and later regretted it.

Dragon lady was more acceptable but just as pejorative as calling her a bitch. Maggie had decided that she was damned if she was going to be dismissed as just some uppity-bitchy broad. She was going to be everything they hated, and wear it as a badge of honor. Rub their noses in it. Make it her own. She would be this new persona and play it to the hilt. Be the lady dragon of Chinatown.

Each click of her heels on the tiled lobby floor echoed louder in the timid silence. As she approached the mat area, the floor slowly emptied as the students backed away. Maggie stepped from the edge of the waiting area to the main workout floor. She removed her shoes swiftly, and in dramatic fashion by standing on one leg, removing one shoe, and then gently placing it on the floor, as she picked up her other leg and repeated the same technique, never looking down.

Walking onto the mat, she gave the customary salute and swaggered confidently to the center of the room. She put her hands on her hips, as she casually looked around at the students standing on the edges of the mat area, letting them see her sizing them up. She looked everyone up and down with a subtle half-snarl that she had practiced in the mirror by imitating a picture of Elvis Presley she found in Emily's record collection. She was becoming more of the lady dragon with each moment.

It wasn't until she stood in the middle of the school that she realized she had created more than an image, but an alter-ego. She felt different than she did in the alley only moments before. Standing alone, surrounded by opponents, she was fed by their energy of anticipation and fear. When she felt completely transformed and consumed by her new persona, she saluted the class and then spoke.

"I am going to have my school here in Chinatown, and I don't care what anyone says about it," Maggie sounded like a military commander. She looked everyone in the eye and studied their body language. This was her challenge address, and as she spoke, she was gauging who would come at her first, who was thinking about it, and who just wanted to get the hell out of there.

"A woman should be able to open a school in Chinatown. It's no one's business but my own. It has nothing to do with you." She pointed roundly and accusingly at the group of students, as she looked carefully for the first signs of attack. She noticed one student, obviously smitten, smiling at her and gave him a knowing wink. Another student, standing next to him, noticed the exchange and expressed a look of outrage before giving his friend a hard knock on the back of the head as punishment for flirting with the invader. Maggie smiled at the incident and continued.

"I know you are going to try me out sooner or later, so I thought I would save you the trip." She dramatically cracked her knuckles loudly in front of her body, accompanied by a wincing look, for theatrical emphasis. She shook her hands as if flinging water from them and quickly flicked her nose with her right thumb. She gave her pants a tug at the knees and slowly settled into a low fighting horse stance.

Her stance was left leg back, right leg forward, right-hand high, left-hand low. Most would assume she was left-handed instead of right, and she would use their mistake to her advantage. Borrowing from fencing, she kept her power side forward. *Be unorthodox, not what they expect.*

She stood ready.

The room was quiet with only the smallest sounds of rustling feet and the student's collective breathing. The tense moment passed snail-like during the standoff. Maggie tilted her head slightly down, protecting her chin, and with her warrior stare, waited for someone to make the first move.

The student's eyes darted at each other in the tense silence before a disembodied voice echoed throughout the school.

"You should leave now."

Maggie searched the pack of assembled students trying to see where it was coming from, then two students stepped aside from the middle of the group to reveal a middle-aged, Asian man wearing a traditional white uniform with black frog buttons. His pants had a crane in flight embroidered on the bottom of the right leg, and the same image on the left breast of his jacket. He looked ex-military. He was stocky with broad shoulders and a crew cut. His uniform was made of a lightweight satin material that hung from his body revealing a muscular physique.

There was no doubt that this was the sifu of the school. Maggie thought from his appearance, that he probably did Shuai-Jiao, a form of Chinese wrestling, as well as kung fu. The school was supposed to teach a Crane fighting style, but she knew that a teacher's experience was not limited to what they teach. The oldest rule of all confrontations continuously proved to be useful advice: never underestimate your opponent.

He was an imposing figure. She tried to hide her involuntary gulp and kept telling herself that she was ready for anything. *Anything.*

214

"I'll leave. I'll leave right now if you swear to me that you will leave me alone. If not, I'll alert the trauma center in Terre Promise to expect new arrivals." Maggie stood defiant, "What's it gonna be?"

The students looked at each other, and Maggie. She could tell by their anxious expressions that they were not eager to get involved in some lady's quest to open her kung fu school. They looked warily to their teacher for his response.

"I won't swear to some dizzy broad who doesn't have the decency to follow the LAW!" The sifu's voice filled the school. "You think you can come in here, into my school, and challenge me? I'll send you back to your fucking dolls, YOU DUMB WHORE!" The teacher's face twisted into a crimson mask of rage as he spat out the last sentence, his fists tightly clenched.

Maggie, though internally shaken, didn't let it show and instead commanded her face to respond with a convincing smirk.

The tense air crackled with expectant energy. Maggie's stomach began to feel queasy with butterflies, but before she could think to quell them, it began.

With a loud yell, a student leaped high into the air executing a flying knife-edge kick. Maggie spotted the attack, and instantly unfocused her eyes, taking in the whole field of vision before her. With multiple opponents, she knew not to look at one, but rather take in the entire room and use her peripheral vision. To her, things would appear to be moving in slow motion.

The flying student's kicking foot snapped at her head, but Maggie dodged it by stepping to the side. The attacker landed behind her in a pile. Without taking her eyes off the crowd before her, she spun around to the fallen opponent, and brought her leg up high, before snapping it down and burying her hammer-like heel deep into the fallen student's abdomen. A high-pitched scream of pain elicited a maniacal smile from Maggie.

The class paused, looked surprised, and eyes searched around the room as if looking for the next volunteer. It was then, that she realized the first attacker was the assistant. There was a moment's hesitation before all of them finally decided to attack. Their collective scream came loudly, as the class advanced on Maggie, each one according to their level of courage. She dodged most of them easily as they streamed forth. With a few parries, head ducks, and subtle evasions of her body, she sent them running into the walls, the equipment, and each other.

Sensing something coming behind her, she spun quickly to her six o'clock position, saw a punch headed straight for her, and parried it away with a slap of her hand. She shifted her head backward, just out of range of the attacker's strike. The attacker threw another punch with his other hand, and she once again parried and moved her head backward out of range. For her attacker, she knew it would be like pursuing a ball downhill, and he would never reach her. The aggressor was forced to over-extend himself and lose his balance. The opponent kept up his pursuit, but now frustrated, he threw a succession of punches recklessly. His body listed forward, and Maggie ducked underneath. She felt his body land sideways across her back, and she added a quick snap and catapulted him into the other students rushing forward. Helpless, he crashed into his classmates like an anvil and knocked them down like bowling pins.

Though all the students were not hurt, it was a good enough reason for some of them to stay down and play it safe. Some slunk away and others backed up to the wall with real or merely dramatic injuries.

Things came full circle. The floor cleared. Maggie stood alone in the middle of the room surrounded by the class.

Though her heart was pounding, and she could feel beads of nervous sweat start to emerge and race down the back of her neck, she ignored it all, standing ready.

The room was almost silent except for the sound of her breath coming in quick pants, and the moaning of some students still laying on the ground.

Time passed imperceptibly, and then she saw the class move as one. She readied herself for the attack, but surprisingly they took a step backward. The group parted, and the teacher came forward. Since the assistant was nursing his abdominal injury, the teacher had to face her. Though she expected it and knew that it was inevitable, she wasn't looking forward to it.

Be ready. No matter what comes. Attack.

The teacher occupied the space between her and the class with the kind of authority that came from a legacy of confrontation. He wasn't going to be a pushover. The teacher took a loud raspy breath, as he closed his eyes and appeared to be focused on some deep meditation. His arms rose and circled slowly as if gathering energy from the empty space before him. His muscles flexed and fists clenched while a sudden calm appeared to envelop him at the end of the ritual.

Maggie had watched as the teacher went through his strange rite, and when all eyes were focused on the sifu, she glanced over her shoulder to see exactly how far it was to the door.

The sifu now appeared ready. His jaw was set tight. The veins in his neck became visible and his eyes bulged wide, full of fire and anger. His face changed from one of indignation to a mask of hatred as he appeared to bubble over from the previous Zen state to a mode of battle.

Taking an adjustment step back, accompanied by a gulp that Maggie hoped no one heard or saw, she cocked her neck sideways producing a loud cracking sound. With a quick roll of her shoulders, she adjusted her body, and then flicked her hands before bringing them back to her fighting position. She settled into her stance.

She did her best to look unfazed by the teacher's theatrical display. Although he was undoubtedly formidable, she knew that an opponent full of anger and hatred is bound to make bad tactical decisions.

Be aggressive, not angry.

It was a fine line, but a fighter could never be emotional. She had learned to antagonize her opponents, so they would slip up, and then she would be there waiting when they did. Her face was a mask of stone that betrayed none of the fear that she felt. She pushed it deep down as if it was only a distraction to her.

The sifu stepped forward. Maggie and the teacher stood opposite each other in the center of the school, on the red matted surface. The class encircled them and waited silently and still. Both fighters were in their fighting stances and studied each other expectantly. Maggie and the sifu eyed each other like two gunfighters waiting for the telling moment, a twitch, or a breath held too long, that would signal that the other was about to make the first move.

With their gazes locked, the sifu's body started to tremble and vibrate. At first, slightly and then violently, his body appeared to build up with rage as if he was preparing to explode.

In an instant, the sifu yelled his fury and launched his body at Maggie. A fierce flurry of kicks and punches streaked toward her as he crossed the floor like a locomotive, his powerful body driving the attack relentlessly toward her.

She dodged and parried his attacks as she moved side to side and back and forth, leading him in a serpentine pattern around the room. She remained just out of his reach and watched as the sifu became more agitated, and angry, as each strike failed to land. Surely, he had seen her use the tactic on his student, and clearly, he thought he would be able to overcome her. The frustration in his eyes told her that despite his experience and rank, he was falling into the same trap.

Stick to the plan. It's working.

The teacher paused momentarily, frustrated, and out of breath. Maggie took the opportunity to take some deep breaths herself. She hopped in place and shook out her arms. She was doing her best to appear full of energy, though she was almost spent.

The sifu closed his eyes and took a step back.

Maggie, thinking he was about to surrender, took a measured step forward and relaxed her guard, but then –

"Aaaahhh!"

The sifu let out a loud yell; his face burned red, and his eyes bulged with broken blood vessels.

The sifu's furious rage filled the room as he fired another attack at Maggie in the form of a wrestler's tackle with arms outstretched and legs driving forward.

Maggie baited him toward her as before and then jumped back a step further than expected letting the opponent's attack come as fast and hard as possible.

Dropping low into a powerful stance, she fired a vicious riposte in the form of a palm-heel strike under the teacher's chin. The sound of his jaw cracking violently shut was accompanied by his agonized expression and the dissonant sound of breaking teeth.

Maggie let loose a combination of three quick punches into his abdomen robbing him of his breath. The teacher flew backward and landed hard on the crimson floor with a bloody mouth, unconscious, at the student's feet.

The room fell silent except for Maggie's heavy breathing. She was sweating, and her body was on fire from the confrontation. Making no effort to conceal her panting, her words came in chunks as she addressed the class.

"I want to be left alone… The challenge is over… I earned my right not to be bothered by you ever again." Maggie looked at all the stunned faces and then had a moment of inspiration. "Do you want to study with me?" she said to the class with a salesman's smile.

The class exchanged looks at each other and a few nodded in agreement.

"Good, come see me next week," Maggie said, as she walked to the edge of the mat and then turned around, "bring cash," she said with a big smile, as she slipped back on her shoes, and walked out the door.

Sunday at the laundromat was going to take some getting used to. Maggie usually waited until she had worn everything twice before she broke down and did a load. And then there was the dilemma of what to wear while she waited. Should she wash her favorite blue jeans, or wear them and know that it will be a week before they are back in the rotation?

Screw it. Wear them, and after the laundry is done, wear them again.

The beauty of living alone was that she didn't have to adhere to anyone else's rules of cleanliness. At least that was what she told herself. Although, in her mind, she could still see Wendy's disapproving look as she asked her admonishing question, "Are you going to wear that again?"

She sorted her basket of colors and whites while she listened to the clunky sound of the first load tumbling dry.

Standing next to one of the laundromat's many large powder blue folding tables, she achieved a Zen-like state as she assiduously folded her clothes and relived the memories associated with each article, like her white button-up blouse that she had worn the day she quit the lab.

In the noise of hisses and hums of washers and dryers and the clanking of hangers and bins, she overheard two women talking. The women were standing just two machines away working with a large heap of black clothes which they were magically transforming into an ordered pile of high-quality kung fu uniforms. Neatly stacked and folded, no starch, she heard them say.

Maggie had kept an ear out, listening while they worked. Though it was difficult to hear over the drone of the washers and dryers, she heard them say that they were laundering uniforms for the Master's Club. The ladies picked up the laundry on Sundays after the master's class. They complained that it was out of their way in the far-off industrial warehouse district.

The Master's Club was a semi-social club of older teachers and masters that Maggie had heard about since she was a little girl. At first, she had heard that it was a secret cabal of teachers exchanging their esoteric knowledge only with the anointed members of the club. As she got older Sifu Chang told her it was just a bunch of old kung fu fighters hiding from their wives on Sunday afternoons. The masters would often have a guest that would teach obscure forms and techniques, but it was more common for them all to get together, eat takeout, and watch the football game on the small black and white TV.

Which warehouse?

During a night of reconnaissance, Maggie went out "gambling." Though she didn't have much money, she could easily stand by a table of distracted players and nurse the same drink for hours while she studied the room. An overly amorous croupier at one of the hidden gambling parlors told her that the highest-ranking masters from Chinatown and Hong Kong would be at the meeting the following week. She needed to be there. She batted her eyes and leaned in close while he pulled in the chips, and eventually, the croupier gave up the exact location where the club met. She smiled and tucked a paper with a phone number into his shirt pocket. The phone number was for a new German bakery in Terre Promise.

Finding the warehouse where the masters met would still be tricky, even with an address. The markings on the buildings were either non-existent or old and faded. Most people that worked there navigated by landmarks and intimate knowledge of the area acquired from working there for so long. Maggie rarely ventured to the industrial side of Chinatown. There hadn't been much reason to.

Once she pulled onto Spring Road, the main boulevard through the district, she was surprised by the stark look of the buildings. It was a far cry from the colorful avenues only five miles away. The potholed streets led to a maze of monochromatic nondescript warehouses, shipping containers, sheet metal fabricators, and light industrial shops.

"You'll see the sign before the address," the croupier had said with a wink and a creepy smile.

She saw the large but simple sign of black letters, outlined in white, from down the street. She pulled around to the warehouse loading dock of Tin City Iron Works. It was off the beaten path, and except for workers during the week, deserted on nights and weekends. The building was painted an uninspired and faded olive drab. The perfect place to share secrets.

As Maggie got out of her car, she checked the deserted surroundings. A quick look around revealed no people and only the sound of the wind moving between the buildings. A row of cars parked between two unattached trailers confirmed there was a meeting today. Surprising herself, she felt a little bead of nervous sweat roll down her back.

Good thing Emily isn't here.

Although Emily had helped many times before, she felt this time might be different. It could be more dangerous. Maggie had left a note for her at the school, on the reception table, just in case. She had written several drafts. Each one had ended with a declaration of her feelings, finally, she decided to keep it simple. The note was brief and explained where she went, but it didn't say how she felt about her. She hoped that it would only be a necessary precaution and that once she got back, she could tear it up, and throw it away.

Get your head in it. This is going to be a collection of masters.

She remembered Sifu Chang's rule regarding titles: "Be respectful, but never be impressed by rank."

Maggie wiped her sweaty palms quickly against her pants, put her hair in a ponytail, and walked up the cement steps to the loading dock. She took a deep breath, let it out slowly, and got into character. She felt different about it though. It was becoming less of a persona and more of who she was.

She pushed up the metal door and the loud mechanical roar announced her arrival. She walked from the warm sun to the cool shadowed expanse of the warehouse. She wasn't sure what to expect, but with a quick inspection, she surmised that it was a typical storage location. There were stacks of boxes, forklifts, and a dirty makeshift office standing dark and lonesome in the far corner.

After she walked past the office the light revealed ten middle-aged Asian men, standing in a semicircle. They were wearing traditional uniforms all in black. The men stood looking at her and didn't appear surprised to see her. They had been expecting her. She thought of the two laundresses. Maybe they were more easily overheard than she realized.

Would they all attack at once?

She expected anything, and as she began sizing them up, a staff flew out of the blackness of the warehouse and landed with a loud snap, as it hit the ground in front of her, and rolled to her feet.

The semi-circle of masters parted, as if by some unknown instruction, and revealed the eleventh master in a white T-shirt and traditional kung fu pants holding a six-foot waxwood staff. He looked about fifty-five, with salt and pepper hair neatly pomaded back. He looked to be in better shape than the rest of the aging masters, with a muscular build that was most likely from working with heavy weapons. As with the other opponents she had fought, they used what they liked.

The master spun the staff quickly, slicing the air with a series of loud whooshing sounds, before he suddenly stopped, saluted, and bowed. He gave a slight nod, stepped back, and took a guard position with the staff pointed at Maggie.

She tried her best not to look rattled by the unexpected eventuality of the weapon and used a quick roll of her foot to kick the staff into the air, and directly into her grasp, without ever looking down. She spun the weapon in an equally impressive display of skill that made the silent bystanders look at each other unable to mask their reaction of surprise and respect.

As she watched, the master shifted his gaze to look on either side of himself. It looked like a warning for the others to back off. Maggie suspected that he had told the others that he could defeat the Lady Dragon by himself. At this point, she knew that whatever technique the challengers came at her with, they had already convinced themselves that it would be the one thing that would defeat her. What they didn't know was that she was an expert in more skills and styles than they were aware of and that Maggie didn't follow their rules.

When this whole drama had begun, since she was one against countless adversaries, Maggie decided their rules of engagement did not apply to her. Her opponents would always be bigger, and stronger, and outnumber her, so she decided that she would take liberties as necessary to even up the odds. She only had one rule and that was to win.

The master stood directly opposite Maggie holding his staff and mirroring her guard position. She was waiting for the master to attack first, and it appeared he was too. A standoff.

Tense gazes were exchanged between them in the dusty expectant silence of the warehouse before Maggie decided to bait the master, by dropping her guard just a little to see if he would seize the opportunity.

A confident smile crossed her lips as she carelessly let the staff fall a few inches lower than the proper position. To her relief, the master fell for the ruse and attacked immediately.

He lunged forward with a long step and brought down his staff swiftly, in a large arc, at her head. Maggie evaded stepping aside and felt the rush of air as his staff whizzed by her face.

The weapon hit the ground where she had been standing with a loud *crack!*

She countered, swinging her weapon in a horizontal strike at the master's head.

He spun his stick back fast and blocked Maggie's assault. They moved across the dusty warehouse floor rapidly. Each striking, counter-striking, and countering the other's counter. It was an even give and take. The cracking sound of the weapons' impacts on each other's staff was loud and served as the only soundtrack to the otherwise silent dance before the ten exalted attendees.

Maggie, being familiar with the tactics of long weapons, took the unusual approach of getting closer to her opponent than would be the normal fighting range. She wanted to invade his space and crowd him so she could use her legs for kicks and trips.

She feinted with the weapon as if to strike her opponent's head, and then shuffled in close, seizing his ankle by hooking it with her foot. She threw a punch at his face.

The master leaned back.

With his ankle trapped he couldn't retreat.

With a quick jerk of her foot, the master's trapped ankle was pulled hard, making his leg extend, pulling him off balance, and making the master fall backward and land flat on his back.

The master hit the dirty cement warehouse floor kicking up a small cloud of dust around him.

Maggie advanced on the downed opponent and pointed the end of the weapon at the master's neck. Before the dust had settled, she moved it closer and pushed the tip deep into his corded muscle. She saw the dour look of defeat and surrender register on his face and knew without equivocation that she was the victor.

Pinned by the end of the staff, the venerable foe's gaze told that he was surprised to be defeated. He looked up at Maggie with hate in his eyes, as his moist brow produced two beads of sweat that ran down the sides of his face. *Or were they tears?*

His hand let the weapon slip from his grasp.

In the hushed space of the warehouse, the only sound was the faint tapping of the staff as it landed lightly on the ground.

Studying their faces, Maggie probed the group for any intent to attack. Once she was satisfied that they had no stomach for any more fights today, she withdrew her weapon and took a step back to allow the master to stand up.

He rose slowly, partially from age and exertion, but also from the added weight of loss. Wearing his failure, he did not attempt to straighten his clothes or shake off the dust that had collected on his pants and shirt. With a small gate and a slow pace, the defeated master stepped back to his original position, between the other exalted teachers.

With her eyes watching the group, Maggie kicked the master's staff, which still lay on the ground, backward toward the door, and out of everyone's reach. She kept her weapon trained on the group in a ready position, and smoothly scanned the warehouse taking in her surroundings.

As she moved toward the exit and felt she was at a safe distance, she bent down carefully and picked up the master's staff from where it had landed close to the door.

The defeated adversary's face twisted up with his obvious disapproval at the audacity of Maggie taking his weapon as a prize.

The collection of erudite gentlemen watched her every step, incredulous, as she walked carefully out of the warehouse door with the two weapons. The group stood silently looking at each other. She saluted once, not waiting for it to be returned, and then walked into the warm sunlight of the bright day.

The warm heated rays of the rising sun began pouring through the large, and recently replaced, front window of the school. The morning light temporarily emblazoned the decidedly generic name, "Kung Fu and Chinese Martial Arts" onto the lobby floor. The black dragon's head with its silent roar at the street below was still threatening ominously from above.

Maggie and Emily were standing next to each other, as if studying some incredible science experiment, looking out the window at the activity on the street. They sipped their tea as they enjoyed the sacred silence. Chinatown awoke before their eyes. The light of day always made everything clear. Definitive. Though she was deep in thought, Maggie could feel Emily's gaze and could tell that she was waiting for her to say something. Something comforting, something profound. She didn't. Not wanting to disrupt the moment with anything that could wait, she kept sipping her tea.

As the sunlight moved across the floor, ran up her body, and then blazed on her face, she closed her eyes. Memories began to flow back to her. Memories of going to school, having a crush on Kathy, and her first experiences with love, trust, and heartbreak.

She was brought back to the present by Emily's voice.

"Tomorrow is the last day. What are you going to do?" Emily asked, and then took a sip.

"I'll tell them no," Maggie continued to sip her tea looking out the window.

"What will happen?"

Maggie put down her empty cup, turned around, and sat on the floor, next to the window, letting the sun warm her back, as she looked intently into the large one-room school. She stared at the open floor with its heavily padded red carpet and imagined lines of students performing drills and sparring. She saw herself, smiling, and walking among them, teaching. Her eyes drifted to the weapons standing ready and visualized herself instructing the finer points of the staff and broadsword to eager students. The large wall of full-length mirrors that now reflected the empty school, was replaced with a vision from her mind's eye, as she imagined a class full of people hard at work, learning, and having fun.

Staring at the space, she dreamed of students bringing her vision of the school to life. She could see herself teaching young girls and boys, men and women. It was a satisfying moment of her true mission, of what she wanted, and why she was doing it all. *Why can't everyone learn what they want?* It was all she wanted.

After contemplating a future in doubt, she was suddenly overcome with emotion. Tears obstructed her vision, before growing large enough to glide down her cheek. She wanted to be left alone, but it seemed like it would go on forever.

Was Wendy right? Was it all a mistake?

Though it hadn't been a long time, it felt longer. The stress of danger had a way of making time stretch out, making the moments deeper, heavier, and harder to take.

She had been taking the fight to the other schools, and she had beaten them all. The nail above the mirror, where she had hung the belt of the first challenger she defeated, had become so overloaded, that she had added another nail, and then finally a box for the sashes and patches of the various vanquished opponents. Her reputation had grown to the point that when she walked in, a pre-chosen defender would approach, and after a short and sweet salute of mutual respect, Maggie would drop into her stance and await the attack. She had fought just about every style of Chinese, Japanese, and Korean martial arts, that she had ever heard of: Hung Gar, Wing Chun, BaGua, Choy Li Fut, Baji Quan, White Crane, Seven Star Mantis, Tang Soo Do, Shotokan, Goju Ryu, Isshin Ryu, and even some more obscure styles that were hybrids. Some fighters used specialized forms taught to assassins who killed for the Triads or fought in underground matches, usually to the death.

When she squared off with a challenger, she never knew what she would get, and she had learned that the style mattered less than the fighter. Some had fought gallantly, some had fought foolishly, some had fought dastardly, but all had fought according to their character. The noble ones were also noble in defeat.

One challenger, after losing, had dropped to his knees and saluted with his forehead on the floor. He had removed his sash and willingly handed it to Maggie. She had taken it with a respectful nod of acknowledgment and a handshake. The next day she had sent him a bouquet from Emily's shop, with a card that read that she hoped they could be colleagues, on better terms, in the future. Along with the bouquet she had included a new sash of the same rank symbolizing their new beginning.

Honorable incidents were rare though, and they had not been the normal reaction. The prideful were crestfallen when they lost. Some made excuses and started rumors that she had used a secret drug to slow their reflexes, or used mysticism, magic, and other ridiculous tales. It didn't matter though, even if Chinatown was a place of mystery to the outside observer, the truth was easily seen, despite the intended deceptions. Those that had taken Maggie lightly had paid the highest price. They were defeated and often humiliated. More than one had been dragged unconscious and left on the sidewalk to awaken in the light of day, bloodied. Conquered.

Emily had been the getaway driver, as she called it, for most of the excursions into Chinatown's martial arts schools. Maggie had enlisted her help by merely asking for a ride once. Emily's surprised and blinking look let Maggie know that she was eager to help but had no idea what she was getting into. At first, Maggie felt guilty, but she made sure to always keep Emily's safety paramount, both because she was a civilian in this war and because she liked her more than she wanted to admit.

All the challengers had been defeated with Maggie only incurring minimal injuries. It was never more than a few cuts and bruises, with the one exception of a sprained wrist. Maggie didn't count it though, since the injury was from climbing into the car after escaping an ambush. A few days later she returned to fight them and defeated them primarily using kicks. Maggie's tactic for the fight had provoked Emily's sarcastic response, "Nice legs, lady," and made them both smile before they sped away to safety.

Maggie's lack of serious injury was a surprise to herself and to Emily who, though she said she didn't like to watch, listened. She said that the fights sounded like a cartoon battle between a mouse and a cat, and the mouse was winning. Though Emily said that she didn't like to watch the fights, Maggie had caught her getting a glimpse a few times from around corners, through peeked fingers or shielded hands pressed against a window. However, it was their unspoken agreement not to point out what they both knew to be true.

Once, in the small bathroom of the school, Emily had lovingly put alcohol on a cotton ball and gently dabbed a series of cuts on Maggie's forehead. Maggie had tried to keep from flinching as the cold liquid burned her wound.

"Does it hurt?" Emily questioned.

"No."

Emily's head tilted even as her eyes widened with a questioning expression at Maggie.

"Well, a little, I guess," Maggie admitted, as she tried not to look into Emily's eyes for fear she would fall into them and never find her way out.

Gently, methodically, Emily moved down Maggie's face, re-applying the alcohol to the cotton balls, and then to the small, almost imperceptible cuts and abrasions along Maggie's cheek and jawline. Each time using a new cotton ball, and each time taking slightly longer than Maggie thought necessary to complete the task. Emily's hands moved in a steady and artistic pattern. Like caressing flowers, or polishing leaves, Emily was careful and attentive as she worked on Maggie like a sculptor in love with their art.

As Emily continued to apply the medicine in the tiny bathroom of the school, Maggie had sat steadily, as a good patient, on the closed toilet seat lid. She studied the Osh Kosh buttons on Emily's worn overalls. She closed her eyes and took in the intoxicating mixture of Emily's scents consisting of fresh flowers, jasmine tea, and imitation Chanel No. 5.

In their escapades together, Maggie had taken on multiple opponents, endured ambushes, and encountered the occasional edged weapon, but when it came to Emily, she felt unarmed and inexperienced.

The way Maggie saw it, they were like two fighters still sizing each other up. Each one was waiting for the other to drop their guard. They had a close friendship, there was no denying that. *Maybe that was all there could be. Maybe that was enough.*

The other schools in Chinatown and the surrounding suburbs had stopped sending challenges. *Was it a respite?* For all she knew, Maggie's idea of taking the fight to the other schools first had worked, but she still had to deal with The Council, and as promised they were making things difficult for her. Unable to defeat her martial skills, as feared, they had used the blunt instrument of city bureaucracy to impede her progress. The school had failed inspection with the fire department, although they couldn't explain why. Utilities seemed to function intermittently for some reason, and her loan at the bank, although initially approved, had now been declined.

She was running out of money. She had borrowed money from Emily and put things in another name, but it seemed like for every hole she fixed, another one opened, threatening to swallow up her life. The Council was dogged in their approach toward her. They wouldn't stop. Ever.

After giving her situation considerable thought, Maggie came up with the only solution she could think of that would end the conflict once and for all: An open challenge.

She would agree to fight whomever they put in front of her. She knew that there was a chance that she could be injured, or worse, and she accepted it. Weighed against a new and possibly never-ending tsunami of violence, she thought it was her best option. She wanted a conclusion: A definitive end to this sadistic ritual. It would have to be an arrangement that they all agreed to. All things would be negotiable, but one thing would be guaranteed, it would be dangerous.

Picking up her teacup purposefully, almost with religious reverence, Maggie drained the small pot into her cup and then threw back her head and gulped down the remainder of its contents. She felt a few stray drops escape from the corners of her mouth and wiped them away with the back of her hand. She studied the lone aluminum ladder, with a drop cloth beneath it, as a standing monument to the unfinished state of the school. The rolled-up bedding in the backroom was visible through the doorway and was a constant reminder that the school was more than a crazy business venture, it was her home. It was all she had. Maggie looked resigned. She croaked out her proclamation to herself, and the four walls, as much as to Emily,

"There will be one more fight, and then it'll be over." Maggie put her hand on Emily's shoulder, and then pulled her close. She looked into the empty school. Emotions were hard to control as she thought of all that had happened and what the future may hold. She tried desperately not to let any tears fall onto Emily's face.

PART III

The Duel

Emily had been asleep on the floor of the school using a kicking shield as a pillow. The calming sounds of Fleetwood Mac's "Dreams" cushioned her slumber when the call to set up the final duel woke her at 10:06 PM. She heard Maggie answer it sounding like her confident Lady Dragon persona. For Emily, it still took some getting used to. She knew that Maggie didn't want to accept that she was becoming very different when she was dealing with anything involving the school, but she was. Her character was beginning to live offstage, as they say. Emily hoped that when it was all over, she would be more of the old Maggie that she knew: Confident, but sometimes unguarded. Vulnerable. She was attracted to the Maggie that she met that first day. The one that was a little awkward and unsure of herself, at least socially, anyway. It was the one that very few people ever saw. It was the one that disappeared or was banished into another realm when she started throwing punches and kicks. Maggie had been so guarded lately, that it made her consider that for all her fighting skills, she was defenseless when it came to love.

Maggie was a master martial artist, she had proven it countless times, but in matters of the heart, she was a white belt. From that first meeting, in the messy school when she had brought her flowers, she felt something between them. It was hard to know what to do about her feelings though since she knew that Maggie had someone in her life already. She resigned herself to let it go.

When Wendy and Maggie broke up, Emily was decidedly careful. She didn't want to be the "rebound girl." She wanted to take things slow, and she was happy that Maggie seemed to agree and wanted to do the same thing. They were starting to become close, and though they occasionally exchanged a peck on the cheek, they were like teenagers in an earlier era. It was certainly unusual for the current times. With the popularity of key parties, wife swapping, and the occasional orgy, the subtlety of small gestures, like the light touch of a hand, a smoldering glance, or standing a bit closer than usual, was easily overlooked. Emily felt a crackle of energy when she was close to Maggie. She hoped that someday she would feel her touch for longer than a moment.

The little bit that Maggie shared with her seemed to indicate that they both had similar upbringings and similar dilemmas. Maggie was an outsider because of the attitude that Chinatown had regarding women and martial arts. Emily felt like an outsider as well, trying to follow her parents' urging and fit into the predominant culture of the upper-middle-class white society of Argent Hills. She was always disappointed though as most of them couldn't get past their racism and homophobic prejudice. She always felt like when she got a chance or any opportunity, she already had two strikes against her. Both she and Maggie were on the outer edges of society, destined to never fit in unless they hid who they were. As a believer in destiny and life's hidden meanings, Emily thought that maybe that was why they found each other.

The break-up with Wendy had been difficult on Maggie, she had seen it. She watched it unfold across the street from her storefront window. Her attention had been drawn to them from Wendy's yelling.

When Emily looked to find the source of the commotion, she saw Wendy beating on Maggie's car window until Maggie got out. From their body language, she knew it was a breakup. It had all the telltale signs. Lots of folded arms, downcast eyes, finger-pointing, and exasperated expressions.

The end of a relationship is like an exorcism, with the demon taking all the memories and understanding between two people down to hell with them as some kind of payment for an infernal debt. Emily kept her distance in those first days and nurtured a close friendship. She tried to be there when Maggie needed someone to talk to or to laugh with. She enjoyed their adventures together, especially driving the getaway car for the challenges. It was so far removed from her daily routine of running the flower shop, that she felt like another person herself. Though they both avoided the subject, Emily knew that it was inevitable that they were going to be more than friends.

"I'm as scared about this one, as I am about any fight, you know?" Maggie declared as she stuffed extra clothes into a red and white duffle bag so that she could change at the auditorium if she needed to.

"This one is different though. At least it seems that way to me. It sounds like a fight to the finish," Emily's face showed her genuine concern, as she handed a towel to Maggie, who grabbed it and put it into the duffle bag along with the extra clothes, athletic tape, a small first aid kit, and $200 in cash.

"To the finish...Not necessarily to the death...There is a difference."

"Really? What is it?" Emily spoke in a measured tone of interest, with her arms folded, as she leaned against the doorway of Maggie's office in the back of the school.

"The opponent is defeated, vanquished...Not necessarily killed...though it could end up–"

"Vanquished sounds pretty crappy if you ask me. *Necessarily killed?* What if—" Maggie held up a finger accompanied by a stern look to emphasize that the conversation must cease.

"I do not deal in what-ifs. This is a challenge to me, and I intend to face it like any other: to defeat my opponent." As if suddenly remembering where she was going, she put her hair in a ponytail, and then picked up the bag she had been packing. She looked around the school, and then at Emily, before she gestured with a tilt of her head towards the door, "Let's go."

On the way to the duel, Maggie had reached across the gear shift for Emily's hand and in her most overt action yet, she brought the hand to her lips and softly kissed it, without ever taking her eyes from the road. Emily smiled broadly at the gesture, and so did Maggie.

In the darkness, the downpour had slowed to a drizzle. The wind still blew briskly, sending loose leaves and branches from the old trees surrounding the park onto the potholed street. The scattered debris across the neglected park and road looked desolate and ominous. The moon's beams fought through the cloudy night sky and enveloped the street, like a veil of unearthly light. Streetlamps glowed with dim halos along empty sidewalks. A single car sped past the auditorium through the littered rainswept street.

The auditorium, dark and foreboding, was curiously constructed as a medieval castle and placed decades ago. It stood alone in the middle of the night-stormed park. The single light several feet from the main entrance was the only sign that it was the agreed-upon venue. Behind the glowing sphere, thin black windows of the castle-like edifice squinted under furrowed gutters and ledges as if questioning the stars with an enigmatic gaze. Two turrets, like horns, jutted out from the sides of the building toward the night sky.

The battlement had crenels for non-existent archers, faux turrets for imaginary sentries, and a sprawling courtyard containing walkways of fake cobblestone to be traversed by invisible villagers. The courtyard contained a wooden stockade on a raised platform, the mannequin prisoner long since removed. As the years cruelly passed it by, each one leaving its mark, the castle became less charming and more of an eyesore.

Chinatown used to end seven miles away from the old theater, but its unchecked growth had enabled the oozing sprawl to swallow up everything in its path. Though it was technically part of Terre Promise, the building had come to serve as a marker for the edge of Chinatown proper.

Maggie parked as close as she could to the entrance of the auditorium and then she and Emily ran up the winding walkway, doing their best to evade the elements of wind, rain, and falling debris. Maggie tugged on the door and felt a combination of relief and anxiety that it was unlocked, as promised.

The two women entered and were immediately struck by the echoey darkness of the entryway. Hearing only the sound of their breathing in the dark space, they both watched as the door's hydraulic mechanism slowly shut and came to rest with a bleak click.

Maggie put down her bag and shook the drops from her sleeves, as she looked around, taking in the dark entryway. Their footsteps echoed loudly off the barren floor and high walls, in stark contrast to the noisy wind that had been blowing in their ears only moments before.

The lonely auditorium made even the smallest and most subtle movements reverberate into the expanse of blackness that surrounded them. The tangible energy of the looming darkness consumed the space. Maggie could feel it. It was heavy, like an oppressive weight, as if the gravity of the moment was causing the event to be carved into reality, making it materialize from the ether and take form.

Emily stood close to the door crossing her arms nervously as if to hug away her obvious nervousness. She opened the door slightly and Maggie saw that she was going to prop it open with a piece of cardboard that she had brought from her shop. Her inquisitive gaze searched Maggie's eyes for agreement.

It was like Emily to think of not getting locked inside the building. After all, she was the "getaway driver". Emily still took to heart her role as the one to get them both to safety. Maggie shook her head slowly and allowed a reassuring smile to broaden across her lips.

Emily, with a disappointed smirk, pulled the cardboard from the door and let it go. They both watched intently as the door slowly closed again, making a clicking sound, as it latched into the steel jam with finality.

Though they had only been in the building for a few moments, it felt longer. Time was passing slowly. The only other time she had experienced such a phenomenon was back when she had tested to become a sifu and had entered the Golden Dragon. When she walked the long hall to the testing room, the solemn grandeur and power of the moment were palpable. This time there was much more at stake.

Though their environment was an impenetrable solitude, she knew that somewhere in the darkness, there were people around them. Though they hadn't shown themselves, The Council would have already arrived with their entourage of assistants, bodyguards, and soldiers. They would be meeting, planning, and discussing what would happen next. They were there and they were probably closer than she thought.

The sound of Emily's stomach growling brought Maggie back from her thoughts to the present. She looked at Emily questioningly, and Emily smiled back with a large grin, shrugging her shoulders. Maggie chuckled and smiled, grateful for the moment of levity. *Should she have come?* Maggie was beginning to have second thoughts about bringing her along. She didn't know what would happen to Emily if it went badly. Although she hoped that The Council would honor their rule regarding civilians and leave her alone, she couldn't be sure.

Codes of conduct were a nebulous thing, despite what people often professed. In practice, they seemed to have more to do with expedience than an unbending code. She couldn't be completely sure about anything.

As Maggie waged a war against her fear and anxiety in her mind and tried to manage her thoughts of disaster and triumph, she noticed the sudden appearance of a large Asian man, as if he had just materialized out of the darkness. She tried to contain her gulp of surprise. He was dressed completely in black and wearing an eye patch over his left eye. His mouth was framed by a well-groomed Van Gogh beard and mustache. A door opened behind him, and the man stood in a newly illuminated triangle of light that shined brightly from inside the auditorium.

Distressed that she never noticed the man's footsteps, Maggie began questioning her abilities. Were her senses not in tune? If they weren't, they couldn't possibly betray her at a worse time. She looked at the Asian phantom's feet and saw that he was wearing those new soft-soled, suede shoes that the neighborhood kids had taken to calling "desert boots." Shoes or not, she still couldn't completely let herself off the hook for not hearing him. She made a mental note to get a pair.

The man dressed in black tilted his head toward the light and then led the way into the auditorium. The two women followed him. With a glance of her peripheral vision, Maggie saw that Emily was noticeably nervous. Her jaw was vibrating as if she were cold. It had to be nerves. *Keep her close.*

As they walked into the large room, staying in the triangle of light, they headed for a partially opened door just off the main auditorium. The man in black was leading them straight toward the light across the large space. Like a trail of ducklings, Maggie followed the man in black, with Emily behind her. Though she tried to peer into the surrounding darkness, it was impossible to tell what, if anything, was lurking there.

Maggie assumed that though they were invisible in the dark, there were probably guards at each exit, and that like their guide, they were wearing black and staying still and quiet. Unheard. Unseen.

The large and silent leader stopped abruptly just a few feet from the lighted doorway. He turned to face the ladies and held his hand up next to his face, signaling for them to stay where they were. Spinning on his heel, he walked on through the partially open door from where the light was escaping and closed it after himself.

With its only light source extinguished, the auditorium was completely engulfed in darkness and a haunted silence. Though she tried, Maggie hadn't been able to see anything in the brief time that the door was opened. She was hoping to catch a glimpse of who was in the room or any bit of information about the duel, but she saw nothing.

She reached out for Emily's hand, and once it was within her grasp, squeezed it tightly. As they stood floating in the endless blackness, Maggie felt happy with Emily next to her, their hands clasped together. Maggie's mind started to look forward to her future with Emily, but then, with the loud clunking sound of a switch at a junction box, the lights came on.

The bright lights of the auditorium showed the complete layout of the location. The women were close to what looked like a stage door. As Maggie walked toward the center of the hall, she noted the black basketball court lines on the polished wood floor. Four sets of folded-up bleacher seats lined the walls. A wooden stage was draped with a lowered curtain, masking the performance area. The bottom of the stage was punctuated with outlets for electrical and audio connections. The wall behind her held a random series of doors. All the doors were labeled generically with rectangular signs: black with white letters: Private, Maintenance, Custodian, and Electrical Closet.

As Maggie surveyed the auditorium, she assessed the advantages and disadvantages of the terrain. After all, it was the battlefield, and *they* were the ones who chose it, presumably, for a reason. Although she wanted to think it was to be fair, why should they be concerned about fairness now? She took a few moments to size it up.

The auditorium was big, it could hold almost two thousand spectators. The floor would allow more than enough room for her and her opponent to maneuver, provided they hadn't decided to pit her against a monster the size of Godzilla. *Although, who knew?*

The space was wide open; there were no obstacles to worry about. She walked carefully, checking the floor's glossy surface by tapping it with the ball of her foot. She was concerned about what would happen when sweat and blood started to fall. *How big of a problem would that be?* She didn't want to stick or slide. She would keep her shoes on.

She breathed deeply and tried to stay calm. It was important to be as centered as possible if she was going to make good decisions. The same principle applied whether in conversation or combat: center, observe, react.

By focusing on the physical, she distracted herself from the endless series of confidence-stealing "what if's" that always popped into her mind when she faced an important moment. She jumped up and down on the balls of her feet, shook her arms loose, stretched her legs, and took more deep breaths.

She could feel sweat starting to form under her arms, on the back of her neck, and in the small of her back.

Damn, I hate when that happens.

She chalked it up to the room feeling stuffy, rather than nerves. *This is no place to show that right now.* She needed a bomb of confidence to go off in her head that was so strong that the fallout would litter the room.

Though she didn't want to think of the moment with finality, she knew that everything hereafter would come down to the outcome of the evening's event.

The lights slowly dimmed. As Maggie looked at Emily's face growing darker, she simultaneously noticed a band of golden light expanding across her cheek. The light embraced her face and bathed the entire space around her in its halcyon hue. Maggie turned to see the curtain on the stage rising. The dramatic and dominant gold light was accented with amber and reddish hues as the stage lights spilled their illumination from their high perch on the rigging above, onto the stage, and out toward Maggie and Emily.

The light revealed the three Council members on the stage, each one seated upon his beastly throne as during their meeting before. It was as if the trio had been transported by dark magic to the new location, bending the world at their will.

Maggie exchanged a look of resolved acceptance with Emily. Feeling the weight of the moment, Emily took a step back. Maggie took a step forward for the same reason and began walking slowly toward the stage alone.

Awash in the golden light from above, Maggie's new uniform sparkled. It was made of black silk and had an embroidered gold dragon coiling downward around the left leg. The pants had elastic gathers at the ankles, not as stylish as the others, but more functional. The black silk top was sleeveless with gold piping around the armholes. It fit her perfectly and it was beautifully made by an unknown woman who had left it for her.

It had been left at the back door of the school and announced with a quick knock. When Maggie opened the door there was no one there, but when she looked down, she saw a white, soft cardboard, garment box, waiting for her. She picked it up carefully, and opened the box slowly, peeking inside, not knowing what she would find. *Was it a trap? An exploding box to finally put an end to her threat to Chinatown's status quo?*

As she lifted the lid and peered into the small opening, she was pleased, and taken aback, by what she saw. Lying beneath a layer of white tissue paper, was a shiny embroidered golden dragon's head. As she pulled out the dragon, she saw that it was stitched into a beautifully made black silk uniform. Who would give such a gift? She looked up thinking that the person that left it couldn't have gotten too far. As she looked around the back of the school and alley, inspecting the area around the dumpster she shared with the other tenants. There was no one.

Walking back inside, she caught a glimpse from the corner of her eye of something near the end of the alley. Where the faded bricks met the sidewalk, a middle-aged woman smiled a knowing smile at her.

The woman was wearing stained faded denim clothes. The white, threadbare, patches on her pants and jacket looked like hand-painted clouds from afar. The color of her clothes blended in closely with the light gray bricks and weathered blue paint of the alley. The woman's graying hair was covered in a ratty light-pink scarf tied below her chin. Her skin looked pasty, but her eyes, though they showed fatigue and worry, shined with an inner light. Maggie knew instantly that she was one of the many sweatshop workers that toiled for a meager existence in Chinatown. They made a substandard wage and worked in horrible conditions. Because they were in the country illegally, they were exploited and their servitude was guaranteed by their overlords with the looming threat of deportation, or worse. Their circumstance had become a permanent and accepted way of life that had gone on for years in Chinatown.

When Maggie saw the woman, and their eyes met, she gave her a bow and salute of appreciation. The woman reciprocated and gave her a salute back accompanied by praying hands. The silent exchange told Maggie that there was support for her in Chinatown, and it was likely growing. She was putting pressure on The Council, and they would have to take her seriously. She knew that they would want to settle the matter sooner rather than later. The Council had read Sun Tzu too, and they knew what he said about a protracted war. She was not surprised when they heard about her offer and contacted her.

As she stood before The Council, she looked her best and was determined to show them that she was different from what they had thought. She was formidable, but she had dignity and grace. She was proud to wear her new uniform into battle. It was made with the qi of not just the one woman who sewed it, but of all the women that had started to believe in Maggie and believe that now could be the time to defeat the corrupt and unjust system that governed them. A landslide starts with a pebble.

Looking up at The Council, she gave the traditional weapon and shield salute with a slight bow. The trio returned her salute. Maggie looked at each of them one at a time, and then quickly glanced back at Emily, giving her a confident wink. Emily, despite her grim expression, returned a forced smile.

Standing tall, proud, and defiant, Maggie crossed her arms. "Let's do it."

The image of Maggie standing alone facing The Council upon their bestial thrones aptly represented her struggle. As she looked up at The Council members, all regally seated, each one acknowledged her with a slight nod. Smoke from idle cigarettes and incense rose from the thrones as if they were a league of smoldering dragons awaiting an appropriate moment to breathe their all-consuming fire.

The stilted silence was broken by a door opening from the back of the auditorium. The sounds of the night storm's rain and wind entered loudly and then were muted as the door hushed quietly closed with a loud click.

Maggie reckoned that it must be her opponent arriving, and her body reacted accordingly. Her heart quickened, her hands became clammy and then there were those damned butterflies.

Footsteps echoed through the silent auditorium. The steps landed hard, but not clumsily against the floor. By their gate, she could tell that the footsteps belonged to a large person, and by their careful precision she could tell that they belonged to someone that had trained in something, some kind of martial art, for a long time. This had to be her opponent: He was big and skilled, of course.

She used her peripheral vision to try to see who was approaching, without turning her head, but the person stopped slightly behind her on her right side. *Crap.* There was no way to see him, without being obvious, which meant that her opponent would know that she was curious about him. She didn't want to give him any advantage. Instead, she wanted him to know that she was going to accept any opponent The Council selected because she was so confident.

I am confident, right? Soon enough, she would know all that there was to know. She kept her eyes forward at The Council and the stage and didn't look back.

The figure stayed close to the shadows behind her, but his bulging silhouette moved slightly forward and became barely visible, just out of sight. Maggie's heartbeat increased, and perspiration started to form and pool on her neck and under her arms, as she realized that the moment she had anticipated and asked for, had finally arrived. She did her best to control her breathing, which had started to become shallow. *Jesus, a full-blown panic attack?*

Though she assumed entirely by the shadowy form and heavy footsteps, she thought it was a pretty safe guess that her opponent was big. It was likely that he was bigger than anyone she had ever fought before. In theory, it shouldn't make a difference, but she didn't put much stock in theories. In theory, she should have been crushed long ago by any number of opponents. As much as she hated to admit it, she was treating this one differently. There was more at stake than losing, despite what she had told herself and even what she had told Emily. As she closed her eyes and tried to convince herself that it didn't matter, she used an old and reliable Qigong abdominal breathing technique to bring down her heart rate. *Inhale. Exhale. Center. Focus.* In a few moments, she began to relax, and even the hot wave of fear had subsided leaving only a moist residue of anxious sweat puddled in the small of her back.

She could accept losing to another opponent's skill, but she couldn't accept losing because of her inability to govern her emotions. Anger, fear, and even joy were all emotions that needed to be kept in check. It was difficult, but she tried to never indulge them. Over time, she had learned that the middle way was best. Balance in all things was necessary to be successful. She brought herself to a better place mentally, even if her mind's butterfingered grasp on reality let an unwelcome thought slip through now and again. She acknowledged consciously, though barely audibly, to herself the one truth she knew. *It won't be easy, but all things are possible.*

DaSifu Dao rose to his feet, with his cigarette held casually in his extended hand. He surveyed the auditorium as a king would his kingdom. He looked to each of the other Council members on the stage with him and gave them a proper acknowledgment of their rank, before finally looking at Maggie and addressing her directly in his soft melodious voice, "I am sorry that we could not come to an understanding. Now we all must accept this outcome, yes?"

Maggie slowly nodded her head in solemn agreement while looking intensely at the DaSifu. She then strained her eyes looking back to see if the opponent had yet come fully into view. He hadn't. She looked over at Emily on the far side of the auditorium. Emily winked, and Maggie winked back. It was their unspoken way to say that everything was all right. Though this time they both knew that the other was lying.

"This is Zhao." DaSifu Dao said declaratively, as he extended his unoccupied hand to the man standing on the edge of darkness. Maggie decided that it was now safe to look back at the mysterious man behind her, and just then, the man stepped forward and walked past her and toward the stage. His large frame made a small draft of air that brushed her skin.

He walked to the very front of the stage, turned around slowly, and looked directly at Maggie, acknowledging her with a slow nod. She returned his salutation with a slow nod of her own, as they stood in silent respect, facing each other.

DaSifu Dao stood on the stage behind Zhao in his same relaxed posture, with his cigarette bleeding smoke into the darkness. He looked as if he were a deity deferring to his disciple, or his chosen demon. This one was a destroyer of cities and worlds.

The reveal was now complete. Maggie looked her opponent up and down, taking him in fully while trying to hide an involuntary gulp. Zhao was an impressive and imposing figure. He stood about six feet two inches tall. He had a chiseled physique visible through his sheer black partially buttoned shirt. His body was taut and strong. He was a formidable opponent, to say the least.

Zhao's reputation was well-known in Chinatown. He could even be called legendary. Well known amongst the population at large but better known by those that dealt in illegal business. His story was often repeated, though few knew how much of it was true, and how much was myth.

He had arrived from Hong Kong at a young age and started as an enforcer for the underworld. He graduated to assassin by eliminating the leader of a Chinatown triad for his first murder. In addition to his career as a soldier in the world of crime, he had been a popular draw in the underground fighting rings. That is until his reputation became such that no one wanted to bet against him. Maggie was surprised that he would agree to this fight since she knew that he had not fought for many years, and she thought he had left Chinatown long ago. She could only assume that his presence was in exchange for something that he wanted. Maybe Zhao was looking to take over a larger percentage of the heroin trade, set up his own organization, or just get a big payday. Regardless of why he was there, her situation had not changed.

The DaSifu blew his smoke up to the gold and red lights and then dropped his cigarette to the floor, taking a moment, and then crushing it out on the stage. He glanced toward the other Council members, who were all as still as statues, and then turned his gaze to Maggie,

"If you would like to reconsider our offer, we will accept, and we will not let it be known that you changed your mind here today. You will not lose face." The DaSifu's eyes widened as he turned his head slightly as if straining in anticipation to hear Maggie's response.

In the hush of the auditorium, Maggie slowly shook her head, shifting her gaze from DaSifu Dao to Zhao and back again. The Council Chairman's face fell as he expressed his obvious disappointment at Maggie's choice.

"Very well, then let's begin with the rules. The fight will proceed until one of you submits or is unable to continue. You may submit by falling to one knee and bowing your head. If you are on the ground and cannot rise, you may raise your fist or hand. If one of you should become unconscious, for any reason, the conscious fighter will be declared the winner. And in the event of death, the duel never took place and history will not record it, though the result of the outcome will stand."

The DaSifu looked at Maggie. "Do you consent?"

"Yes."

Maggie's stomach was betraying her outward façade by turning, twisting, and generally moving around involuntarily. Her abdomen was full of the dreaded butterflies of fear, and they were taking their poisonous flight through her body, with the potency of a scorpion's sting.

DaSifu Dao looked to Zhao for his response.

"I consent," he said, and removed his shirt.

He was naked from the waist up, save for a silver claw-shaped pendant that he wore. It was the legendary talisman from which he had taken his name Zhao, the Claw.

He tossed his shirt in front of the stage. His body displayed a large tattoo. A tiger crouched and clawed his flesh on the lower right side of his torso. It looked like the tiger was clawing from below his waist. A black and silver dragon was flying in a serpentine "S" across his left chest. The two beasts faced each other fiercely at his solar plexus in the classic yin and yang symbol.

As he turned to remove his watch and bracelet, leaving them next to his discarded shirt, Maggie saw that the dragon's body continued scrolling and twisting over his shoulder and across his back. In addition to the grand tattoo, Zhao's body was marked with numerous scars, presumably, from his many previous encounters, both in the underground fighting ring and as an enforcer and assassin.

He had earned his status and reputation in Chinatown with his skill as a fighter, his cunning, and his ambition. The fact that The Council chose to put Zhao against her meant that they were not taking her lightly, and they wanted a definitive outcome. She was at once flattered and scared to death.

DaSifu Dao sat down on his throne purposefully and snapped his fingers. As if by black magic, a hand produced another cigarette for him. He held it aloft for the attentive valet to light. The Council Chairman put it to his lips, and then took a long draw. Taking his time, he adjusted himself on his throne and crossed his legs as casually as if he were telling a story to a group of children. With the fighters waiting, hanging on his every movement, he took his time before blowing out the smoke.

"Begin!"

They both moved away from the stage with their eyes fixed on each other and walked to the center of the floor. Zhao saluted Maggie. Maggie returned the gesture. Her eyes were locked on him. The formalities were brief. They approached each other slowly.

Maggie tried desperately not to look scared as she stalked cautiously. Her mouth was dry, her hands were clammy, and her heart was racing. Despite how she felt, she did her best to project nothing but confidence toward her opponent. The battle had begun, there could only be thoughts of victory.

She did not rush at Zhao, and he remained a cautious distance though their spiraling orbit would soon put them close enough for combat. They both appeared to respect the other's abilities. She figured that he had certainly been briefed on her recent victories and knew that a feeling-out process was the best course. She did the same. Maggie knew that he would not be overwhelmed easily. And it was clear that Zhao was a true warrior, not underestimating his opponent like the others that had underestimated her.

Her mind raced analyzing, observing, and looking for opportunities as she circled him with alternating patterns both clockwise and counterclockwise. She kept her guard up and her legs bent.

Though he seemed impregnable, she tried to remind herself that everyone has a weakness, and the mind must be unfettered to uncover and exploit whatever that weakness might be. *Control fear. Seize all opportunities.*

Given Zhao's size, she would not try to stand in front of him, she would evade and strike. She would be a mongoose to his cobra. She was smaller and more agile. She could outmaneuver him. He had size and strength. She would take away his advantage by refusing to fight him head-on.

Though she had been watching, she didn't notice how subtly Zhao had closed the distance between them until he exploded forward with a powerful snap kick of his right leg, followed by a straight punch with his right fist. He was even faster than she had thought!

She was almost caught by his blitzkrieg attack, but as the weapons approached, she faded her head back and twisted her body in a spiraling motion, deftly parrying the kick and the punch. She continued spinning and swung her leg around wide to sweep him. She took out his back leg, sending Zhao down hard, flat on his back, with a loud thud.

Maggie wasted no time as she swirled her body upwards and then descended in a deadly corkscrew, bringing her heel down with a sledgehammer's force toward her opponent's abdomen.

Zhao's eyes grew wide as he saw the impending danger plummeting toward him. He rolled away from the strike, springing to his feet like a jungle beast.

Re-engaging with Maggie, Zhao threw a combination of rapid-fire punches at her head. His fists fired like spears and maces of bone and flesh. She parried and slipped them all moving away just out of reach.

Evasion was the one strategy that had worked every time in all of her fights. As she stepped backward and continued to fade her body away from danger, she appeared to falter from the pressure of his attack, but she remained on her feet as if leaning on the air in her unorthodox Mongoose style. She parried, blocked, evaded, and slipped away from all of Zhao's punches. His eyes narrowed and his jaw clenched with frustration at not being able to hit or get a hold of her.

Zhao, she thought, was having difficulty sizing her up. More than once, he had tilted his head inquisitively, like a wolf studying unusual prey. Maggie's head was rolling away from the fearsome strikes as if it were not fully attached to her body. Her torso elongated and twisted as if her spine were supernaturally supple.

To him, it was like trying to hit an illusion or grab a handful of smoke. As with most of her opponents, Zhao started to get impatient. The clock started for her. At some point, he would make a mistake, and that is when she would pounce.

Zhao pursued her across the floor relentlessly. She continued her evasions and moved in a series of circular zig-zagging patterns like a skater making figure eights on virgin ice.

While Maggie thought hers must be an impressive display of technique and skill to still be standing against the martial colossus, their violent waltz could only postpone the need for contact between the two. Though she was a skilled defender, Zhao was the aggressor, and if Maggie was going to win, she would have to strike him, and it would have to be devastating.

The DaSifu watched with rapt attention. He looked to his right and left taking a silent poll from the other two members of The Council. He received two silent nods of assent from SiGung Hen and Sifu Shou. It was unanimous. All of them were impressed with Maggie's abilities. Though he had heard of her prowess from her other challenges, he now realized that she was truly exceptional.

Skill aside, DaSifu Dao was surprised to see that someone still taught the Mongoose style. It was a rare technique and even rarer to find a practitioner that could apply it at the level Maggie did. The unconventional use of being off-center was often too strange for most fighters to adapt to, but she had embraced it wholeheartedly. Given her smaller size, the choice of the Mongoose was not just apt but inspired. Sifu Chang had done his work well with this one.

He watched her movements smoothly flowing in what could often be a clumsy transition of a person's weight shifting rapidly from one extreme to the other, as she routinely fell and caught herself at the last moment. It was like watching a martial contortionist.

It made sense now. DaSifu could see how she had beaten so many of the other martial artists in Chinatown, they would not be expecting anyone, especially a woman, to be so unusually skilled.

DaSifu Dao glanced again to his left and right, offering a questioning gaze. In return, he received looks of concern from the sifu and SiGung Hen. DaSifu Dao realized that he had made a big mistake, in the beginning, by underestimating her. She was good, better than they thought. He had to admit that Zhao would have a difficult challenge on his hands, but he also knew that Zhao would win. He had to.

In the cat-and-mouse exchange of the fight, Maggie was always moving, always just out of reach. Punches sailed by speedily, as she evaded with a sink of her body and a twist of her head. Kicks flew at her abdomen like steel battering rams, but only exploded next to her like flash grenades. Zhao's claw-like grasp reached for flesh but only wrapped around empty air. With each attempt she made him pay a toll: A chop to his ribs, a punch to the jaw, an elbow to the spine. His face registered each strike's damage with a wince or a grimace. Though he was throwing bombs, she was a sniper, picking him off a piece at a time. The strikes from Maggie would become cumulative. *They had to add up. He was human, wasn't he?*

Zhao countered one of her parries and quickly spun unexpectedly into her ribs with a piercing elbow, robbing her of breath and energy. Maggie felt the sharp shock of pain shoot through her body, as she instinctively grabbed her stricken ribs and recoiled from the crushing hurt. The impact of the strike knocked her back more than a few steps. Zhao, capitalizing on Maggie's stunned response, grabbed her by the neck with his right hand, pulled her close, and with both of his muscular arms around her, began to crush the life out of her in a bestial hug of death.

"I think this is the end, tricky one." He breathed a gasping whisper into her ear.

Though the corded muscles of his arms squeezed tighter, Maggie realized that this was her best opportunity to strike. She was close to him, and with his arms occupied, she wouldn't have to worry about taking any strikes. *Think fast.* She rolled her eyes into the back of her head, let her neck droop, and her body go limp. *Play possum.*

Zhao, thinking victory was at hand, loosed his grip and raised his arm to strike with a fist. It was all she needed. In an instant, before Zhao realized she was conscious and could tighten his constrictive grip again, Maggie dropped hard and fast, like a sack of cement, below Zhao's arms and then fired her knee mercilessly into his groin and then his abdomen before grabbing his head and firing one more knee into his face.

As Zhao staggered backward, his eyes squinting with pain, Maggie leaped like an acrobat and flung her legs, like a boomerang around Zhao's neck. She locked her legs tight in a triangle choke and squeezed as hard as she could. He stumbled out of control trying to stay upright with the added weight of Maggie's entire body in a death hold around his neck. With his claw-like hand, Zhao tried to push Maggie's legs away from his neck, but as he pushed, she allowed his right arm to slip through, letting it fill the space necessary to make the choke tighter. Zhao's expression revealed that he realized the consequence of his mistake.

Adrenaline streamed through Maggie's body. She felt her energy and spirit lift as she realized she was in the dominant position. She squeezed ever tighter both legs against his neck and arm. Zhao would be feeling the pressure of her choke on his carotid arteries, as they slowly restricted the blood flow to his brain. Even though the situation for Zhao was dire, she knew that he would not panic. Like Maggie, Zhao was a warrior, and he knew to keep calm when in danger.

Maggie hung on relentlessly with her legs wrapped in a death lock on Zhao's neck. Like a helpless animal stuck in a trap, Zhao continued to tug and pull at her legs to try and break free of her choke. Her body rotated and hung from his neck squeezing with every ounce of strength that she could muster to keep the choke in place.

Her face was twisted into a tortured mask as she called on every fiber of her body to provide enough power and strength to bring defeat to the massive opponent. She saw his face was turning dark red and veins were starting to appear on his forehead, temples, and neck. He struggled and resisted with a tenacity that was only matched by the determination Maggie was using to keep her hold.

A feeling of anticipation came over her, as she could feel Zhao beginning his escape. He swiftly rocked his body backward in a big arc. Maggie knew what he was going to do. He suddenly reversed his direction and rocked forward to slam Maggie's parasitic body down to the floor head-first before him. Anticipating his counterattack, she quickly released the triangle and used Zhao's rocking momentum to propel herself through the air, somersaulting once, before landing on her feet in a deep crouch.

She spun around and assumed her ready position, with her left leg behind her, arms raised, feeling her body full of fire in her low crouching fighting stance. Her legs were throbbing, and she had a Charlie horse in her calves and thighs from torturing her muscles relentlessly through the choke.

Ignore the pain.

Though her legs were aching, she kept herself low to the ground and ready to spring into action. No matter how much pain she felt, she would never show it.

Clumsily, like a drunken tiger, Zhao staggered around to face Maggie. His large body was heaving, as he tried to catch his breath and let the blood flow freely from the near-fatal choke.

Sweat rolled from Maggie's face, as it did from Zhao's. His hair was wet and stuck to his head as if adhered by a slick glue. Maggie's eyes studied Zhao's expression. She could see his hatred, anger, and frustration, but she also saw new respect in his eyes. The one thing she knew was that neither one was going to submit to the other. This one was going all the way.

It was clear that it was going to take all her skills, an iron will, and a little luck to defeat Zhao. However, she noticed that while she had been able to remain calm and poised, Zhao's frustration was taking a toll. He was getting angrier by the moment, and that was good for her. She tried to cultivate her calm as she took deep abdominal breaths and shook the blood back into her cramped legs. If she could keep her distance until the fatal moment, she had a chance.

After a few deep breaths, Zhao looked up at The Council in a silent exchange of dire looks. Maggie could see that Zhao appeared to be questioning whatever deal he had made with the lords of Chinatown. She could almost hear The Council say what was inevitably said by all of her challengers: *"It'll be easy, she's a woman."* Now they all knew that it was going to be harder than they thought.

Zhao's attention returned to the fight, and he began stalking her again, but with his guard held low and his eyes filled with hate. Something had changed in him. His frustration had gotten the better of him. His emotions made him unpredictable.

Never take your eyes off him.

With eyes burning red with rage and consumed with fury, Zhao's gaze bore into Maggie. His bulging arms squeezed his hands into stone fists, and he let loose a yell that shook the walls of the auditorium, "AAAAHHHH!"

Maggie watched as The Council members pushed themselves back further in their chairs and Emily turned away covering her eyes.

A wailing rage trailed behind him, as Zhao jumped into the air like a tiger and pounced on Maggie, taking her down to the floor in a tackle. She fell hard with Zhao landing on top of her. Her ribs flexed painfully from the impact. Zhao's massive body weight sat like a full-grown gorilla on her chest and sapped her air and strength, as she lay pinned to the floor on her back.

Struggling with great effort to get a better position, she tried to wriggle and slip out from under the immense fighter. Maggie's breath was slow to return, and she was still stunned by the impact of the attack, but she knew that she had to get off her back before it was too late.

Zhao crawled like a snake onto Maggie and then sat atop her in a mounted position with his legs straddling her sides. He raised his massive mace-like fist high in the air to drop down in a crushing blow to her head, which would surely be death.

One chance.

In one swift move, Maggie fired her arms up with her wrists crossing to make an "X" and block his strike. She pushed with her legs and hips to bridge her body up high and roll Zhao off her. The larger opponent rode her body like a bucking bronco. His arms reached uselessly for something in the air to stabilize himself.

His guard was down.

This is it.

Maggie stabbed her thumb into Zhao's right eye. A howl of shock and pain escaped, as his body recoiled involuntarily from the strike, making Maggie's maneuver easier. The duo rolled over quickly with Maggie now assuming the superior mounted position. She sat atop her imposing opponent, still stunned from the strike, and straddled his body, determined to remain dominant as she rode his squirming torso.

Inexplicably, Maggie felt a spiritual transformation take place within her as the universe suddenly aligned in her favor. She leaned close to his body, adhering to him, and feeling his hot breath burn into her skin. Her arms snaked around his neck forming a chokehold. As her hands found purchase and formed a solid grip, she squeezed her arms hard together against his thick muscled neck. Contracting with an almost supernatural force, she resisted Zhao's talon-like fingers as they ripped into her flesh trying to tug her arms free. Her grasp held firm. Every part of him resisted, writhed, and struggled against her. Riding Zhao like a python coiled around its prey, the two spun and spiraled endlessly on the cold floor. After an unceasing struggle, she thought she could begin to feel him weaken. *Could this be it? Hold tight. Tighter! Don't let go.*

The muscles in Maggie's arms strained past fatigue. It was happening. Zhao was weakening. *Don't let go.* She waited for his signal of submission. He would raise a hand, tap, or give some kind of signal for her to release the choke. He must. His body began to fade. She felt the resistance was less. He was going to make her put him to sleep. It was inevitable. The brain starved of oxygen would shut down and so would his body. She waited for a sign of surrender, but then – Like a light breeze or a lapsed moment of daydreaming, she could feel he was gone.

My God!

Maggie threw off her arms with a flick of her hands as if to shake off the deed, and rolled herself off the massive warrior. She jumped to her feet, and stared down at Zhao, her eyes big with disbelief. Percussive gasps of horror filled the auditorium. The Council members stood before their thrones, stunned. The guards closed in making a circle around the pair. Looks of incredulity passed between the onlookers as they alternated looking up at Maggie and down at Zhao. As if sensed in unison, they instinctively started to back away from the tragic scene. Maggie was left alone. Viewed from the dark corners of the auditorium, it was a devastating spectacle. One stood tall looking down at death.

The air held the eerie quiet of a mausoleum. Only the sound of Maggie's labored breathing rose above the stillness. Her body began to chill as the sweat from her exertions caught the cool air. The clammy perspiration brought by the anxiety of knowing she had killed Zhao, slowly started to evaporate. Her body was processing the effects of the previous moments as her mind struggled to catch up. Lost for a while in the confusion was the prize: It was over, and she had won.

Her mind played the moment over again and again, as she felt the time to release her hold come and go. She wanted to be sure, to win. She did, but it was a Pyrrhic victory. Hollow. Maggie felt as though she had lost something of herself, but what choice did she have? They, The Council, Chinatown, and mankind, had forced her into an extreme position and forced her to make a blood sacrifice for what should have been anyone's right. *Why did it have to go so far?*

She had to live with the consequences of winning and live with the knowledge that there was a part of her that was darker than she realized. Could she see herself the same way anymore? *How would Emily see her now? Where's Emily?*

Maggie saw that she was where she had been before the fight started, by the wall of the auditorium. Emily was peeking through her fingers. *Did she see it all?*

Laid bare, Maggie felt naked before her. Though she wanted to run to her and know that everything was all right, she would have to stow her concern and deal with the aftermath later. On the stage, The Council had retaken their seats and were facing her on their thrones, each one expressionless. They looked like frozen images stuck in time.

Feeling a need to bring the event to an end, she reached down and plucked the silver claw necklace from the spiritless warrior's neck. As bad as she felt, she needed to be mindful of the danger of the situation. She glanced around the quiet venue once again, to make sure there were no more opponents, no rushing of guards, or double-crosses, and that it was truly over. Once she was satisfied that there was no one else coming, she held the necklace aloft, her fist shaking with tremors of exhaustion, as proof to The Council of what they already knew.

The light reflected off the silver claw necklace of the vanquished foe for all to see. She rolled it up in her right hand and saluted The Council with it firmly wrapped around her fist, watching their stony faces.

As the other two pushed themselves further back in their seats, DaSifu Dao rose and walked to the edge of the stage. He waited for a beat and then looked back to Sigung Hen and Sifu Shou to rise and follow him. All three stood before her. Sifu Shou was the first to salute, then SiGung Hen. As they followed by rank from lowest to highest, DaSifu Dao was the last to salute Maggie.

"Our business is concluded." DaSifu Dao's voice bounced delicately off the walls of the auditorium as if coming from the heavens. "It is the verdict of The Council that you may open and run your school, on your own, and as you see fit. No man will be over you. No further challenges will come. You will have the same opportunities as any other school in Chinatown."

Maggie nodded her head. And though her eyes were stinging with sweat and blood, they never left DaSifu Dao. Her breath was returning, and her sweaty skin revealed a draft nearby. She could feel gooseflesh forming, and a soft shiver, as her body powered down.

"This matter is closed. No vengeance will result," DaSifu Dao said loudly, for all to hear, and then looked at Sifu Shou for acknowledgment.

The sifu nodded slowly and reluctantly at The Council Chairman, and then he looked at Maggie with a gaze of malice so fierce, that it could burn down a forest.

"We will move forward," DaSifu Dao said, as he dropped his cigarette, and squished it out with the slow twisting of his foot. Before turning to leave, he gave Maggie a crooked smile.

The morning sun burst through the overcast sky and set a righteous light upon the city. The air was cool as nature began to reveal the coming of fall. The streets of Chinatown were already busy with traffic and the sidewalks were filled with pedestrians. Shop owners carefully moved their merchandise outside and onto the sidewalk, with bright signs elaborately illustrated, telling of low prices on everything from shoes to pork buns. Large chrome racks were filled with clothing and stationed carefully in front of the shops that sold them. Signs told of great values on jade sculpture, rosewood furniture, and one-of-a-kind pieces of calligraphy.

The denizens of Chinatown busily headed to their day's work. Buses, cars, bicycles, and pedestrians streamed past the newest kung fu school on the block. Most people walked by with their heads down, deep in thought, and didn't notice the two women working in front of the school. One woman was high atop a ladder and the other was holding it steady. They were partially obstructing the sidewalk, and like a rushing stream evading a large stone, the people flowed around, skirting the ladder on both sides.

Maggie was working patiently on the removal of the black dragon's head. She looked down to be sure that Emily was holding the ladder steady, while she worked diligently at the two remaining screws that held the dragon's head in place.

The irony was not lost on Maggie that she had hung it up with Wendy and was now removing it with Emily. She saw that Emily was surveying the area around her cautiously, if not a bit suspiciously, as she dutifully kept her hands around the ladder's steel legs. The look on Emily's face was anxious as if she were waiting for something to happen.

"It's over," Maggie declared from the top of the ladder. "The hard part anyway. Now, I just have to get some students, and convince them that they should study with me." Maggie worked carefully at the remaining screw holding the head in place, "The Council isn't going to bother us anymore. We won."

"We?" Emily looked up, shielding her eyes from the sun.

"Yeah, *we*. We kind of did it together, right?" Maggie craned her head down to see Emily's response, her hair tousled by the breeze.

"I just drove the getaway car a few times and held your bag with all of your...stuff, ya know? I didn't fight anybody. Although I did give you those flowers pretty cheap that time. Remember?" Emily joked, looking up at Maggie. The night of the victory, Maggie could not shake the feeling of taking Zhao's life, and it had been Emily that reassured her that if she hadn't held on to the choke, Maggie wouldn't have seen the next day.

Coming down the ladder, carefully, Maggie tossed the black dragon's head onto the sidewalk, where it landed with barely a sound. A passerby, a woman dressed in a black evening gown and red stiletto heels, sidestepped the dragon, never slowing as she deftly negotiated the disturbing symbol.

Maggie was delighted to see a few people stop and peer curiously through the window of the school. They were followed by a few more. The people gathered around each other, gently nudging those closest for a better position as they looked through cupped hands into the window.

It was as if removing the dragon's head had lifted an invisible curtain, obscuring the school from view, or had released positive energy that had been stifled by its dark presence. Or they could all be following up on the rumors that had started circulating about her recent victory, slightly exaggerated as they were, about her fighting prowess. It was amusing for her to hear how she had defeated a legion of Hong Kong's deadliest enforcers, which were imported to put an end to her insurrection. They had all been defeated with ease and aplomb. Upon hearing the tale, Maggie did nothing to clear it up.

The city was moving all around them, but still, Maggie felt as if they were all alone. She stood next to the ladder, holding it with one hand, and looking at Emily as she stood similarly on the other side. Their eyes found each other's, and Maggie's gaze refused to let go. For a moment, time froze. With a timid step, Maggie moved closer to her, reaching for Emily's hand.

"I remember. I remember everything. Thank you," Maggie reached out, and gently pulled Emily close to her. She watched the sunlight dance on Emily's face from the reflections from passing cars. She looked at Emily and saw, for the first time, someone she truly loved. She moved closer to her and then their lips softly touched.

They stood as immovable as pillars, locked in their embrace on the bustling sidewalk. They held each other tight, and kissed intensely, tasting each other fully for the first time. Their senses abandoned them, and the cacophony of the Chinatown streets went quiet, the sunlight faded, and the world fell away for one majestic moment.

When the moment subsided, as all moments do, the world came back into being, bringing them both back to a new, and shiny, present. They still held each other closely and looked into each other's eyes, one not wanting to release the other from their magical interlude. They stood looking at each other. Maggie's eyes glossed and shined with happiness.

People walking by, saw two young women holding each other closely, in front of the newest martial arts school in Chinatown "The Lady Dragon Kung Fu Academy."

Listed on the door were the hours of operation, class times, and the name of the proprietor: Sifu Maggie Long, *"The Lady Dragon of Chinatown."*

The End

Noel has been studying martial arts since 1990 and writes about Qigong and martial arts-oriented material in both fiction and non-fiction.

Printed in the USA
CPSIA information can be obtained
at www.ICGtesting.com
LVHW031814210823
755846LV00003B/247